Eat the Moon

Breda Joy

POOLBEG

Published 2018
by Poolbeg Press Ltd
123 Grange Hill, Baldoyle
Dublin 13, Ireland
E-mail: poolbeg@poolbeg.com
www.poolbeg.com

1

A catalogue record for this book is available from the British Library.

ISBN 978-1-78199-8014

Typeset by Poolbeg Press Ltd
Printed by CPI, Group, UK

www.poolbeg.com

About the author

Breda Joy is a Kerrywoman living a stone's throw from Killarney National Park in her native town. She has a son, Brendan.

A winner in the ESB National Media Awards (1997), she has worked as a regional journalist with *Kerry's Eye* and *The Kerryman* newspapers for over 30 years.

She holds an MPhil in Creative Writing from Trinity College Dublin. She was one of twelve finalists in the Green Bean Novel Fair 2016 at the Irish Writers' Centre and was shortlisted for the Francis MacManus Short Story Competition (2011). Her poetry has been published in literary journals and has won two national awards. She has published three non-fiction books, with Brandon Press and Mercier Press.

Eat the Moon is her first novel.

Acknowledgements

In the beginning there was a short story, the kernel from which this novel grew. The initial encouragement came from my friend, Liz O'Brien, who read the story and said, "I want to hear more".

The novel might well be an eternal work in progress but for the motivation furnished by the Irish Writers' Centre Green Bean Novel Fair (2016) to get it across the line. I am infinitely grateful to the IWC for this opportunity which was tailor-made for the 'Queen of Procrastinators'.

I owe so much to the members of my Killarney writing group who have been a creative community and a sounding board for me for so many years.

Inspiration doesn't come from locking yourself away from the world. My book would not be a reality today but for two community groups that exposed me to crucial influences:

Through the Kerry Education Training Board, I met adult learners whose determination in taking on mountain-high challenges made me reassess my own capabilities.

The Killarney charity, 'Be Aware Prevent Suicide,' set up by Deirdre Fee to nurture mental wellness, introduced me to outstanding speakers who personified grace in the face of adversity (an expletive-charged grace at times). The focus of *Eat the Moon* grew from this experience.

They say that the landscape of a book is a character in its own right. While the plot comes from my imagination, the setting draws heavily from the home farm of my late mother, Mairead, in Carrignamuck, Coachford, County Cork. My happiest childhood memories were forged on summer holidays there. My late grandparents, Michael and Mary O'Shaughnessy, and all their family, will ever hold a special place in my heart because of those summers.

Writing thrives in allocated spaces or residencies where time is given over exclusively to imagining and crafting. I am thankful to the Arts Office of Offaly County Council and to the Tin Jug Studio, Birr, for awarding me a week-long Birr Writers' Residency in 2015. Thanks also to Rosalind Fanning of Tin Jug Studio for looking after me so well during that fruitful sojourn in the Georgian town.

As always, Killarney Library staff provides a working space where I can escape from the distractions of my busy home. The same is true of the Somerville family and Ken and Theresa Rogers in Castletownshend in West Cork where the spirit of the late Edith Somerville is never far from my thoughts.

Thank you to Alice Taylor, Nora O'Dwyer Vogelsang and Ray Ryan for being such astute readers of my manuscript.

The light of *Eat the Moon* would yet be confined within the manuscript pages but for the faith and tenacity of my agent, Jonathan Williams, who guided it to safe harbour at Poolbeg. Heartfelt thanks to you, Jonathan, for your piloting and for your forensic editing.

The fact that Poolbeg Publisher Paula Campbell appreciated what *Eat the Moon* is about has meant the world to me. Likewise, the affirmation of my editor, Gaye

Shortland, was a priceless endorsement. Thank you both for recognising the value of my work.

Much of this book revolves around horses. I want to thank my father, Brendan Joy, for sharing his 'horselore' with me. The writing of the late Dáithí Ó hÓgáin on the horse in Irish myth and folklore also informed the material.

Writing is the bedrock of my life but my truest sense of purpose comes from my son, Brendan. Sound man, Brendan.

Thank you to my family, friends, colleagues, neighbours, lodgers, and to Brendan, Eimear, Liz, Valerie, Ann, Deirdre, Mike and Milo, for being there. The world would be a lacklustre place without you all.

For Brendan,
my finest creation

"For he would be thinking of love
Till the stars had run away,
And the shadows eaten the moon."

W.B. YEATS "The Young Man's Song"

A horse is unpredictable; he can bolt at any time. The simplest thing. The unexpected. A lorry or a bus or a tractor, he might never look at. A horse could shy from his own shadow, or a pool of water. He shies sideways actually and that's what makes a person fall off. It depends on the fright he gets. Some only travel a small way. Others keep on going for a long distance. Very often people are thrown off. If you were ready for him, it wouldn't happen at all.

A lot depends on their eyesight. At times they can see too much; you have to put blinkers on them. All horses aren't the same. A young horse can be giddy. With age and work they quieten down.

The thing is, some are naturally very quiet. They're bred that way. There's the odd one you'll always have to watch. It's in the breeding of them too. Like people.

But mark my words: when a horse gets it into his head to bolt, neither God nor man will hold him. You could have twelve men behind him dragging on the reins and still they wouldn't halt him. Any horseman will tell you that.

1

Sally

My mother hated Nixon with a passion. There was no sense to the set she had on him that I could make out, given that she was living 3,000-odd miles away from him and had never encountered him gallivanting around any boreen in our neck of County Cork. When Watergate emerged, she greeted the news as an endorsement of her reputation as a woman with a sixth sense. She had spotted the signs of the chicanery in those "shnakey eyes of his". 'Chicanery' was one of Mammy's fancy words, more about that later. But Watergate and all those shenanigans were way down the track from the July night we sat up late in the kitchen waiting for the astronauts to leave the *Eagle* and take their stroll on the moon that, aptly enough, was gleaming outside our kitchen window in crescent form.

"As sure as anything, that Nixon will go poking his nose into this and it having nothing on the red earth to do with him," Mammy said, throwing a filthy look at the television set.

A man called Kevin O'Kelly was giving the commentary. His voice, if they could only cork it in a bottle, would make a great cure for those nervy city wans who couldn't sleep, Daddy said. My head nodded and nodded until it sank down on my arms on the kitchen table. I thought I was still listening to Kevin O'Kelly when Kieran pinched me and I woke with a start. It was at least half three in the morning by then and I was so tired that Neil Armstrong might as well have been stepping off the half-six bus from Macroom for all I cared.

Nana was convinced the astronauts were going to sink down through the powdery surface never to be seen again. She was fingering her rosary beads as she sat on her throne beside the old black range. The glow through the range bars had dwindled to ashes, and the kitchen held the coolness of the early morning.

"There's no call for them lads to be going up there at all," she said. "Them Yanks are away with the fairies. All that good money wasted and half the world starving. If God wanted men on the moon, he'd have put them there himself. It will come to no good."

Nana was a self-appointed prophetess of doom, according to Mammy. When the first few blue-skied days dawned in April or May, she used to pronounce "That's the summer for you now".

Daddy and Kieran were deaf to the remarks of my mother and Nana as they scrutinised the screen to collect any extra information they could about the mechanics of the big *Apollo* rocket, the *Columbia* which was the bit of it that would circle around the moon, and the smaller machine called the *Eagle* that they were going to land in. You'd swear Daddy was going to build one himself. I wouldn't have put it past him. He had a cut at building a small plane when he was a young fella but it came to grief in a bog. What more could you expect from a flipping motorbike engine? He was known in the parish as the man who could fix anything, but flying was a bit beyond him.

"When all else fails, Con Mahony is your only man," the other farmers used to say.

It was a marvel to me that he had left behind the shed and all its machinery to sit in the kitchen for hours on end to watch the *Apollo* coverage because he had no time for the telly apart from the news. If they had the space mission on all day and all night, there would have been no budging him. Clane mad he was about it. And why wouldn't he be, since there was a man with a great Cork name and roots in County Cork itself in the driving seat of the *Columbia* – Michael Collins? Neil Armstrong and Buzz Aldrin were only in the tuppenny-ha'penny place compared to Collins in Daddy's estimation. All that changed when Armstrong succeeded in safely bedding down the *Eagle* though they were four miles away from the planned landing spot. Armstrong impressed Daddy no end with that display of driving skills.

"Wouldn't Armstrong be a mighty man to back a tractor out of a tight corner?" he said, eyes glued to the screen.

Our London cousin, Tamara, was scarcely a week in the house the night we sat down to watch the moon landing. It was her first visit over to us. We were just about getting used to the fact that she never opened her mouth. Of course, she did open it to eat and yawn and cough, all the normal activities you would associate with a mouth, except for the small matter of spitting out words. There were no two ways about it: my cousin was a bit of an oddity.

There was a fierce smell of oil and Swarfega off my father and Kieran that evening. Swarfega was all the go back then. The greeny jelly look of it and the dizzy smell of it would nearly make you want to eat spoonfuls from the tin. Daddy could have used buckets of the stuff but it

Breda Joy

would never shift the black rims from under his nails. Nana said the pair of them would be struck down for working of a Sunday but Daddy told her that they had to put in a couple of hours to finish a job. He said he'd go to Confession – a likely story. They had been rooting in under some old Major tractor, and didn't bother changing their clothes before plonking down in front of the telly.

Armstrong and Aldrin had yet to venture out of the craft but my father was already wondering how the *Eagle* was going to manage to rise off the moon surface.

"That ascent engine must be a mighty piece of machinery to get them back up to the command module again," he said to Kieran. "I'd give my eye teeth to get a good look into the belly of it."

Kieran had two big black rings under his eyes, and his black hair was as tousled as if he had just got out of bed.

"What if it's not powerful enough to rise it?" he replied, swallowing a yawn. "They'll be rightly shanghaied. Imagine being stuck on the moon."

The idea terrified me. We had a picture in the parlour of a great big stag bellowing under a dark sky in a scary place that wasn't too different from what we could make out the moon surface to be. Nana had told me ages ago that the deer was crying because he couldn't find his mammy. She was never a woman to let the truth get in the way of a good story – he was a huge hulk of a beast with antlers as big as trees on him. Looking at the *Eagle*, I felt a shiver run down my spine at the thought of the astronauts being stuck up there for ever and ever, looking down at the rest of us.

Kieran wasn't a bit worried. Nothing was a problem to our Kieran. Up and at it, he'd say. He had been obsessed with the *Apollo* for weeks. Now that the time had come

6

for the astronauts to step out of the capsule, he was out on the very edge of the kitchen chair.

"Hey, Sally, Tamara, in another ten years or so we could all be striking off for the moon," he said. "Holidays on the moon. What do you make of that?"

Tamara looked at him blankly. For once, her expression didn't annoy me. Her tired face was as milky as the moon itself. The only time she had shown any real interest in the landing was when Mission Control had a joke with the astronauts about looking out for a lovely Chinese girl with a big rabbit on the moon. The girl called Chang was supposed to have been banished to the moon four thousand years earlier because she stole her husband's pill of immortality. That pill must have been fierce tack altogether, whatever it was. Maybe Tamara thought she was like Chang because she had been sent over from London to live with us for a while. Collins said they'd look out for the 'bunny girl'. I hoped we weren't going to be stuck with our 'bunny girl' for too long.

"How far away is the moon?" I said, shifting my sorry arse around on the polished seat of the chair. "How long would it take us to get there?"

I had my doubts about taking a hike to the moon. Even the bus to Killarney made me sick. The shame of the last time I had made the return journey was still with me: the desperate feeling of the two pinpricks near my cheekbones, the sick rising up my throat and the mortification of puking into a brown-paper bag handed to me by a kind woman. The nice part of the journey had been the flat brown cardboard box of chicks on their way from a hatchery in Clondrohid. The lid was pierced with holes as big as a silver thruppence, and when I put my finger through the holes, the chicks pecked at it. But they would hardly be sending chicks to the moon. And I'd have to find something else to pass the time.

"It's 240,000 miles away," Kieran said. He had a fierce head for figures. "But give them another few years and they'll have the journey down to nothing. Start saving now, Sal girl, and we could be celebrating your twenty-first up there in nine years' time."

"Don't forget there is a dark side to the moon," Nana warned. "Nobody knows what's lurking behind there."

Mammy threw her eyes to heaven. "Ah, will you let the boy dream, Mother dearest! You don't have to be throwing cold water on everything."

My father was not as convinced as my big brother about the possibility of excursions to the moon for us. He rubbed the grey stubble on his chin thoughtfully. "I think we'll wait and see how these lads get on. They're not home and dry yet."

But I knew that Kieran was already slipping away into a world where great white cities had sprung up in space and people were zipping around in contraptions that were like cars except for the fact that they floated instead of being driven on the ground. I was all up for one of those and I could imagine myself gliding along in a shiny bubble, as light and as free as a bird. But there would have to be horses up there as well. Moon horses, pearly as Mammy's mother-of-pearl rosary that came from Knock. Our Kieran wouldn't last candlelight anywhere without a horse.

Waiting for the astronauts to step out and walk on the moon was every bit as bad as the evening before when we were waiting for the *Eagle* to land. You could have cut the tension in the kitchen with the old bow saw. My father was afraid that the craft would explode when it hit the surface. My mother was convinced that the spindly little lunar module would be sucked away by some sinister galactial current (her words). My grandmother said the little green men would come out from their white dusty burrows and 'ate them without salt'. I was ating my nails with the worry of it.

There was no picture of the *Eagle* on the screen when it actually landed around nine o'clock that Sunday evening. All we had was the voice from Mission Control. The man behind the voice was Charles Duke but the astronauts called him 'Houston'. The voice said, *"Thirty seconds"*. Even my mother was silent as the reports dribbled out a couple of words at a time with silences between them until, finally, we heard, *'Houston. Tranquillity Base here ... the Eagle has landed.'*

With that declaration, we jumped up and danced around the kitchen like mad things, except for my father – he sat there with a smile as wide as the crescent moon printed like a transfer from a lucky bag on his tanned face. Kieran stamped on Sam's paw by accident. The collie had been christened Samantha by Mammy who got the name out of some Mills and Boon romance she was reading when my father brought the pup home years before. No plain old 'Shep' for the Mahonys, I'm telling you. Old and deaf and retired from action, Sam had been sleeping on the hearthstone while the whole drama was going on.

"I told ye not to be bringing that dog into the house," Daddy had said earlier. "The kitchen is no place for dogs."

"Ah, but the cratur isn't long for this world," Nana said. "She deserves her bit of comfort."

"Well, I'll be helping her along if she doesn't hurry up," he'd answered.

In case you're getting a bad impression of Daddy, he wasn't always a sour puss but you wouldn't want to be any cratur that outlived its usefulness on our farm in those days. And you had to keep an eye to being useful yourself. Mammy used to be telling us to say 'creature' instead of 'cratur' because Tamara would think we were talking about craters on the moon or in volcanoes, but I wasn't going changing my way of talking for someone who had left her voice behind in London. Anyway, elocution classes were bad enough in school without having to be all posh at home.

Mammy went over to the dresser and took down the coloured china plate with the picture of John F. Kennedy and his wife, Jackie, and kissed it. Their head and shoulders were set against a halo of blue and the plate was edged in gold.

"God bless you, Jack – you did it," she said, crying. What the dead president had to do with the moon landing was beyond me, but Mammy was a divil for crying. Happy or sad, she could turn on the waterworks at the drop of a hat.

The same tension that went with the moon landing was back in the kitchen again in the early hours of the next morning. No one could see Armstrong on the screen but he was crawling through the open hatch to stand on the *Eagle*'s porch. When the first fizzy images of the self-same man setting foot on the moon appeared on the screen, I was puzzled.

"How come he is getting out before Buzz Aldrin?" I asked.

There was a chorus of mad '*shhhs*' and Kieran gave me a sharp dig in the side with his elbow. No need for that at all. That great moment for mankind was to be forever tinged with a sense of outrage on my part. Couldn't a girl even ask a straight question without being attacked?

Armstrong, cautious as my father, tested the surface before surrendering himself to it. He didn't disappear.

"That's one small step for man, one giant leap for mankind . . ."

He was bouncing gently, much too gently for my liking. I had expected him to take off with the giddy gait of calves when they are left out of the shed for the very first time in spring.

But the kitchen was alight with excitement, and I forgave Armstrong and Aldrin for their lack of bounce. Even my father stood up awkwardly. Kieran punched the air. We couldn't have been as happy for the astronauts if they had been from the next parish.

Nana clapped her hands together like a child and recited *"Hey diddle diddle, the cat and the fiddle, the cow jumped over the moon"* so often that Mammy told her to stop or people would say she was doting.

Nixon appeared on the screen saying, *'Because of what you have done, the heavens have become a part of man's world.'*

I stole a look at Mammy but she seemed to have forgotten about old 'shnakey eyes' in the power of that special minute.

We had all forgotten Tamara, who was staring at us with such lonesome eyes that you'd think she was a desperate distance away from us all, if not on the moon with a bunny rabbit, then on some other planet.

Looking from one face to the next, I saw happiness shining as brightly as Nana's luminous green statue of Our Lady. Tamara was the odd one out. Apart from her, the little world of my family had never felt cosier. Little did I realise what was flying towards us, the same as a comet bursting out of one of those scary dark stretches of space and frozen in a picture in the big mildewed *Reader's Digest* book that Mammy kept down in the parlour with all her other fat books – books that Tamara was killed from reading, the show-off.

2

Tamara

Every night, in the bedroom that smells of damp, you set about conjuring up home. You can't wait to bury yourself under the duck eiderdown your nana has given you and to sift through memories like pieces of the jigsaw of a thatched English country cottage half-assembled on the table of the cold room they call the parlour.

Start with the steps leading up from the basement door to the narrow street and, minutes walk away, the river of traffic throbbing on the Earls Court Road: big red buses, black taxis, cars, delivery vans, motorbikes, sleek chauffeured cars with tinted windows. Remember the blonde girl driving a red sports car, an Old English Sheepdog sitting upright in the passenger seat, the old lady with a goat-like beard gazing into the past from the top of the bus, the Afghan hound you reach out to pat on the traffic island and he pulls back ebony lips to bare his fangs. *Oh, the things you see when you haven't got a gun.*

But you're getting ahead of yourself. Come back to the steps rising from the basement, the patch of grass inside the railings, discarded pages of *The Sun* blowing in from the pavement, the pots of withered geraniums. Think of the magnolia tree growing in the centre of the grass, its sumptuous petals pink and white like bars of Lux soap.

You are told that the flowers blossom while the branches are still bare. This is one of the things you absorb and store away. And the blossoms come loose and fall to the scruffy grass, rest beside soggy newspaper pages, paper that one day was part of trees itself, a long, long way from here. This is another thing to consider.

She has a new rota at the pharmacy, and she has to leave earlier on Mondays. She trains you how to walk to Earls Court Station on your own, how to avert your eyes when sitting on the Tube. When you're walking along Earls Court Road to the station, look neither left nor right. The druggies and the prostitutes hang around the gaping station entrance, but they won't bother you. And, anyway, there's always a bobby there. Just walk up to the bobby and you'll have no problem. Look ahead to an imaginary spot. Seal yourself tight inside, away from the one pair of searching eyes that could pry you open in a second. Walk fast. Listen for the leather thwack of your shoe-soles against the pavement. You are a statue, a walking statue. They cannot touch you. You are invisible, hidden deep inside this uniformed figure they see flitting past. You're a big girl now. Three stops only to your school in Hammersmith. Don't tell the teachers. They wouldn't understand. You tell Daddy how you managed when you talk to him on the phone. *Not a bother on you, what did I tell you?*

He guesses the kind of people you see on the Tube. The tourists on their way in from Heathrow. Stern-faced, well-off women with expensive handbags, backpackers with rucksacks. Young couples talking to each other softly. Everyone else looking into books, into newspapers, into space. There are stray dogs who ride the Moscow metro, even know where to get off. He reads that out of the paper one weekend when he's home. *Well, doesn't that bate all?* He tells the story then about Lilac, his harrier. Harrier, a strange word. Is it a bird, you wonder, some kind of a hawk? Lilac was one of the pack of dogs owned by the fox hunt and kennelled on different farms, he explains. The day he left to take the boat, she began to keen. The others all keened with her. As if they knew, as if they had sense about these things. *So they did, every last one of them howling.*

On the Saturdays he is home, you go to Holland Park with the two of them. You see dogs, lots of them. *Dogs in coats, faith then.* Lots of children too. With their nannies, their au pairs. There's a little girl in a bright red coat with black trimmings. She has a black fur muff to tuck her hands in. You crave that muff, dream about it. All the lights are on in Kensington High Street when you're going home. They stop to look in a travel agent's window. They are reading out all the names of the destinations as if they were dishes on a menu. Mombasa, Singapore, Hong Kong, Melbourne. Her shoulder brushes against you, and she looks at you as if she has seen a stranger.

"My goodness, you're almost up to my shoulder. Will you look at her, Jack?"

He buys Indian take-aways on the Earls Court Road. Remember the smells, the spices. Feel the heat when you come in out of the cold which is making the exhaust fumes smell keener in the dark of late evening. She thinks the man behind the counter is like Omar Sharif. He has the whitest of teeth when he smiles at you. He should have the Colgate Ring of Confidence. You would like to see the Colgate Ring of Confidence appear in front of you, like the shining halo in the church on Kensington High Street when you go there and light candles.

"What's carrying you to a church?" he says jokingly.

She tells him it's only for the candles but he knows that already.

You don't have to go to the church to light candles or to see angels. You have dozens of them at home. *Angels and candles coming out of our ears, so they are.* She has been collecting the angels since she was a little girl. Her godmother, Edith, started the collection, brought them back from Venice and Rome, from Prague and Vienna, wherever she travelled. Angels made from stained glass, porcelain, straw, ebony, even biscuits. They have alighted on the mantelpiece, the sideboard, the window pelmet. There is a glass cabinet of them. They have even fluttered into the kitchen. He has banned them from their bedroom. Well, apart from the tall slender one blown from Murano glass, all red, yellow, gold. It's so strangely shaped he feels it doesn't really qualify as an angel.

She sets the foil containers of curry on the coffee table, and he switches on the two-bar heater with the artificial coals. There's a smell of burning dust when the bars turn red. She lights the candles and he brings in the plates.

These are special Saturdays when he is at home, when he is on a break from his work on the oil rigs. Smells of candle wax and curry, the light running through the artificial coals, the sparkles of the angels glinting in the candlelight. *Our own little heaven, so it is.*

And this is the night he saves for his stories – stories from home, stories of fairies and the púca, and, if he has had a few beers, tales of the man with the cloven feet, all accounts he swears are true. You can still feel the magic of his voice wrapping the wonder of those stories around you.

"The fairies were still in the memories of the old people when I was young. My grandfather told me he heard the story of the chieftain from his own grandfather, and that the telling of it stretched way way back like a chain with no sight of the beginning. It went like this.

There was a man of our family walking the road one day when a big wind rose from the direction of the lake and swept a stream of leaves past him. He turned in the direction of the wind and saw a line of horsemen coming for him, the tallest of them riding a white horse out front.

He knew it was the Chieftain, risen from the drowned castle on the bed of the lake as he did every seven years on the first day of May. This was known as surely as Christmas came every December. And the man had no fear.

As they drew nearer, he saw that the horses were wet with the lake water and it was streaming from the deerskin boots of the bearded men. He drew in close to the ditch to let them pass. When the horses lifted their hooves, he could see their silver shoes. Silver shoes that made no sound as they struck the stones. But he could hear the horses snorting, eager to stretch their legs on dry ground after seven long years in their watery stables.

When the last horse passed him at a canter, its left back hoof hit a sharp rock with some force. A silver chip broke off and struck the man on the cheek. When he put up his hand, he caught the fragment as it fell. They say it was in the family for years. But I never saw it. It must have been lost long before my time."

These stories are your Saturday jewels, glinting in your mind's eye. They are the prism you look through every night here in the coal dark that falls so absolutely, so differently from home where the street lights and the car lights quench only when their watch is over and the daylight returns. When you came here first and woke in the night and pulled back the curtain, it seemed as if there was an invisible black-out sheet draped across the window. You reached out your hand but met only the glass pane. The very first time this happened, you panicked: you were afraid you had gone blind.

The light shining from the open door and the windows is no match for the inky darkness overwhelming the house, cloaking every living thing except the stars. Yes, this is the first thing you notice here, the way the night hides everything. You are crossing the concrete yard to the milking stall with Sally to bring milk from the dairy. You look up – your head stays tilted back as if you will never look down again. You practically fall over Sally. She doesn't know what has got into you. She thinks it's yet another example of you being barmy. The starry sky reminds you of a black lurex jumper that Mu . . . that she wore on special occasions. But the night sky is only an everyday pullover in Sally's eyes. It doesn't merit a second glance from her, hardly a first glance.

You are in the dairy, a chilly little room set at least four feet above the yard. Kieran is pouring a bucket of milk through the strainer into a milk churn. Some sort of a machine is humming in the background. Sally is hosing down the concrete floor, the milky water running out over the big step and down onto the ground.

The dairy is just off the stall where the last couple of cows are being milked.

The cows are named for their colouring or for their former owners: Daisy, Snow White, White Stockings, Strawberry, Kerry, Moriarty, and more names you are still learning. These names are daubed in white paint over each of their spaces in the stall.

Every morning and evening, they file in from the fields

and peel off into two lines, their heads passing through two wooden posts in each allotted space, their rough tongues rasping the ration from concrete basins in front of them. The posts rest slackly until the cow is in place and then they are closed and held together by a binding at the top. If one cow, usually a younger one, goes into the wrong space, the cow who should be there will butt it out with her head.

Sally tests you like a teacher about the cows and the farm, gets you to write down your answers in a writing book, makes regular reports of your ignorance to Kieran. You are still not used to it.

Imagine Tamara doesn't know the difference between a plough and a harrow! She doesn't know how many times a day the cows are milked. She doesn't know that sugar comes from beet, that potatoes have to be dug out of the ground, that a bird will forsake its nest if you touch it.

Some of the time you think they are speaking Gaelic. It takes you weeks to realise that 'ating' means 'eating' and that 'mate' is 'meat'. So often 'e' sounds like 'a'. The 's' words take getting used to also. They speak about a 'basht' when they mean 'beast'. When Daddy told you all the stories about Cork, it was like a familiar world but it can actually feel like a foreign country. There is so much to grow accustomed to.

You never knew how green cow dung is, how badly it smells indoors on the wellingtons in the kitchen, but not so bad out in the plain air. You never knew it crusts like a pie in the fields and that when you stand on it, barefoot, the green splurges up through the crust and oozes in between your toes.

Kieran makes a joke of it all but you still flush, still wish you could say that you might as well have landed on

19

the moon that day back in July when they collected you from the airport.

This evening Sally picks a new topic.

"Guess what?" she says.

"What now?" Kieran says with an air of resignation.

"Tamara hasn't seen the dawn. Imagine that."

"You haven't seen the dawn," Kieran says. "Well, we must set that right. You haven't lived till you see the dawn."

This time, you don't feel so bad. The way Kieran talks about the dawn, it sounds like some sort of a magic place. Sally shoots you a look. It's not turning out as she expected. But she will have more opportunites to draw from your bottomless pit of ignorance. You could add another one to the list right now: you never knew what milk smelled like until you were enveloped in the warm, cloying smell of it in the dairy where your father's name is spelled out on the ceiling-boards with crunched-up paper strainers that come out of the milking buckets. How he did it you don't know, but the once-wet paper balls are studded to the ceiling, spelling out a yellowed J-A-C-K that must have been there for years. It's like a charm, this sign that he was in the dairy before you. You are not alien to this place. *Jack*, you think, turning the name over in your mind, the hard sound of it. *Jack*. It clangs off another word jumbled in the same cell of your honeycombed store of words. *Forsake*.

3

Kieran

There was a lot going on at home that summer. Sally was getting way too big for her boots. She kept giving me cheek. Said I had a big head just because I was good at hurling. Then Tamara landed in on top of us. Sally didn't take too kindly to her arrival. She was cock of the walk and wasn't too happy about sharing her patch. I had no real complaints myself. Just turned eighteen, I was playing with the parish senior team, which meant that a gaggle of girls from the village were cheering me from the sidelines. But I had eyes only for the wan girl.

"If you keep going like that, you'll soon wear the Cork jersey," the trainer told me.

That's what every family wanted in those days – their own Christy Ring on the hurling field or a priest on the altar. And if you got the two, so much the better.

Mammy wanted me to go on to college, to 'make something of myself' before I settled down to life on the farm. I heard her tell Nana once that she wanted me to take the chance she never had. Mammy had her nose in a book any spare minute she got. The parlour shelves were stacked with Agatha Christies and *Reader's Digests*. There were other books too by men called Walter Macken, Frank O'Connor and Canon Sheehan. The only book by a woman was *The Turf-Cutter's Donkey* by Patricia Lynch. Mammy read that to Sally when she was small. Sally bawled her eyes out the night she came to the last page. I wanted her to read out *The Ginger Man* by J.P. Donleavy next but she said that it was only for 'big people'.

I wasn't inclined to kill myself with the schoolbooks. I did enough on the farm to keep my father off my back. Helping out with the milking and the machinery repairs was about the size of it.

I was nuts about horses. I used to borrow one of the Donovans' horses in return for working around the stables. I wanted to keep one of them in the Screen Field. Balthasar, a big mountain of a black horse. But Daddy blew a gasket whenever he saw the horse darkening the lane.

"Haven't the Donovans enough grass of their own down there without that monster demolishing what grazing we have?" he'd say. "There won't be a blade left for our cows by the time that yoke is finished."

"Take him away, Kieran, or I won't have a minute's peace," Mammy pleaded.

I think she would have liked Balthasar to stay. She had a great way with him. Whenever I went to put the bridle on him, he would toss his head to the sky, so I had taken to standing on a wooden butter box to put it on. But when Mammy went out with the bridle, a gentle word and a cut of bread, Balthasar stood for her like a lamb. She stayed there with him for a while afterwards, patting his neck and stroking his face.

"A horse will get to know you and do things for you if you're nice to them," she said. "Not like some people belting them and hitting them. People I could name but I won't. A lot of them think you need to hit a horse to get him to do things. If they get afraid of a lorry or a tractor or something, some people get an ashplant or another class of a stick to try driving them past the thing that's frightening them. But there's no point in telling ignorant people that's the wrong way to go about it. Some people only know the stick. If you talk to horses, they understand you. They have their own sense. People think they're dumb. They're not as dumb as a lot of the people at all. A dog is the same."

The Donovans had the big house down on the far side of the river. The father, Timmy, bred a few winners but whatever came in from the prize money took flight again in gambling and drinking at the race meetings in Mallow, Limerick and Killarney. He was known all over the place for it. Timmy the Thirst he was called. Not to his face, you understand. Only for the earnings from the grain and the tight hand of the wife, Kathleen, they would have had to sell out. I was up there a couple of nights a week, riding out the horses. This drove my father spare because he expected me to be doing more work around our own place. That's not to say I was doing nothin' but there was no plasin' him no matter how much I did.

"Wisha, I think it's more than the horses he's after," Nana said one evening. "There must be a girleen taking his eye." She was watching me as I put a crease in my hair at the mirror beside the kitchen door.

There was a grand smell of Brylcreem and the green Palmolive soap I'd lathered himself with in the red plastic pan filled with hot water from the urn on the stove.

"Will you hark at her, and there were people thinking she was beginning to dote," Mammy said.

Between the two of them, I was gone as red as a beetroot. "Will ye lave me alone!"

There was a family of five sisters in the Donovan house – like steps of the stairs they were, all beautiful and as different from one another as the flowers in the garden. Mammy said they looked for all the world as if they had been shaken out of a mixed-seed packet. Their hair ranged through all the colours of barley, rabbit-brown, coal-black, whitethorn blossom. Their skin was like cream on the top of the churn, or golden as toast. They came in assorted sizes: thin as laths, lumpy as cushions, long and short.

Kitty, the eldest, was the one age to me. Like myself, she was mad for the horses. A pure lunatic, in fact. She was a sight to see high up on the big chestnut mare with her goldie-red hair flying in the wind. Lady Godiva, my father called her. She was tall and wiry, fearless clearing ditches and banks rising before her as high as the garden walls of the big house. Even the crackest horsemen in the hunt couldn't get over the chances she took.

The few times Kitty had been up in our kitchen, Mammy had taken her a bit cool like. She thought Kitty was grand in herself. I never saw her like that. Kitty was sound out once you got to know her.

"I can't make my mind up about her," Mammy said afterwards. "It's hard to read her green eyes. Were they laughing at us in our houseen or were they just naturally dancing in her head?"

Our house might be small compared to the Donovans' but there was more room in it since our two grown-up sisters, Tess and Sheila, had emigrated to New York where they were working in an ice-cream parlour called Schrafft's. I was dying to visit them.

I was six or seven years younger than the sisters. There was a big gap too between Sally and myself. The pram had been well and truly retired when she turned up under another head of cabbage, moryah. Nana used to call her '*dríodar an chrúiscín*' or the 'remains of the jug'. Work that one out for yourself.

I slept downstairs in a bedroom beside the parlour. It was the coldest room in the house. And it gave off a fierce smell of damp in the winter. Nana would have slept there but for her chest. There were three bedrooms upstairs: the two big ones for Nana and my mother and father, and the small poke of a gable room Sally had to share with Tamara. You should have seen the puss on her when she had to make room for the little mouse of a cousin.

Our house was up on a height looking across the valley. It looked lovely with the grove of dark trees rising up behind it to break the wind. A stream ran off the slope behind us and tumbled over stones at the end of the orchard. The upstairs bedroom windows overlooked the orchard and, as Mammy was killed from saying, they let in the stream's music. Mammy was embarrassed that we were still saving up to build a proper bathroom but Daddy used to say that a plastic pan and a white enamel po under the bed would serve us fine for another while. Maybe the lack of a bathroom made her nervy when Kitty was around. Daddy said Kitty could go down the field and find a dock leaf if she got a call of nature while she was visiting.

"The flow of talk out of her – does she know how to listen to a person at all?" Mammy sniffed after one of Kitty's visits. "Like her mother, with the touch of grandeur about her."

"There's nothing grand about Kitty at all," I said. "Just because you couldn't get a word in edgeways yourself."

If my mother liked to do anything, it was to talk. She approached silences like she did the holes in the heels of our socks or in the elbows of our jumpers, darning the lulls with statements, stories, opinions. When Daddy didn't hold up *The Cork Examiner* like a ditch for shelter from her chatter, he dozed to the sound of her voice, waking always to find she was still going strong.

"At least I'm not talking about myself all the time," she said.

Well, she was right about that. Kitty was always clacking away about her school, her friends, her horses. But she had a lovely way of talking. I could listen to her all day. 'Twas aisy for me too. There was no call for me to go bothering my head making talk. I could just let her spout away.

"Ah, Mammy, we can't all be as fascinating as you, with all your book-reading," I said.

I was halfway out the door when she spoke again, in a lower tone not meant for my ears, but I did hear her.

"This will end in tears," she said. "I feel it in my bones."

I turned in the doorway. "What's that you said, Mam?"

She said nothing.

"Why didn't you catch it when it was flying?" Sally said, cheeky out.

I whistled away to myself going down the lane. There was a dance in the village hall. All the lads were going. Kitty might be there too. Mammy and her tears. Where was she getting those quare notions from? If she wasn't talking, she was thinking. And if thought could make a fool of a man, the same was surely true of a woman.

4

Sally

Tamara had been with us a few weeks before she copped on about Kitty because she had been up with her cousins in County Meath for a holiday. I remember the day she first found out about Kitty and the fact that Kieran was like a sick calf whenever he was around her.

It was a Sunday afternoon, hot, airless, not a branch or a blade of grass stirring. The hum of an invisible swarm of bees sounded as loud as the milking machine. Kieran had taken down my grandfather's fishing rod from where it rested on two nails on the kitchen wall. Poor old Sam was stiff with arthritis but, at the sight of the rod being brought down, she lepped up and down with the excitement of a pup. Well, she gave a fair good imitation of lepping anyway. If I had a tail myself, it would have wagged as much as Sam's because I loved those afternoons down by the river with Kieran. I was bulling that Tamara would be coming too but the sun was out and, with the thought of an entire lazy afternoon with my brother stretching ahead, I said to myself that I would cut her some slack. At least she wouldn't be at home reading more boring *Reader's Digests* or another *Nancy Drew* or *Just William* book from the library, making Mammy and Nana think that the sun, moon and stars shone out of her arse. It wasn't as if she was some class of Einstein or anything. I didn't know what all the fuss was about being able to read a few mouldy books.

We headed off down the laneway, Sam trotting ahead of us with that rocking-horse gache of hers, the stiffness of her spine mocking the way the poor cratur used to be able to fly along. But she was happy to be heading for the river and that was the main thing. At the other side of the road, we climbed the stone stile into the long beet field and, from there, down the grassy boreen running beside the walled garden of the old mansion owned by the filthy-rich Dan Mulhall. He had a big clothes shop in the middle of Cork city. Old money, not that useless bank money, Daddy said. Dan was convinced that the end of the world was going to land in on us ever since the Cuban Crisis. I couldn't tell you much about the Cuban Crisis only that it must have put the fear of God in half the parish because they were still talking about it seven years later in the summer of '69. One of the local girls who worked as a maid in Mulhall's house said there were enough tins of food in the cellar to feed an army, and that the mice had bellies like barristers from enjoying royal feasts on big bags of rice and flour before they were thrown out on account of the mice ating holes in them.

"Mad as a March hare," Nana said, whenever Dan's name was mentioned.

His English housekeeper, Dorothy, tried her best to keep him in order. There had been a lot of people talking out of the sides of their mouths about Dorothy in the parish when she'd arrived about three years before but most of it was lost on me.

"'Tisn't for winding the clock he hired her," remarked one of the men leaning against the chapel wall after early Mass one Sunday.

"The older the goat, the giddier," said another.

When I questioned Mammy about these remarks, she changed the subject. Daddy smirked.

Out of Dan Mulhall's determination to survive if everything happened to be blown to smithereens around us was born his decision to buy the mansion with a small river dam that generated electricity, not alone for the house but for a woollen mill downstream. The dam was one of my favourite play areas, all the better because it was dangerous and out of bounds unless Kieran was with us. But Kieran let me do nearly everything I wanted. Good job Mammy didn't know the half of it. The dam itself was barely two feet wide. On the upper side of it was the pond with a low-roofed boathouse tucked in under a steep laurel bank. On the other was a drop of about twenty feet down to a concrete basin, foamy white waterfalls crashing into it from two or three sluices. The waterfalls merged into a river flowing parallel to a by-road running above it. The sheer height of the dam scared the life out of me but I always concentrated on putting one foot in front of the other as I walked across the narrow wall that held the pond back.

A machinery shed with a galvanised roof was set against the dam, and a channel flowed out under this shed. Kieran, Tamara, Sam and myself went down the rough concrete steps to the channel which was full of perch so hungry they would swallow practically everything we dropped in. It was the nearest thing to a pirhana pit I could imagine this side of the Amazon. Alright, books can be good for something.

"Look, Tamara," Kieran said, dropping the line with a silver metal lure into the dark water. "This is the Mepps. Watch it go to work."

A pack of shadows shot towards the bait on cue. He swung the line out of the water and dropped the writhing fish onto the concrete. A fan of spikes rose on its back as it thrashed. Tamara screamed. I wasn't a big fan of perch myself but I kept silent. Secretly, I was sorry for the poor, starved fish. 'Twas a wonder to me how they weren't ating each other. Maybe the spikes were putting them off.

"Naw, that's too way too aisy," Kieran said, unhooking the fish and dropping it back into the water.

Away from the sound of the crashing water and the hum of the machinery, the ground opened up into a grassy area where the river from the dam flowed on one side and the water from the canal full of perch made a separate passage. The briars were weighted with blackberries and we stopped to pick some. I showed Tamara how to judge the good ones by the white spot the size of a crumb where the fruit joined the stem. If there was no white mark, they were no good. Soon our lips and fingers were stained purple. I located a squashy one with a fine, white maggot nesting where the good spot used to be. Tamara wrinkled her nose in disgust before running ahead of me. She had a lot to learn, that city girl.

The main river flowing out of the dam beside the main road passed on under a curtain of trees. Mammy was always saying things like that. 'Curtain of trees', I mean. Some of it rubbed off on me and the teachers used to be delighted when I said anything fancy. 'Twasn't too often they were delighted with me then. Shiny lengths of fishing gut had snagged on the lower branches. Kieran selected a branch from an alder tree, and whittled it down to form a fork to hold the rod when he stuck it in the ground. He took three balls of lead from his pocket, ran the line through the fold in the middle of each and pressed them close to hold the line. Next he took a slimy worm from the wriggling heap in the tin can, and pulled the hook through the soft flesh in two places until it was kind of crucified – not that I was thinking it was anything like Jesus, in case I'd be struck down. I loved the way Kieran could do it so quick and handy, like, without spilling the worm's guts out.

Tamara's lips shaped a perfect 'O' of horror. Would she ever toughen up? I had my work cut out for me.

Kieran cast the line and the worm disappeared beneath the surface. He rested the rod on the fork in the stick and the line hung taut.

"Now we wait until we see something like this," he said, tapping the line to make it twitch. "Then we'll be in business."

Tamara and myself sat on either side of Kieran on the grassy bank. Sam had finished sniffing the territory and lay down behind us. The sun was hot on her coat. Bees buzzed on their way past. The afternoon drowsed. I felt as if I would doze. Kieran's eyes had a faraway look – far away with Kitty probably. I picked a long blade of grass and began to chew the juicy stalk. Tamara did the same. I picked another wide blade, placed it between my thumbs and demonstrated how to blow a squeaky sound from it until Kieran told me to stop or I'd frighten all the trout away.

"I don't know if I come fishing for the fish or just for the excuse of sitting down here doing nothing," he said. "It's a pity what the fish have to go through for this peace and quiet."

"And the worms," I said. "Couldn't you just come and sit down here anyway?"

"Ah, it wouldn't be the same," he said, turning his gaze

31

on Tamara. "Have you anything like this over in London? Maybe in one of those big parks – Hyde Park or Kensington Gardens? Do they have rivers? Ponds maybe. Yeah, ponds I suppose with goldfish as long as your arm. Savage goldfish raring up like sharks and swallowing entire ducks with a gulp."

Kieran had this habit of asking Tamara questions and answering them for her, rambling on as if it was the most natural thing in the world, inventing the maddest stories.

"Am I right, Tamara?" he asked. "Enormous duck-eating goldfish that'd swallow a child alive if the go-car tipped over and landed them in the water."

She shook her head vigorously and smiled.

Kieran said, "Arrah, I suppose I'll have to invent an answer until you're ready to enlighten us. Will that be any day soon?"

This nudge surprised me as much as it did Tamara. In fairness, I think he caught himself on the hop too. More often than not, we were content to hold our peace about Tamara's silence. And he was usually down on top of me like a ton of bricks me when I tried to get her to talk. "I'm not tormenting her," I used to say. "It's for her own good. She can't be waltzing around like a dummy all her life."

Well, surprise, surprise, he was the big tormentor himself this time, so he was. Tamara dropped her gaze and the green stalk fell from her mouth, a trail of spit hanging from it. She blushed and wiped her mouth with the back of her hand. I felt sorry for her.

"Don't mind that buck ape," I said. "Come on, I want to show you something."

Poor Sam was so deaf she didn't hear us leave. She was lost in a doggie dream, her paws quivering as if she was off running somewhere.

We followed the lazy, brown river downstream to a shady spot where it elbowed into a deep pool with a bank of washed gravel beside it. There I taught Tamara how to skim flat stones. The more we practised, the farther they made it across the water to the overhanging trees. She was right good at it. I think she got about five skims before long, maybe six even. That was mighty going. There was some hope for her.

We moved further downstream to where the grassy valley dipped and gave way to a stony plateau set below the main river that had been channeled through a mass concrete casing at that point to divert it down to the old mill wheel. 'Plateau' – that was one of Mammy's words. Daddy says her words are getting so big he'll have to bring them up the haggard and chop them up with the hatchet. Anyway, there were deep pools set into the rock, a grand place altogether. It was a watery world, hidden away from everything and filled with the sound of racing water. The channel that began with the starving perches at the dam continued on a separate course from the river and entered the lower side of the plateau through a tall grille set upright and checking its flow. The grille had become choked with twigs and dead leaves, backing up the water until it formed a deep pool with a bank of gravel at its edge. I found two strong sticks washed up on the gravel. I took one and began to poke at the grille, forcing the stuck stuff out the other side and letting the water run more freely. Tamara watched me for a few minutes, the way one chimpanzee will learn from another. Then she took the second stick and attacked the grille with it. We worked together, dislodging pebbles, twigs, leaves and other rubbish until about half the grille was clear, the torrent of water was increasing and the pool beside us had shrunk to a small stream. It was satisfying work, but our clothes were damp from it and the air was growing cool in the shade.

Kieran was still sitting in the sunshine when we got back to him, but the evening shadows were lengthening.

"Any luck?" I called.

"Shut up," he hissed, putting his finger to his lips. "Do you remember anything I told you? Mam's right. In one ear and out the other."

"Sorry."

Kieran was always drilling into me the importance of approaching the riverbank silently. But silence wasn't always enough, he'd explain. You had to watch for the light as well. If the sun was in the right position and your shadow wasn't cast over the water, you could observe the trout, holding their place in the current beside the streaming green weed, motionless except for their beating gills. It took a few minutes for the eyes to adjust so you could see them. Any sound or shadow from the bank and they darted out of sight.

"Can we go home now? It's way past teatime and I'm starving," I said.

"I want to try for one more to keep that fella company," Kieran said.

I summoned Tamara and we went to inspect the trout. There he lay, cold and slimy, eyes glassy, his body dotted with rainbow spots above the white underbelly.

"Watch this," I said, running my fingers down along the body until two brown worms of his you-know-what shot from his underbelly like ointment from a tube. I got the desired result when Tamara squealed.

"For feck's sake, Sally, I told you to keep quiet!" Kieran said.

34

"That was her, not me. Anyway, I told you, we're starving. And we're cold."

"There's nothing stopping you going home on your own. On second thoughts, I don't trust you. Just sit down there and hold your whisht until I'm ready."

The entire bank was in shadow by now. I sniffed my hands. The smell of the trout was on them. I shoved one under Tamara's nose and she made a face. I pulled out tufts of grass and rubbed them between my fingers until the juice stained them green. I sniffed my hands again. They still smelled of fish but more faintly. I hugged myself with my arms to keep warm. Tamara did the same. Our eyes were on the line. I prayed for it to twitch. But it slanted there taut, the whole world contained in every minute. My stomach rumbled. I shivered. Downstream, a heron stood like a grey watchman.

"See that fella," I said to Tamara, and pointed to the heron. "We call them birds 'Johnny the Bog'."

Suddenly Kieran gave a low whistle. The line was twitching. Tamara's eyes were glued to it. The line circled and the top of the rod bent. Kieran began to reel it in. A trout broke the surface, flicking this way and that as if it were a single muscle. Kieran swung the rod towards him but before the line reached the bank, the fish slipped the hook and fell back into the water with a plonk. I was glad for the fish.

"Damn it," Kieran said. "Come on. I've had enough."

We walked home in the half-light. Bats swooped low over our heads, hunting the clouds of midges. Every so often we had to stop and wait for Sam.

The Donovans' house was set back a little from the main road, in a big field not far from the turn-off for our own house. A light was gleaming from one of the upstairs windows.

"Here, take this for a minute," Kieran said, landing the fishing rod into my hands.

He climbed up on the ditch and stood behind an ash tree. He cupped his two hands in front of his mouth and made a strange calling noise, a bit like one of the Indians in a cowboy film.

A silhouette of a girl appeared in a lighted upstairs window.

"*Is that you, Kieran Mahony?*" she said.

Once she spoke, I knew it was Kitty.

Kieran said nothing but repeated the same warbling cry.

"*I know it's you, Kieran!*" she said, leaning out into the dusk.

I kicked a loose stone into the ditch.

It was nearly dark by now and a cut of the moon was lighting up. Tamara was taken up with the Romeo and Juliet antics of the pair of eejits.

Even when I mimicked Kitty in a high tone, she didn't laugh. We were only about ten minutes' walk from home but I didn't want to continue on my own. Kieran was still doing his imitation of a lovesick owl and Kitty was simpering in the square of light. Well, my eyes couldn't see so well in the dark but what else would she be doing with Romeo cooing at her?

Tamara tugged at my sleeve and pointed to the window with a questioning look in her eyes.

"That's Kitty Donovan," I said. "We think she's his girlfriend, but we don't know."

Tamara looked downcast. She wrapped her skinny arms around herself. Neither of us had brought cardigans with us.

Kieran was still doing his stupid yodelling. He was cracked as the crows. I stepped towards the ditch and poked him in the behind with the fishing rod.

"Come on home, we're perished with the cold."

"*Good night, Kitty!*" he shouted.

"*There. I knew it was you, Kieran! I knew it all along!*"

She retreated into the room and closed the window.

I hoped a pile of moths and midges and even the odd bat had flown in while they were yapping.

Kieran was seriously losing it if he thought she really liked him. I had seen her at the hunt the winter before, laughing and talking with the twin Callaghan brothers who were off in boarding school in Kilkenny. I wouldn't like to be the one to tell our Kieran that. Mild as he was, he had a vicious temper when roused and I wasn't going to be the one to take the brunt of it.

5

Tamara

They call the big cow Bernard. You wonder why a "she" is given a man's name but you can't ask.

"Go for the cows and bring Tamara with you," Auntie Jenny tells Sally.

Sally sighs. Her mother frowns.

"Give over that sighing. What a big job I'm asking you to do!"

"We'll miss *Flipper*. It's on soon. We'll never be back in time to watch it. You know it's my favourite programme."

"It's far from dolphins you were raised. If you went back the land the first time I asked you, instead of catfarting around the place, you'd have plenty of your *Flipper*."

"You're always giving out to me," Sally says.

This much is true, you know. But Sally has an answer for every criticism. You admire this in her.

"If you did what you were told the first time you were asked, then maybe I wouldn't be giving out to you so often. Put the skids under yourself now. Your father will give you *Flipper* if he's waiting too long to start the milking."

Going 'back the land' for the cows is generally Kieran's job, but he has a hurling match this evening and he's going through the fields with you both before taking a shortcut down through the Hilly Field to the main road and on to the village. Hurling must be something special. You have gathered by now that it consists of men running around a field very fast with sticks. It's a lot like hockey really, except the sticks are thicker. No excuses are taken here for missing out on the work, but Kieran is let off without a problem for this match. They all laughed when, at first, you thought he was a hockey player. You drew a picture of a hockey game.

Kieran is always fooling around with the hurley when he gets a spare minute. The hurley and the strange little ball with all the ridges.

"Look, Tamara, this is the shliotar," he says. "Catch it if you want."

Shliotar – I later discover there should be no 'h' at the start of the word but they pronounce it as if there is. A strange word for a strange little thing you can hardly believe is a ball.

You touch the hard ridge running around the leather surface.

"Imagine getting a belt of that on the side of the head," Sally says, as you both watch Kieran strike it straight into the middle of the field with the hurley.

"*Come on, you slow coaches, race you to find it!*" he calls.

The wind is tugging at you as soon as you leave the shelter of the farm buildings.

Kieran turns to you. "Can you feel it? Can you feel it in the wind?"

You stretch out your arms out and whirl around, coming to a stop with your face turned into the wind, your hair streaming behind you. But you are puzzled. You don't know what you're supposed to be feeling.

"It's the rain, Tamara," Kieran says. "You can feel it in

the wind. I can't describe it. You have to feel it for yourself."

You hold your face into the stream of air coursing past you. You wait. How is it different? Cooler, a hint of moisture hovering. You feel it, or are you wishing you do? The swallows are slicing low over the grass, lower than you've ever seen them fly before. It's as if they are escaping something in the sky, dropping down beneath it.

"See them," Kieran says. "That's another sign. They feel it coming too. That's why they're dipping low."

The Stall Field climbs a slope towards the highest part of the farm. It's full of prickly thistles with purple flowers that bees love. The thistles scratch your legs as you weave your way through them. You crash one foot through a crusted pie of cow manure and the khaki-green feeling oozes out – that smell! – but you're wearing wellingtons and you're racing on again. You want to find the sliotar first. Your eyes tracked its flight towards the ditch. On you fly, faster than your cousins. If there is one thing you can do well, it's run. At the ditch, you kick the grass margin with your wellington toes, searching out the hardness of the ball – well, what passes for a ball. Kieran and Sally have begun to do the same.

A foot away from you, you glimpse the faintest of tracks in the grass. Above it, the earth is bare, and nesting at the mouth of a hole is the sliotar! You grab it and jump up and down, waving it.

Kieran reaches you first. "Good girl yourself. You ran like the wind, didn't she, Sall?"

Sally pretends not to hear him. You catch her scowling before she turns towards the ditch. Your elation dims.

"Look what I found," Sally says. "I never knew they were out."

She extends a palmful of yellow berries to Kieran and, you gather, you are not included in the offer to taste. They look like raspberries except they are yellow instead of pink, yellow like the pineapple chunk sweets sold out of jars in the village shop. Kieran takes one. Sally offers you the other one – for shame's sake or are you wronging her? These are wild raspberries and they're sweeter than any raspberry you've ever tasted. Summer explodes to the very roof of your mouth. The three of you search out more of the lemon berries hidden behind the green canes on the ditch.

You keep eating until Kieran says, "Come on, or there'll be a search party out for you! I have to high-tail it down the road to the pitch."

The herd is grazing in the Primrose Field. You can't see any primroses but you know it's the right name. It corresponds with the map you have in your head, a map woven from the stories Daddy told you in fits and snatches when you were stopped at traffic lights on the Edgware Road or sitting on a sunlit bench in Holland Park, or on winter evenings when the rain slid down the basement window. The Lough Field, The Small Lough, and on and on until here you are now in the Primrose Field, not as you imagined it studded with yellow clusters, but filled with enormous black-and-white cows grazing between the purple-topped thistles and clumps of white and purple clover. The clouds are grey today, whipped along by a lively wind cutting through your blue Crimplene dress. You're sorry that you didn't wear Sally's hand-me-down anorak.

Sally begins to shout, *"How how how!"*, and the cows lumber slowly into a line.

You begin to giggle. How what? you ask yourself. How

now brown cow? Only they're not brown. Sally stands beside you, close to the gap leading out of the field. The cows are following a narrow path of beaten earth in the centre of the field.

One hulking cow is leading the procession that follows in single file along the length of the field. Their great udders are swinging. As the big cow passes through the gap, she pauses and turns her limpid eyes to meet yours exclusively. They are dark, glossy pools. What does she think of you, a small-eyed skinny creature, you wonder.

"Hello, Bernard, my lovely lady," Sally says, stepping forward and leaning against her barrel belly. "Lean up against her – she doesn't mind. We're old friends."

The cow's body is warm against your cheek, your arm, your hip. You sway with her, mesmerised by the warmth, the rhythm, by Sally's voice telling you that her father named her for Saint Bernard who looks after animals, that she is their leader, that no other cow dares to take her place at the head of the line, that it's her job to lead them all through the fields along the well-trodden brown ribbon of path down the Stall Field and into the stall, that Bernard is her father's favourite and her mother swears he would have Bernard in the bed with the two of them if it were possible.

The concrete set in front of the great gaping door of the stall is mottled with cow dung. You stand back with Sally as the cows file in past you. One cow stops, lifts her tail high and rigid. You watch a stream of yellow pee cascade down and hit the ground frothing.

"It's not something you'd see every day in London," Sally says to me.

The stall is fashioned from corrugated iron – walls, doors, roof. The roof is low and slanting with skylights set

43

here and there in it. The smell indoors is a blend of the sweetness of hay and the sharp tang of fresh cow dung. You come in the side door, the door that scrapes off the stone floor when it is pulled out at night. Do all doors have to scrape here?

Sally begins to help your uncle settle the cows. Each one is eager for the measure of ration in the curved trough at the head of every byre. Sally walks down the inside, putting scoops of ration in the troughs. The ration looks like flour but has a rougher texture.

The wind is rising outside. A loose sheet of iron is shuddering on the roof. Soon, the rain is drumming on the sheet iron, filling the space inside with a percussion that's competing with the ticking of the milking buckets. They tick like a clock, like the equipment in the hospital where she . . . The hospital you don't want to remember. You lean up against the warm belly of a cow called Primrose, absorbed by the comforting heat, the milky smell. The bucket ticks away underneath her, milk streaming through the four cups attached to her udder.

Uncle Con comes to detach a full bucket from the cow beside you. This cow is called Snow White, according to the letters daubed in white paint on the wooden post. Two cats are following him on dainty paws, tails rigid as pokers, held high.

"Time to give the piscíns their supper," he says.

"Show her Pangur's trick before you fill their pan," Sally says.

"I will so I will," he says. "It's so long since I've tried that one that I've nearly forgotten it. It will be a test for Pangur's memory as well."

He crosses to the other row of cows waiting to be milked.

"*Pish pish pish*," he calls to the white cat, who suddenly gives him her full attention.

Familiar with the signal, she opens her mouth just in time for him to direct a jet of milk straight into it from the cow's teat. You clap your hands.

"And some people doubt the intelligence of four-legged creatures," he says. "Pangur and more of these piscíns would leave the two-legged creatures at the starting blocks."

The warm smell of milk wafts from the bucket he carries down through the passage. Sally follows him and so do you.

In the wide space before you come to the dairy door, he stops, puts down the milk bucket, and shakes stray wisps of hay from a battered and dirty white enamel dish. He splashes some milk in. The two cats stick their heads into the dish. As if by magic, four more cats drop down from the big wooden Ford crate nearby. He pours a little more in between their heads, splashing them, but they continue drinking without taking any notice of their milky christening.

"I shouldn't be pouring my profits away on those mangy old cats. Every cat in the parish will be lodging here if they spread the word about the good feeding."

"Mammy says they earn their meals as rat-catchers," Sally says.

"The rats will be dancing polkas of delight if we keep on filling the cats' bellies," he says. "They'll think they're in a holiday camp. A cat will never be a good hunter if she's not hungry."

Sally begins to walk out the stall door.

Her father calls her. "Where are you off to, young missy?"

"I'm going down home for a jumper," she says. "I'm cold."

"Well, come back up straight away because I need a hand washing down the dairy, with Kieran away at the match winning glory for the parish. Jack Murphy is calling for his pump tonight and I have another bit of work to do on it. Go down with her, Tamara, and get a jumper or an anorak for yourself too."

You stand beside Sally at the open door. The rain is already pooling in the haggard. Sally gives a backward glance to make sure her father is out of sight before she sprints across the yard to the hayshed You outstrip her. You love the hayshed, the perfume of the hay, the cocoon between the top bales and the roof. Kieran says you climb like a piscín. Up the fragrant wall of hay you shimmy, digging your toes into the crevices between the bales, grasping fistfuls of hay as you go, reaching in to grab the baling twine when you can. You know Sally is doing her best to gain on you but you are half a body-length ahead when you pull yourself over the final row and into the barrel-vault of the metal roof where the rain is still drumming away.

"I am sick to the back teeth of all this work," she said. "We may as well be slaves."

You try to draw up a list of conditions that would qualify Sally as a slave but concrete examples are sorely lacking.

She is lying back, her hands folded behind her head. She continues in the same vein, listing all her jobs, becoming most vehement when she reaches cleaning out the henhouse. She wrinkles her nose in disgust. "Hens' shit. The smell of it. I don't know which is worse – when it's hard-packed in the ground or when it's freshly made, soft and green like snails."

You know that she is scarcely aware that you are beside her. You chew on honeyed wisps of hay, still slightly green.

She is still droning on when you hear the sound. It's hard to discern the source, given the rain and Sally's voice. You might be imagining it. You relax again until you hear a faint half-cry. You touch Sally's shoulder. She flinches.

"Jesus, you put the heart crossways on me. What's the matter with you, as if you would bother telling me?"

You put your finger to your lips and then next to your ear.

She sits bolt upright. "You're spooking me."

There's silence. You're sorry you caught her attention. The rain has receded to a patter. You feel foolish. She will have ammunition for the night at least. But then you both hear it. Crying. A weak mewing, but audible to you both. Sally's eyes light up. She reminds you of Kieran's harrier Trouncer, when he comes alive at the scent of a fox or a rabbit. She follows the sound back into the bales where the light is dimmer. There, in a bowl-sized depression in the hay nestle three black-and-white kittens, eyes closed and snuffling together. They could be cast from gold bullion, Sally looks so pleased. You are too. She picks up one tenderly, cups it in her palms and holds it under her chin. You do the same. It snuffles against you, pink nose and mouth, tiny claws, a tight ball of life. You hold it to your cheek, feel the vibrations of it.

"They must belong to Maid Marion," Sally says. "I knew she must have had them and hidden them away somewhere because her belly was gone flat again."

Sally places the kittens back in their hay bowl, more tender than you've ever seen her before. You replace your kitten and watch the three of them blindly seeking each other. The words of 'Three Blind Mice' are in your head.

You can hear Uncle Con calling from the haggard.

"He'll have my guts for garters," Sally says. "Come on, we'd better face the music."

6

Sally

The idea came to me during the rosary, not wonderful timing I'll admit. We were all kneeling on the red earthenware tiles, elbows on the kitchen chairs, eyes staring through the spindles like monkeys in Dublin Zoo.

There was Mammy, Nana, Kieran, Tamara and myself. My father was still out in the shed, dismantling a Dexter.

'Holymarymotherofgodprayforussinnersnowandattheho urofourdeathamen.'

The words swirled over the range with the water urn on top, past the shiny green press that Mammy always knocked on the door of to frighten the mice before opening, and over the table where the freshly made pots of crabapple jelly were the colour of diesel. Nana had a half-smile on her face looking at Tamara, who knelt there, lips pursed.

Kieran had told me that Tamara was Nana's way of getting Uncle Jack back to her – well, the piece of him that was his daughter. Granddad, a hot-tempered man that I could barely remember, ordered that Jack was not to get as much as a red penny, a boggy acre, not a single, sickly bonabh. He signed the farm over to my mother for fear Nana would go soft in the head when he died. Nana wore him down until he agreed to put a thousand pounds aside for Jack – on condition that he stayed over in London with that 'London wife' of his. That he did, even when the 'London wife' died and he needed Tamara taken care of until his latest turn on the oil rigs had finished, until he could make arrangements. That was how she arrived in our house. Minus her voice.

"*To thee do we cry, poor banished children of Eve*," my mother recited.

I wondered if the words hit home with the poor banished child in front of me.

Two beetles, as black and glossy as liquorice, emerged from the ashes under the range to scurry around the floor with a purpose known only to themselves. They made this excursion every night during the rosary as if the prayers were a signal for their appearance. I swooped and caught one between finger and thumb and deposited it on top of Tamara's fair hair. Sensing the weight, she put a hand up to check it out. The alarmed beetle fell on its back on the chair in front of her, legs flailing. She tipped back on her heels, wailing like a banshee but sadly uttering no intelligible sound.

My mother hit me a stinging slap across the face. "Sally, have you no conscience? And during the rosary. You have the heart scalded on me."

There was no need for them all to make such a big fuss about it. All I was trying to do was to get her to flipping say something. Anything. Shock therapy. Like giving someone a fright to make them stop hiccoughing. That's how I explained it. Not that anyone was listening to me – they were too busy consoling 'poor Tamara'. I was sent to bed like a baby while the evening light went on for ever and ever outside the window.

But the shame of my punishment all but disappeared

with the arrival of the combine harvester to start the barley harvest the following day. When I got to the Lantern Field, I was winded from the run. The rusty gate was thrown to one side in a tangle of briars. Tamara was trailing behind me, wearing yet another Crimplene dress from the blue suitcase that had arrived with her. This one was rose-pink with a band of rainbow at the top. A rose-pink like the icing on my birthday cake when I was twelve in June. I was standing beside a furze bush at the edge of the gap when Tamara caught up.

The combine harvester was growling in the distance. The heat shimmered over the island of rustling barley, soon to be devoured by the hungry red Massey Ferguson. Kieran was perched up behind the driver on the Massey, as he called it when he was acting the big man. Tamara had never seen such a beast before. She was more used to the red double-deckers in London, I imagine. Not that she was likely to tell me. I could have asked her but I was tired of the nod-of-the-head, shake-of-the-head business. She was constantly on my heels since she arrived the same week that the black-and-white moon surface flickered on our telly in the kitchen. One small step for man, one giant pain in the behind for me.

The sun was a blowtorch scorching my head. Tamara followed me across the stubble. You could see the stones and the dusty earth in between the shorn stalks, like the scalp showing between the crease in my father's hair when he slicked it down with brilliantine. Tamara was like a barley stalk herself. Five months younger than me, yet she towered over me by a head. Four weeks out in the breezy high fields under the summer sun had barely put a blush on her cheeks. She looked like someone who came out only at night: a vampire feeding on my days.

51

"Mind her now, Sally," my mother had called, hands deep in the mixing bowl as we left the kitchen. "None of your cod-acting, I'm warning you. Keep well back from that machine."

The combine was down near Driscolls' boundary when we reached the grain trailer parked beside the ditch. I scaled the trailer's mustard-yellow sides and dived into the cooling masses of barley. There was nothing but blue sky above me until Tamara's face appeared over the side, her spindly arms dragging her up and over. She hunkered into a corner.

"What are you looking at?" I asked.

As she dropped her gaze I felt bad. It's not that I meant to be nasty to her, but she just brought it out in me. She was such a copycat. The combine rumbled closer. I could smell the warm diesel fumes, the cooking rubber of the mill-wheel tyres. The machine pulled up beside the trailer and the long arm of the chute extended above me. Grain poured out.

It began as a game. I jumped in and out of the shower of barley. The trailer was just about half-full, so I knew Kieran and the driver couldn't see us over the high metal sides.

"Come on, jump in," I told Tamara.

She shook her head. I wish she had stayed back in the kitchen with Mammy and Nana, or back where she belonged in London. The barley cascaded from my head, flowing under the neck of my check shirt. The pointy grains were pricking my skin. I jumped away and shook them from my hair. The bed of cool, flinty beads moved under me when I threw myself down. The combine moved to even the load and the chute poured the grain onto my legs like water gushing from a drainpipe in a thunder shower. The tide flooded my thighs and my stomach with a speed that took me by surprise. It advanced across my chest and I struggled to get up. Another gush hit my face like hail. I tried to turn my face away from it.

"*Help!*" I screamed before I lost sight of Tamara's scared face behind the beaded curtain.

My lungs were going to burst. The roar of the combine was muffled. I tried to shout but my mouth filled with the raw taste of barley. I couldn't move.

Suddenly the engine sounded clearer, the light was brighter on my smarting eyes and my mouth was free to gulp the air. The flow continued but Tamara's bony fingers were drumming frantically on my face to keep it clear. Even if she shouted as loudly as my father herding the cows, they would never hear her above the roar of the engine. My own words had been sucked out of me, the terror and the grain rushing in to fill the space they left behind.

The trailer was more than half full and the barley rising fast. Tamara was digging like a thing demented. Her hands moved like pistons and the grain rained over the trailer and into the field. My face covered, cleared, covered.

There was a thump beside me. I could make out Kieran's voice somewhere above my burial mound.

"*Tamara, you eejit, what are you doing with the good grain?*" he shouted. "*Where's Sally?*"

Just as I felt I was going to smother, my face was clear again. I gasped for breath like a fish on the riverbank.

"Christ almighty!" he said, as his eyes met mine.

He dug for my arms, grabbed them and pulled me up and up until I rose from the depths, spluttering and choking.

There was no end to the post mortem across the sea-

53

green formica table at teatime. What could have happened but for the grace of the Good God and His Blessed Mother, and the intervention of Tamara and Kieran. The entire rosary was given over in thanksgiving for my deliverance from death by drowning in barley.

My head hurt and earlier, in the spattered bathroom mirror, I looked as if I had chicken pox.

Nana had the telly on at full pitch.

"Is there no off-button on that thing?" my father enquired with a fake mildness.

A pot of small potatoes boiling for the hens filled the kitchen with steam. I needed air. As I sidled through the kitchen door, I felt someone watching me. Tamara. She was waiting for a signal. The old annoyance prickled but I nodded. She was off the chair like a greyhound.

Up in the haggard, we climbed onto the flat corrugated iron roof of the calves' shed built against the barn. I sat leaning back against the barn slates that still held the heat of the day. I closed my eyes and let the warmth seep into me.

Tamara nudged me. What next? Why couldn't she let me alone just for this once? I opened my eyes. She was offering me a stick of barley sugar. She reminded me of a sheepdog pup hungering for a soft word, a pat on the head, yet fearful of a kick.

I remembered my near-burial. I broke the stick in two and gave her half. We sucked the orange twists of boiled sweet. The sun was a Massey-red disc balanced on top of the Stall Field. Second by second, it sank like a fiery coin that God was thumbing down into the hill. Minute by minute, the fire of the clouds cooled until they were the colour of barley sugar. We sat side by side, watching the evening sky and crunching the sweetness.

54

＃

7

Tamara

You stay up all through the night in the kitchen with Kieran and Sally, to wait for the dawn. They teach you how to toast grains of barley with sugar under the grill of the gas cooker. It's sweet, sticky and hard as grit between your teeth. It's a primitive popcorn. They get a packet of oxtail soup and boil it up on the gas. The smell of gas gives way to the smell of soup that makes your tummy rumble. You dunk white bread in the bowl and spoon up the soft, spicy mouthfuls. They get out the cards and teach you how to play Pontoon and Thirty-One. Or *try* to teach you. Your eyes are smarting – it's an effort to keep them open and you want to go to bed. Finally, even though it's still pitch black outside, they put on their coats and you put on yours. Even Sam doesn't want to leave the hearthstone in front of the range at first, but then she rises stiffly and stretches out her front legs.

You walk past the line of palm trees bordering the Screen Field across from the stall, putting one foot carefully in front of the next on the stony path. You pass into the grassy laneway bordering the Stall Field which leads you out onto the hilltop. You walk through the high fields where the barley stubble has grown softer underfoot. Sam is sniffing every rock, every tree, and especially every rabbit burrow you pass in the ditches. Two or three times you have to tug Kieran's jacket and point back to her so that they will wait for her.

"Remember the day in the trailer?" he says to Sally.

She throws him a dagger look. "I don't want to remember it. It's enough to have it coming to me in my dreams."

There's a cool breeze blowing across the hill. Bushes and saplings are shaking. Some of them are casting strange shadows. Your two guides get ahead of you and you are terrified they will disappear. They scramble up onto a ditch overlooking the next field where the cows loom out of the gloom like dark islands. You pause to give Sam a helpful push up the ditch. She rewards you with a growl. When you follow them down the other side, you see what they are looking towards – a silvery crack on the horizon.

"Here she comes," Kieran says. "Watch."

The silver band grows wider and wider by the minute. Banks of grey cloud are broken apart by bars of brightness. A pinky light grows deeper. It spills across the sky but one grey lake escapes the colour. Crows are crossing the pearly sky, their black wings reminding you of loose stitches called tacking. A rooster crows far below in the farmyard. Birdsong is rising too. The pigeons sound chesty.

A sound of barking comes from way off in the distance. Sam yaps back. One of the cows, lying on the dewy grass, lumbers up on her front legs but then seems to think better of it and settles down again. The sound of the distant barking rises once more.

"You think that's a dog?" Sally says smugly.

By her tone, you know she holds some secret card. Do you nod or shake your head? Before you decide which, Kieran speaks.

56

"It's a fox," he says.

Sally breaks in as if she is the teacher addressing the class.

"He's barking to find out where the dogs are," she says. "When he hears a dog barking in a certain farm, he won't go there that day."

The light in the east is spreading. Now the birds begin to sing all around. They remind you of the parks in the squares between Earls Court and Kensington, of glossy laurels and trees burgeoning behind the railings, of the invisible choirs of city birds creating their own mini-world beside the traffic, the concrete, the fanlights set above elegant doors. A pang of loneliness steals up on you like a mugger on a half-lit street.

You follow Kieran and Sally across the damp grass of the field where you hear the cows chewing the grass with a steady rhythm. Sally skips ahead and calls to Kieran. She is holding up something small and white between her fingers. When you catch up, the two of them are doubled over, picking white lumps from the grass. The smaller lumps remind you of an opal ring *she* used to wear. An Australian opal she got from an old boyfriend.

"Come on," Sally says. "Help us pick them."

You mask your puzzlement to prevent another episode of what Tamara doesn't know. But Sally is so preoccupied with her task, she doesn't notice your ignorance. The three of you fan out across the field. You pick up one of the little globes, and hold it to your nose. It's a mushroom. The pink pleats fanning out underneath the white cap are more perfect than you have ever seen in a shop at home. You imagine what she'd say if she were here. *It's a work of art.*

Kieran takes off his jumper, lays it on the damp grass

and places the mushrooms he has collected in the centre of it. Sally deposits her collection with his. You add yours to the white pile. All the cows are on their feet now and the daylight has flooded the field. Pink clouds are billowing way off to the west.

"Plenty for ourselves for the breakfast with more to spare for auld Mulhall," Kieran says.

You are heading out through the gap into the next field when a furze bush on the ditch catches your eye. The bush has a white lacey covering and it's sparkling with little drops of water that could pass for diamonds. The beauty of it stops you in your tracks. Kieran glances over his shoulder and doubles back when he sees you standing there.

"Oh but the city girl sees things with different eyes, doesn't she?" he says. "Sally and myself walked right past that."

Sally has turned back also. You can feel a nature lesson coming on but she's surprisingly silent.

"I always think it's lovely," she says, "but you have to be up so early in the morning to see it. When we were small, Mam used to tell us it was the lace for the fairies' dresses, but it's the spiders' webs. We call it gossamer. There's loads of it."

She points to the other bushes back along the ditch, a chain of diamanté cloaks draping them all.

Back in the kitchen, the house is still quiet, apart from the clock ticking on the dresser. The metallic hen on its face is pecking away at tiny grains of corn as she always does. Kieran fills a small saucepan with mushrooms, a dab of butter and peppered milk and sets it to simmer on the black range.

He pokes the ashes between the grill until the fire

58

reddens again. A few sparks from a re-ignited stick fly towards him. He rubs his hands gleefully. "That's money on its way to me."

Tiny bubbles soon ring the edge of the pot, the milk wrinkles on the surface and the butter dissolves into a golden skin. Kieran takes three blue willow-pattern bowls from the dresser and divides the mushrooms. You spoon up one mushroom, soft and juicy, tasting of pepper and the earth. Soon nothing is left except the buttery milk the mushrooms have simmered in.

"Finish it like this," Kieran says, lifting the bowl to his mouth.

The three of you put the bowls to your lips. The milk holds the flavour of the mushrooms.

Kieran and Sally wipe their mouths with the backs of their sleeves and you copy them.

The two of them begin a debate on how much Dan Mulhall will pay for the remaining mushrooms they have arranged in a nest of grass and wrapped in a double sheet of *The Southern Star*.

"A penny each. That'll be two bob for the lot."

"If he's on the gargle, maybe a shiny half a crown."

"Go away, you gom! Do you take him for a pure stump of a fool altogether?"

"But what if he's off it and he's as cranky as a bag of cats?"

"We won't even get a smell of a sixpence if he's in one of those moods."

"What did he give us last year? I'd swear it was half a crown."

"He must have been well on the batter."

"Don't count your mushrooms before they're paid for."

You can picture the bronze and silver coins while

they're talking: the greyhound on the sixpence, the bull on the shilling and the horse on the half-crown. Your favourites are the hen and chickens on the big copper penny and the halfpenny with the sow and the piglets. You remember Daddy's mock astonishment when you came home from school talking about piglets. *Where are you going with your piglets? Doesn't everyone know they're bonabhs?* The bonabhs are probably the nicest thing you have seen since you came here: the cosy way they all snuggle in together under the red lamp that keeps them warm, their snuffles, their eyelashes, the very tang of them. And the mother sow. What a good mother she is, grunting and snuffling when they all lie under her and drink from her. Who says pigs are dirty? They have their own separate toilet area in the shed. How Sally and everyone else can sit down to the kitchen table and eat bacon and rashers, you will never understand.

The morning is flying by on wings. Milking is over and Kieran is itching to get away down to Mulhalls' with the mushrooms. Sally and himself are still pinning their hopes on making half a crown for their white treasures.

"Don't count your chickens before they're hatched," your aunt says as she passes through the kitchen with a bucket of eggs. "Now, a job for you two madams before you take off."

You are summoned with Sally to the big white enamel sink to wash away the green and brown smears from the eggshells. Some are still warm to the touch. Pieces of straw have stuck to one or two of the eggs that a broken egg has spilled over and stuck to like glue.

"Yuck," Sally says, picking up one of the dirty eggs. "Have they got the scutters or what? Why doesn't Kieran have to do any? It's not fair."

"That's little women's work," Kieran says.

You bend your head low over the egg you are dabbing because you know he has provoked her.

"You're not escaping either, my boy," your aunt says, flicking the blue-and-white tea towel in Kieran's face. "I've been waiting over a week for you to clean out the henhouse."

"*Nah-nah-na-nah-na!*" Sally chants.

Kieran protests in a half-hearted way but goes off to do the job.

You can't blame him for his reluctance. The stench of the dark henhouse is revolting. Sally tells you how she put her hand into a laying barrel one evening and her hand closed around something soft and furry instead of the eggs. A dead rat. You shudder. You have a fascination for the snail-like whorls the hens excrete in olive green and white but the fascination doesn't extend to coming into close proximity with them. How some of the eggs emerge so clean, you can't imagine. You like hunting for the nests of the ones who have escaped. These are the hens who are 'laying out', the ones taking their chance with the marauding fox. To discover a dozen or so eggs hidden deep inside a clump of nettles or buried in the fragrant hay is so different from gathering them from the straw-filled boxes in the henhouse. It's like a treasure hunt.

Kieran is back and taking the paper parcel of mushrooms from the dresser when your aunt accosts him.

"Sure there's no need for you to go down there. Let the girls off with the mushrooms," she says. "You know your father will be looking for you to give him a hand when he gets back from the creamery."

"Ah, Mam, we won't be that long, and Dan Mulhall mightn't give the girls a fair price," he says. "Himself won't mind if he thinks I'm making a few bob. Wasn't it enough that I cleaned out that stinking auld henhouse for you?"

Your aunt's face darkens. This is one of the shadows you have sensed since you came here: the conflict between Kieran and his father.

"How many times have I heard you promise to be back in time for some job?" she says. "I'm the fool landed with the job of telling him that you're not a lazy good-for-nothing. I'm growing tired of it, Kieran."

"Well, you won't have to be making any more excuses for me if I take the boat to England, will you?" Kieran snaps.

Stung by his words, she turns her back, takes the eggs from the draining board and places them in a yellow bowl.

You look at Kieran, your mouth open. Even Sally is shocked. You are glad Nana is still in bed and doesn't have to listen to Kieran's outburst.

The ticking of the clock fills the kitchen. The cock crows outside across the yard in the hen run. *Up she flew and the cock flattened her.*

Kieran storms out the kitchen door. You want him to come back, to tell her he is sorry, that he didn't mean it. You are shocked. Kieran leaving. How could you last here without him? He is like the pink comfort blanket with the lemon rabbits that you carried everywhere when you were little. He is the one who jokes with you, who keeps you going when all that country-night darkness feels as if it has seeped inside you. When you and Sally wake the morning after he has been to the dances, you slide your hand under the pillow to find the box of Smarties he had left there while you were sleeping. He is the one who has never tried to force you to talk. He is the one who keeps Sally in check when she is needling you. How will you last here if he leaves?

"Take those blasted mushrooms and follow him, the two of you," your aunt says, her back still turned. Her voice is full of tears. *Keeping the good side out like the cracked jug on the dresser.* She is letting the mask slip and this is new to you too.

Sally is in a daze. You take the parcel of mushrooms and hold it lightly between your hands. You catch Sally's eye and she follows you. At the back door she hesitates.

"Are you sure you're alright, Mam?"

My aunt doesn't turn around but she raises her right arm, as if she is dismissing us.

The roadway, two long fields and a grassy laneway running beside the high orchard wall lie between the farm gate and Mulhalls' cobbled backyard. Kieran is below at the roadside, head bent as he scuffs the gravel with his boots. The sky has clouded over and there is a light drizzle. No one speaks when you reach him and the three of you continue over the stile and into the first field without a word. Beyond the orchard, four beehives are set in a small grassy enclosure fenced off with barbed wire. The bees terrified you at first but now you are used to them. Beyond the hives there's a big stone outhouse with a weighbridge in front of its arched doorway. To the right, the ground falls away to a concrete path rounding a bend and dropping down to the backyard. All these sights are familiar to you as far as the bend because it's the route you follow down to the dam that provides electricity for the big house. On your fishing expeditions with Kieran, you have always turned left at the beehives into an avenue shaded by palm trees. To turn right and head for the yard is new to you and, as you follow Kieran and Sally, there is

63

a strangeness about the high stone storehouses set around the cobbled yard.

You turn the corner of one of the buildings and the back door is ahead of you. Between you and the door there's a small donkey. He ambles towards you, his long tail dipping towards the ground and curving up. Then you realise it's a dog, bigger than the Afghan hound that snarled at you in Knightsbridge. You drop the parcel of mushrooms in fright and dart between Kieran and Sally. The dog walks over and sniffs the newspaper but Kieran swoops in and grabs it before the dog can inspect it further. The cloud seems to have lifted from over him. You are relieved. He pats the dog on the head.

"How's tricks, Bran, old pal? Come out here, Tamara, and rub him. Poor auld Bran wouldn't hurt a fly."

You come and rub the wiry, grey hair on the head of the wolfhound. It has come to you that this is a wolfhound because you have seen pictures of one in a book of Irish fairy tales that Nana posted to you in Earls Court for your seventh birthday. They were the hunting dogs of the Irish kings, though Bran seems so gentle you can't imagine him hunting anything. He drops his stately head and sniffs at Sam, who is pointedly ignoring him.

"You know this poor old giant will kick the bucket when he's about eight," Kieran says. "It's the breed. And the bigger any dog is, the shorter his lifespan."

You feel sad for this big old dog with the soulful eyes. This day isn't living up to the bright promise of the dawn.

The three of you descend a flight of steps to the back door. Kieran raps at the blistered wood, and a young woman comes out. She flushes when she sees Kieran. Sally elbows you in the ribs. Later she will tell you that Mary Flynn was in Kieran's class in primary school but left early to take a job in Dan Mulhall's kitchen to earn some money to help her parents rear the brood at home. Mary was always sweet on Kieran.

"The boss is keeping to the bed these last few days but I'll get Miss Simpson," she says.

Even you, in your short time here, know that Miss Simpson alias Dorothy is mean. *She wouldn't give you the mange.* What the mange is, you have yet to discover, but you have a feeling it's nothing good.

The minutes tick by in the dusty yard. Out the housekeeper comes, thinking she is disguising her disapproval, but the smile she affects is as artificial as the brown make-up caking her face above the snow-white neck.

Kieran opens the newspaper to show her the mushrooms. You feel bad about this. You remember those door-to-door salesmen she was always trying to avoid at home in Earls Court.

"Splendid," the housekeeper says, pretending to be pleased. "Just the medicine to coax Mr Mulhall's appetite back. Let me get you something."

She disappears into the kitchen, and hopes rise again.

"It won't be as good as if Dan himself was there," Kieran whispers, "but she can't be that stingy."

It's Mary who returns to the door, so embarrassed that her eyes are turned to the ground. She stretches out her arm and thrusts a packet of Lemon Puff biscuits into Kieran's hand. Before he can react, she retreats and closes the door.

"*Well, bad cess to her!*" Kieran says, hurling the packet of biscuits on the flagstones.

"*Shhh,*" Sally says, picking up the biscuits. "She might complain about us at home."

"A grand reception she'll get for her griping, if she does," Kieran hisses. "The robber! Come on."

The tension is back again. You are not used to Kieran being like this. You hate the uneasy feeling that has crept up on you. The big house is so important, built on a cliff looking out over the brown river cutting across the flat fields, but all she can trade for the mushrooms is this miserable packet of biscuits.

The three of you retrace your steps up out of the yard and turn into the avenue leading down to the dam. You sit together on the wall and dismember the biscuits. You eat the honey-coated dry biscuit and throw the sickly cream filling into the water.

"That feckin stuff will poison half the bleddy fish in the pond," Kieran says.

Sally finds a light plank floating near one of the grilles, places a biscuit on top and propels it off out into the lake.

"Away you go on your voyage!" she says with a mock salute.

Her larking about is infectious, and Kieran smiles.

You are happy again.

8

Tamara

Balthasar is missing. Kieran has called Sally and yourself out to search the fields with him. He is frowning. You know he wants to find the horse before Uncle Con and the Donovans discover that he has broken out. The three of you start out from the Screen Field where he left the horse loose the evening before. The big green space stays totally empty, much as you want Balthasar's black shape to appear out of some corner.

"Why didn't you bring him back to the Donovans' last night instead of leaving him here?" Sally asks.

You can't imagine how she dares question Kieran because he is as tense as a wire.

"It doesn't matter why, does it?" he says. You can only guess that he is touchy because he stayed out riding late and took a chance on leaving Balthasar in the field overnight. "All that matters is that he's gone. Just don't say any more to me till we find him."

"There's no need to be so cross," she says. "I was only asking. It's not our fault. And we're trying to help you."

"It was nearly dark when I got back," he mutters. "I thought I'd be up early enough this morning to have him back down to Donovans' before Daddy saw him in the field."

Sally is wise enough not to comment on this. Early

Breda Joy

mornings are not Kieran's thing.

"We'll divide up," Kieran says. "I'll take the top fields. Sally, you go through the Small Lough and the Big Lough back to the Hilly Field." He turns to you. "Tamara, you know the Primrose Field and the Crabapple, don't you?"

You nod. You knew every one of those fields in your mind's eye before you ever set foot in this place. Your father recited the list of names so often you had them off by heart. *Primrose Field. Crabapple Field. Hilly Field. Upper Hilly Field. Mushroom Field. Small Lough Field. Big Lough Field. Upper Langtry Field. Lower Langtry Field. Stall Field. Top Field. Screen Field. The Well Field. Back Stack Stable Field. The Bog Field. The Lantern Field. The Coolach. The Fairy Fort – a place set apart.*

He drew a map in one of your copy books and marked in every last one of them for you. He sketched all the features with bare pencil strokes – the spring bubbling at the top of the Upper Langtry Field, the fairy rock hidden in the furze bushes in the Hilly Field, the stile leading to the Driscolls' farm, the crabapple tree with its bitter fruit, the wild mint growing at the edge of the Bog Field, the Ordnance Survey marker in the ditch in the Top Field, the big iron tank hidden in the heart of the Coolach which wasn't really a field at all but a marsh bordering the road.

"Are you listening to me?" Kieran says. He sounds exasperated. "Go right back through the Primrose Field and the Crabapple Field as far as the ditch of the Bog Field. I don't think he'll have gone that far, but we have to check everything. Just stand on the ditch and look in to make sure. But I know he's headed for the greener grass and not the bog."

Sam starts after Kieran when he begins to run but he sees her and shouts and waves his arms at her. It's like sign language for deaf dogs but you know there's no time to

68

laugh. Sam puts her tail between her legs and slinks back to the gate. She pauses there and looks mournfully over her shoulder for a long time. Her normal habit is to make a second attempt to follow but even she seems to sense the gravity of the situation and pushes herself stiffly under the lower bar of the gate.

You run through the fields as fast as you can. Most of the blackberries, so luscious and plentiful a month ago, have disappeared from the briars; the remaining ones have shrivelled back among the brown, curling leaves. The briars scratch your legs as you climb the last ditch into the Bog Field but you don't care. You are determined to find Balthasar. You want to do it for Kieran. He will be so delighted. You can see his face already. You can hear him thanking you. You can feel the importance of being the one who helped him. But this field is the last one, a boundary field. It's your last chance.

A thicket of scrawny trees is obscuring your view of the lower half of the field where no grass is growing because of the wetness of the land. You have heard your uncle talking about it in the kitchen.

"Better men than me have tried and failed to bring good out of that swamp," he said. "All the drains in the world wouldn't make a difference. There are too many springs bubbling underground."

The same night, he lifted his gaze and addressed Sally and yourself across the room. "And don't let me see either of the two of you within an ass's roar of that big drain near the boundary ditch. If you end up inside that, you won't stop sinking until you reach Australia."

You are heading straight for the drain now. Your feet are growing colder in your wellingtons as they squelch into the boggy soil. Deeper and deeper they sink until the water is coming over the top and filling them. Your stomach is churning but you keep forging ahead until, over the sucking sound of your wellingtons pulling clear of the mud with every step, you hear another sound. A thumping or a splashing up ahead.

. You head in the direction of the sound but you are making slow progress and there seems to be no end to the thin trees you are pushing yourself through. But you keep on going, dragging one wellington after the other out of the water until, without warning, you are clear of the copse of trees and there is just a narrow band of rushy ground between you and the drain. It's so full that it is almost flush with the field. And you see something rising and falling at the edge of it, some unidentifiable beast. Not a fox. Maybe a badger. Or a hare. It's thrashing and splashing as if it's caught in a snare and trying to break loose.

How long have you been stopped in your tracks looking at it? Twenty seconds? Thirty seconds? How long has it taken your eyes to register that this is Balthasar's mud-slicked head beating against the edge of the bog as he vainly struggles to rise out of the drain that has swallowed his great body whole. All that is visible is the disembodied head that could for all the world be operating as an independent creature only that your brain tells you that his body is submerged in the drain and the head is the only part of him capable of maintaining the desperate fight to keep from drowning. How long he has been in there and how much longer can he can hold on? You sink on your knees beside the trapped horse and stroke his soaking head. He pauses but the head rises again with another frantic motion, striking you under the chin and throwing you backwards on the ground. Your head hits a sharp stone. You put your hand to the spot and when you pull it away there is scarlet blood mingling with the mud on your fingers.

The sight of the blood triggers some wild emotion in you. Balthasar will not die. You are not going to allow this magnificent creature to quench like a candle in that dreadfully cold water, his head beating his last breaths into mud. You sit back and pull off your wellingtons, the same way that Kieran pulled them from Sally's legs when she was in the barley trailer. You are on your feet and running, ignoring the stones, the briars, the pain and the piercing. The alders are slapping your face as you race through them, scratching, biting. All you see is Balthasar's head. It must not sink. It's up to you. If you run fast enough, he will be saved. If you are not fast enough . . . You cannot think of this. You think of her and you ask her to help you, to do this for you if she can never do anything else again for you in your life.

You are clear of the bog and you are running across the Primrose Field. Your eyes are scanning the ditches, hoping for a glimpse of Kieran. Nothing. On you go into the Mushroom Field. And then you see Uncle Con and Kieran coming through the gate ahead of you. You wave your arms frantically. Kieran is the first to reach you. Your breath is coming in gulps, your lungs fit to burst. You point back in the direction you have come.

Kieran's questions are tumbling out one after another. "Have you found him? Where is he? Is he alright?"

Your uncle looks at you, the mud, your bleeding feet. You know he knows.

"He's in the Bog Field," he says.

You nod furiously.

"And it's not good," he says.

Scalding tears course down your face.

"Go back there and do what you can," he tells Kieran, his voice without reproach. "I'll get the tractor and round up some of the neighbours. Come back with me, Tamara, girl. You're in some state."

You shake your head and start back after Kieran. But he is half a field away from you already, running as if the hounds of hell were on his heels. It is outside your control. You walk, you feel the pain, you feel the cuts. But they are worth it. You have done your best.

You sit beside Kieran at at the edge of the drain. Balthasar still lifts his head every few minutes but very feebly. Is he calmed by Kieran's presence or has the fight gone out of him? You don't know. Your ears are straining for the sound of the men coming. Sometimes you imagine you can hear them but then the silence falls again. Finally, you hear shouts and a tractor in the distance. Kieran shouts back.

You can make out at least eight men around you, all action and hullabaloo. They have left the tractor at the far ditch. Two of them are carrying a bale of hay between them. Another has an armful of potato sacks. Sally has arrived too. Uncle Con orders you and Kieran to stand to one side. He takes out a penknife and cuts the string holding the bale of hay together. The men set to work packing the hay deep under the horse's chest in the murky water. The coarse sacks are weighed down along the bank of the drain with heavy stones. Two men lie on the sacks at either side of Balthasar's head. They reach deep into the muddy water to pass the ends of two thick ropes behind Balthasar's forelegs. The waiting men take their positions in separate lines. They dig their heels into the wet ground and lean back on the ropes like tug-of-war teams. They are sliding and falling until they are covered in mud themselves. And still Balthasar does not budge.

"Look, I will suffer the loss of him," Donovan says. "It's nobody's fault. The only thing is someone is going to have to put the poor beast out of his misery. I won't let him die like that."

My uncle is red in the face. Red as a turkey cock, as Nana would say. His chest is heaving and his words are separated by gasps.

"We're not going to give up that aisy," he says. "That whoring drain is not going to get the better of me. And that brave heart didn't hauld on this long to be lost. Come on again. For Christ sakes, men, put your backs into it."

"The drinks are on me in the village tonight if we can shift him," Donovan says. "And there will be shteaks in every pan of yer houses the next time we kill a basht."

And so they put their backs into it. Every last one of the men pulling and straining and farting and shouting, falling and rising, swearing, sweating, plastered with muck and earth, until Balthasar finally begins to budge. With every inch of movement, Kieran packs more and more hay under the emerging legs to help the horse rise onto the bank. His two front legs gain purchase on the sacks but slip backwards again.

"That's the man!" Donovan gasps. "Come on, help us – keep coming, keep coming! Come on, lads, one last almighty pull!"

To a man, they haul the ropes until Balthasar's front legs hold and his rear quarters suddenly shoot from the water like a cork from a bottle and with an unearthly squelching sound.

"*Pull like the bejasus!*" Uncle Con shouts again.

And there is Balthasar kneeling on the bog as weak as a new-born foal. Your uncle steps forward then with a whiskey bottle quarter full of a clear liquid. One of the bigger men wrenches Balthasar's jaws open and Uncle Con pours some of the liquid down his throat. You learn later that he has given the horse poitín, an illegal whiskey that can put the life back into half-dead lambs or, in this case, a feeble horse. Minutes after the burning liquid has gone down Balthasar's throat, he gets to his feet on the bog and shakes himself like a dog, showering you and every last one of the laughing, cheering men with stagnant water that has a whiff of sulphur about it. He shakes his head and snorts and coughs.

"You can't bate the mountainy men around Ballyvourney for the quality of their poitín," Uncle Con laughs. "It never failed me yet with an ailing basht."

Kieran rubs Balthasar's long face. When he turns around, his face is muddy and his eyes are fastened to the ground. You know he is ashamed. You want to tell Kieran it's not his fault. You want one of the men to say it for you but no one does.

Suddenly a leaden tiredness is sweeping over you. Your head is light, the field is swimming and you begin to sink towards the ground.

"*Catch her, Kieran, for the love of God!*" your uncle shouts.

Kieran reaches out and does just that. He carries you up the field to the tractor and lifts you up into the cab. You smell the oil and the chilly metal. You look back and you can see Donovan leading Balthasar through the gate. Your uncle follows him with Sally. The men file after them. They throw the soaking ropes and the sacking into the transport box at the back of the tractor. They look as if they are returning from a war. You feel like they look. Kieran touches your shoulder. His eyes are full of gratitude. He leaves you sitting there and jumps down from the cab. Your uncle swings Sally up onto the other side of the tractor from you. He climbs in and revs the engine.

"Now, my two madams, I think ye've had enough excitement to last a lifetime," he says. "And I hope I've seen the last of drowning horses around this place. The next horse that puts its nose up the lane will get the high road to the factory."

9

Sally

According to my grandmother, Our Lady of Fatima was the woman to sort out Tamara. As the heavenly being charged with the conversion of Russia and securing world peace, finding a child's voice would be a thing of nothing for the same woman. And so to the mighty trimmings of the rosary was added the invocation 'Our Lady of Fatima, please help Tamara to speak again'. As part of this crusade, Nana set out to remedy the lack of religious knowledge of her 'little pagan' who had been raised without religion in 'godless London'. I was recruited for back-up in the sessions of religious instruction.

"Now, Sally, tell your cousin the names of the three shepherd children," Nana began, her voice affecting the posh tone she used when reading aloud or ordering from waitresses on her rare excursions to the city.

She was distracted for an instant by the droning of a fly passing her nose. She grabbed the bright-red plastic fly-swatter from the kitchen table and whooshed it vainly through the air. "Bad cess to you for a fly!" she snapped, her voice switching back to her normal accent.

I was well-used to her fly attacks and held back my response until she had calmed again.

"Go on, girl," she said, as if nothing had happened.

"Francisco, Jacinta and Lucia," I chanted. "Our Lady appeared to them while they were out on the mountain minding the sheep."

The fact that the three of them were children who came from a farming background gave me something in common with them but, more than that, certain details of their story struck terror in me.

Like myself, Nana was delighted with her role as a mock schoolmistress.

"Very good, Sally. Now tell your cousin what happened on the thirteenth of October 1917."

"Francisco, Jacinta and Lucia were in a big field." I said. "It must have been very big with no ditches because seventy thousand people were waiting there with them for a sign to show they weren't telling a pack of lies about seeing Mary."

"Our Blessed Lady," Nana corrected me.

By now, I had almost convinced myself that I had been in the field myself when the terrifying events unfolded.

"The sun twirled and twirled around the sky like a big tractor-wheel left go from the top of Patrick's Hill inside in Cork. It shot across the sky in mad zig-ags, bucking and lepping like a stallion that was fed too much oats."

I must confess that the comparisons to Patrick's Hill and the stallion were fancy bits donated to me by Mammy but Nana didn't know this. She thought they were my own invention. Eyes closed, she tapped her palm gently on the armrest of her chair, keeping time with the rhythm of my voice.

Tamara's eyes were as wide as the buttercup-yellow Belleek saucers in the glass case in the parlour. Could I coax them even wider? I was going to give it my best shot.

"What happened next but didn't the sun begin to fall out of the sky. Down, down, down it came spinning directly towards the frightened people who were ready to take leave of their senses with the terror of it all. There was pandy-monium –" another donation from Mammy but one that I wasn't quite sure of the pronunciation of, "They were roaring and screeching. For all the world they were convinced that they would be killed stone dead."

I snuck a look at Tamara. Her hands were gripping the edge of the polished table, knuckles white. Yes, I was thundering past the winning post. Next stop, the stage of the Opera House.

"Dazzling colours – every shade of the rainbow – were shooting out from the burning disc of the sun as it came closer and closer –"

"Finish up now." Nana had the cheek to put a stop to my gallop in my finest hour. "You're scaring the life out of myself, never mind Tamara."

Hurt by the interruption, I wound up my story at speed. "And then it stopped dead in its tracks and shot back up to where it had started out from. I think that was God yanking it back up like a yo-yo." The yo-yo was my own invention, a flourish I was very proud of.

Nana moved along a little too briskly for my liking and began to elaborate on the Three Secrets of Fatima with an authority that would have done a university professor proud. I was well up on expounding on the conversion of Russia myself, but she wouldn't leave me. She wanted to get back to her own part of the session with the Penny Catechism.

Nana's concentration regularly wandered from the lesson on account of her obsession with the execution of flies. She kept one eye on the textbook while the other carried out roving inspections on the flypaper hanging from the kitchen ceiling.

"*Who made you?*" Nana asked.

Tamara wrote down the answer, '*God made me*', on the copybook with the blue and pink lines. Nana looked at the neat script, and read the answer out with a posh twang.

Kieran kicked me under the table. "I thought we were all found under heads of cabbage up the haggard, Nana. Does that mean God dropped us in among the drills of cabbage?"

"Shut up, you cheeky pup," Nana said. "It would be more in your line to get up off your behind and count those flies on the paper for me."

Kieran ignored the request. I turned my head away so that Nana wouldn't see me smiling at the thought of God strolling through the cabbage drills and setting babies underneath the green leaves. We had a first-hand education of the source of all life from observations of the farm animals – the bull and the cows, the cock and the hens – but knew to keep our gobs shut about it at home and, especially, at school where the 'townies' were at a distinct disadvantage from us when it came to these facts.

"Now, Tamara, next one, please," Nana continued. "*Why did God make you?*"

Kieran gave the flypaper a look of disgust and nominated me to undertake the fly-count in his place. I pulled my chair over to the long strip of toffee-coloured cellophane pinned to the ceiling by a thumbtack at one end and weighted at the other by the waspish yellow cardboard cylinder from which it had been unfurled.

"Some of them still have their legs moving," I said. "Yuck."

"It's not half good enough for the dirty things," Nana said. "The blackguards, in and out of every last bit of food, spreading disease and dirt around the place."

78

Tamara had a look of sheer disgust on her face as she watched me count the flies trapped on the sticky ribbon, but Nana rapped the table with a wooden ruler to make her concentrate on the study.

"Twenty-six," I said, coming up with what I imagined was an acceptable number.

"Are you sure?" Nana said suspiciously. "Did you take note of every single one of the dirty things on both sides?"

"Of course I did," I lied.

Nana turned her attention back to her scholar, repeated the question and read out Tamara's answer with a twang. *"God made me to know him, love him and serve him in this world, and be with him for ever in the next."*

There was one more great truth to be dispensed for that lesson.

"In whose image and likeness did God make you?"

Before Tamara had a chance to put pen to paper, I sang the response out like a parrot. *"God made me in his own image and likeness!"*

Nana glowered at me then closed the green cover of the book containing the answers to all the deep mysteries of life. Reverting to her own Cork accent, she turned to Tamara. "You're a great girl altogether. We'll have Sister Dominic ating out of our hands before we're finished. And she'll never have guessed that you arrived over here to us a pure pagan."

Now that Nana had done her turn for the advancement of the Catholic faith – every footsoldier counted in the great crusade for the conversion of Communist Russia – she was free to turn her full attention to the business of fly-killing once more. She took up the fly-swatter again.

"He has some set on my forehead," she said, swatting at one kamikaze pilot buzzing around, unaware that he

had entered the death zone. "He's pinching my forehead."
She swatted the air wildly, addressing the fly as if he were
a personal enemy. "Oh then, you'll be no loss if you're
gone to your Maker, boy!"

The stupid fly started banging and buzzing against the
window pane, even though the window was open on the
other side of him.

Nana enlisted Tamara. "See if you can hunt him out the
window, child of grace."

"Child of grace made of butter," I said.

Tamara began the hopeless quest to keep Nana happy.
Herding a wayward fly out of an open window was as aisy
as herding mice at crossroads, but Nana had to be
humoured. My gaze tracked Nana's as she studied
Tamara's thin frame beneath the cotton dress with a small
blue check pattern dotted here and there with minute
golden daisies.

"Oh, Tamara, we have a job ahead of us to fatten you
up," she said, "but fatten you up I will if it's the last thing
I do."

Tamara gave up on the fly who had zipped back into
the room. She sat down on a stool, rocking gently, the legs
of the stool tapping on the floor.

The heat was making me lazy, and I had no inclination
to walk all the way down to the river as I had planned. It
took me three attempts to persuade Nana to tell the story
of the fairy shoe.

"Haven't I told you that auld story a hundred times?"
she said. "I'm kilt from telling it."

I persuaded her that Tamara had never heard her tell it
– a blatant lie, but it worked. Off she went, catching us
both in the spell of the story I never tired of.

"The fairy shoe was found in the Bantry mountains a

good hundred years ago by a small farmer on his way to get the doctor to come and visit his wife, who was very poorly. The farmer gave the shoe to the doctor, hoping that it might be valuable and might knock a few pounds off the bill because it was wintertime and funds were low.

The doctor gave the shoe or brogeen to his daughter. With this marriage and that marriage down through the years, the tiny shoe travelled from one house to the next until it ended up in a big house on the other side of the village.

When I was about five I was brought on a visit to that house. It was like Buckingham Palace to my eyes. It was the size of the windows that took my attention. Every window was about as big as our gable. I was brought into this lovely room with all these Chinese things in it. The lady of the house was old by then. She was bent almost in two, and she had a shock of white hair. I was afraid of her at first but she gave me a small cake with pink icing to win me over. Then she took a silver key from the mantelpiece and brought me over to a glass case by the window. She opened the door and took out the tiniest shoe and rested it in the palm of her hand to show me. It was hardly the size of an almond.

The heel of the shoe was a biteen worn. The old lady said that was because the fairy had done too much dancing in the moonlight. The story was that after the old lady died, the shoe was put into a bank in Skibbereen for safekeeping, along with pieces of jewellery. It was not long gone when the cows on the farm began to sicken and the hens stopped laying. The people of the house sent for the shoe to be brought back and the farm prospered again."

Tamara began to clap as soon as Nana had finished the story and I joined in. It was only right. She told beautiful stories and the one about the fairy shoe was my favourite. The telling of it had made me sleepy, which suited me fine because we weren't supposed to wander far from the house.

Mammy was going on the bus into Cork city – her monthly outing and her treat. She was upstairs getting ready while we were having the session with Nana.

"Let you and Tanara mind the house and mind your grandmother," she whispered to me as she busied herself around the kitchen before she left. "If ye're good, I'll bring the two of ye something nice back from Cork."

I told them that I was only going to give a walk around the garden when she saw me strolling out the door. Sam was stretched on the flagstone. I stepped over her. She thumped her tail without raising her head from between her paws. The only time she lifted it that afternoon was to snap at any flies that strayed around her head. She was Nana's ally in this. The rusty-coloured hens had buried themselves in dusty cocoons of cinders and ashes in the flowerbeds where scarlet and lemon-coloured dahlias bloomed above them. As pretty as the flowers looked, I knew their heads were havens for earwigs. The hens tilted their heads to this side and that as if they were trying to figure out if some piece of gossip they heard earlier was true or not. They paused in their chit-chat every so often to rustle their wings deeper into their bath of ashes and dust. Their crooning reminded me of old women making a feast out of a great scandal.

"Mind yer grandmother!" Nana snorted from inside the kitchen. "As if I needed minding."

"I thought you were going deaf, Nana!" I called in the open door. "Mam only whispered that to us!"

"Don't you be giving cheek to your grandmother,"

Mam said, emerging into the brightness of the yard. "Remember, you have to –"

"Respect your elders," I said, finishing her sentence.

Nana's voice carried into the open air. "Whatever happened to the days when children were seen and not heard?"

Out there in the sunlight, I was suddenly overcome by a wave of affection for my mother, who looked so different without her trademark apron. She was wearing a mint-green summer dress and coral lipstick applied from a golden case she told me was as old as myself. In her 'good clothes', she seemed younger, almost girlish, to me. Mixed with the affection, there was a feeling of sadness. Maybe I thought she deserved more out of life. I don't really know.

"Tamara and myself will walk you to the end of the lane," I told her, adding in a mock whisper, "if Nana can survive five minutes on her own."

We walked down to where the lane met the road. One gate pillar was freshly whitewashed, a bucket and a broad brush standing beside the other.

Mammy's face, so bright and carefree a few minutes before with the expectation of her day in the city ahead of her, clouded over.

"Can I ever rely on Kieran to do one blessed thing that's asked of him?" she sighed. "He must have gone skiving off to those blasted horses again. And I'll be coming home to find your father with a head like a pig on him."

The resentment welling up inside of me was only beginning to catch hold when the three of us were startled by a shout from above us.

Tamara pointed skywards. The top third of the palm tree was swaying over and back with the weight of Kieran, whose head and shoulders appeared just then like a sailor on a mast. His blue shirt was a mirror of the blue sky above him.

"Will you come down off of that for the love and honour of God before you crack your neck!" Mam called.

Her voice was stern but I could tell that she was relieved that the threat of another row was lifted, and I was happy that she could escape to the city without worry.

"Ah, Mam, you can't blame me for wanting to see a bit of the world," Kieran said.

He disappeared and flashes of the blue shirt between the branches signalled his descent. He burst from the bottom branches, sprinted to the pillar and began to paint furiously with the antics of a pantomime character.

"Happy now, Mother dearest?" he said. "I'll have the pillars done to perfection and the lane wall glistening the whole way up to the house before your day's gallivanting is over."

"Make sure you do," she said, her eyes full of kindness. "And the two of you misses, be sure and stay around the house for me."

My shadow and myself stood for a while to watch Kieran whiten the pillar with the bristles of the broad bush. Dipping it back in the bucket lightly, he took it out and flicked it towards us, spattering us with flecks of whitewash.

"*In nomine spiritus sancti*," he intoned.

We raced back up the lane laughing, Kieran chasing us with the brush. We burst into the kitchen, Kieran on our heels, Sam jumping out of our way with all the speed an arthritic dog can muster. In his hurry, Kieran's head struck the end of the fly paper, sending it into a mad orbit.

"Jesus, Mary and Saint Joseph! Ye're after taking leave of yeer senses altogether," Nana said. "Wait till herself comes home and I tell her about yeer antics."

"Ah, don't mind us," Kieran said. "I'm dying of the drought. Will you wet a pot of tea for us there like a good woman?"

"Don't you 'good woman' me," Nana replied primly, but I could tell she was secretly pleased to be fussing around Kieran. She would have gone to the moon and back for him.

I cut big chunks of the white curranty cake that Mammy had baked in the cool of the early morning. We dipped the knives into the jar of blackcurrant jam and smeared the jam on the layer of butter. The teapot was brown as turf, a blue band circling the top of it. Kieran carried it from the range to the table.

"Ye won't be long scattering if himself comes in and sees ye lazing around the place at eleven o'clock in the day," Nana said.

"Every working man needs a break," Kieran said. "What are you two damsels doing to earn your keep?"

"They're supposed to be minding me," Nana snorted. "Did you ever hear the like of it?"

Sam had moved from the flagstone to her usual spot in front of the range. In her slumber, she didn't hear the hen make her cautious way through the kitchen door, placing one leg and then another so carefully in front of her that she could have been testing for landmines under the tiles. Nana opened her mouth as if to shoo the bird away but Kieran put his finger to his lips. He threw some crumbs onto the floor. The hen's caution melted immediately and she began to peck.

"Just like the hen clock," I said, pointing to the dresser.

Kieran dropped the crumbs closer and closer to Sam until the hen was practically between her front paws.

Tamara was silently laughing so much that her shoulders were shaking. A mouthful of the bread went with my breath and I began to cough. I took a swallow of tepid tea to clear it. Kieran threw down another handful of crumbs, some of which scattered over Sam's head. The hen began to peck at the sleeping dog. Sam woke with a start, made a drive at the intruder who rose into the air with an alarmed squawking and a flurry of loosened feathers. In her hurry, Sam's claws slipped on the floor and, while she was running on the spot, the hen made her getaway through the open door.

Nana wiped the tears from her eyes with the corner of her apron.

We soon finished our tea but no one wanted to move. The heat of the day and of the range had made us drowsy.

Kieran finally broke the silence. "I'll go at the whitewashing again soon, Nana, but read the tea leaves for us before I do."

"Yerra, I don't want to be bothering with that old carry-on today," she said.

"Ah go on, Nana," I said, pushing back my chair and going up to her with my cup. "What do you see?"

"Get me my glasses off the dresser there, or I won't see a blind bit."

I took the glasses from their place beside the pecking hen clock and handed them to her. She peered at the black leaves pressed against the side of the cup.

"Do you see it?" she asked us.

"See what? I said, standing beside her and looking into the cup. Up close, I could smell her familiar aroma of Silver Mints and Vicks VapoRub.

"The ship in full sail – the pole there running through the rigging," she said. "You'll be crossing the broad

86

Atlantic yet, Sally girl, 'pon my soul."

Tamara's eyes, sharp as a needle, were riveted on us. I called her over to see the outline of the ship. Her eyes widened. She didn't have to be asked twice to bring her own cup. Nana took it from her and held it this way and that.

"This is a hard one," she said, twisting it one more time and swirling the dregs of the tea to dash the leaves against the side of the cup. She held it up to catch the light from the window.

"I think I see a stack of books," she said. "You could be a great scholar some day yet, Tamara."

Tamara glowed with pride. Herself and her stupid books. What did I care anyway? I never wanted to be a swot. All those lines of black letters crawling along like ants. I didn't need them crawling around inside in my head. I squirmed in my seat. We had been indoors too long. I longed to be down by the river under the cool of the overhanging trees, my feet dangling in the water that smelled of green weed. We would have to wait until Mammy got home – an eternity.

Kieran should have the whitewashing finished by then. He had gone very quiet in the last few minutes. He was looking into his own cup, swirling the tea around. A frown creased his brow.

Nana was watching him. She looked serious too.

"What do you make of it, Kieran? Give it here to me."

"Don't mind it," he said. "It's only codology. It's alright for the little girls here but I don't hold with it at all. Anyway, I'd better get myself down the lane or herself will have my guts for garters."

"Ah come on, what's ating you?" I said. "We had ours read. You might get a ship or a plane. That would suit you. Are you afraid or what? *'Cowardy, cowardy custard! Fill your mouth with mustard!'*"

He shot me those cobra eyes he used when a rare and frightening flash of white anger possessed him.

My stomach flipped. I had pushed him too far. It wasn't my fault that he drew a different line between joking and getting insulted.

"Alright so, you smart aleck," he said. "Don't be so fast at shooting your mouth off. See if your silly games bother me."

He leaned across to Nana and banged the cup down on the table.

All four of us sat there in the tension of the silence. Even Nana seemed unable to resume her chatter.

"We'll leave it altogether," she said, pushing the cup away from her. "I haven't a good feeling about this. People need to want to do this of their own free will."

Kieran pushed the cup back towards her. "No, go on. We'll finish what we started."

Nana picked up the cup as reluctantly as if she was grasping a time bomb. She studied the leaves. I couldn't see them but there was no mistaking the change that came over her expression. Her lips drew into a tight line, her eyes darkened and she held her breath for an instant. The clock ticked on the dresser, the hens crooned in the garden, a cow lowed in a distant field. Still she didn't speak.

"What is it?" Kieran asked.

"Whisht a minute," she said, turning the cup to the left and then to the right.

"Ah Nan, it's only old tea leaves, not the front page of *The Cork Examiner*," I said. "There can't be that much reading in them."

Kieran shot me a poisonous look. "Spit it out, Nana."

"I see a horse's head," she said carefully.

"And?' Kieran probed.

"There's something else in a cluster beside it but I can't really make it out," she said, her voice trailing away.

"Well, a horse is good enough for me any day." Kieran's voice was artificial, forced. He pushed back his chair, the legs screeching on the tiles.

I knew he was acting as if he didn't care, but I clung to that act, convincing myself that it didn't matter.

"Yerrah, don't mind me. My old eyes aren't what they used to be," Nana said. She sounded as if she was trying to shrug off some bad feeling.

Deeper and deeper it was getting. Tamara was biting her nails. Not a good sign. Why did I ever ask Nana to read the tea leaves?

Kieran left the kitchen abruptly. The sound of an alarmed squawking and the beating of wings sounded through the doorway. In a flash, Tamara darted from the stool and grabbed the cup from Nana's hands. She studied the inside for an instant. The cup slid from between her fingers, blue and white fragments scattering on the earthenware tiles.

10

Tamara

You grow so accustomed to the traffic on the Earls Court Road that you don't actually hear it except when ambulances scream or bus-brakes creak or motorbikes roar. Isn't that rather peculiar when hundreds and thousands of cars are flowing past you? Becky, a girl in your school, lives in an apartment block beside the railway tracks. She says she never hears the trains unless they have visitors and the visitors say silly things like, "Oh, how can you live so close to the trains?"

Daddy used to try and explain to me how peaceful it is to live way out in the country with nothing but the birds twittering. "The birds there are like the cars are here. After a while you don't even hear them unless it's a five-o'clock-in-the-morning job and they're all up singing about what a grand place this world is. At least, I used to be telling myself that's what they were chirping, especially if I was on my way home from a dance and full of the joys of life. Holland Park is the closest thing in London to the silence of our farm at home but, even in the park, the noises of Kensington High Street come to find you."

You have become like everyone here on the farm, ears finely tuned to any engine noise from a car or a tractor sounding through the screen of palm trees at the end of the garden or floating through the lane entrance where the iron gate is never closed but always thrown back against the mossy wall. You assume the selective awareness of the rabbits studding the fields like brown stones or garden ornaments. They nibble away unconcernedly at the grass until a sudden noise makes them lift their heads and their slender ears become twin sentries standing to attention. Everyone here pricks up their own ears at the least sound of an engine purring on the boreen, willing it to slow down and turn into the laneway, bringing with it a visitor or some excitement to ripple the stillness of the place. Every car that drives on by is a dreadful disappointment, especially the false alarms that sound as if they are slowing so much that your hopes lift only to be dashed when they pick up speed again and the engine hum fades away around the bend of the road.

On the boreen. You said that in school in London one day and the teacher, Miss Rogers, pushed her half-moon glasses farther down her nose and surveyed you as she might a little creature in a lab experiment.

"Is that another example of your Irish dialect?"

More than once you noticed her writing down something you said. Maybe something like 'míle murder'.

"The Irish dialect, my arse," Daddy says. "Does she think we're some sort of tribe or what?"

You have learned from Sally and Kieran how to assess the likely visitor-potential of a car on the boreen. They are the experts. They can identify exactly what person's car or tractor is passing. This is because they usually belong to locals since strangers rarely have any business on this narrow road they call a boreen.

A boreen, I knew from Daddy, is not a small bore even though most words with 'een' at the end of them refer to a

small version of someone or something. Well, it does mean
a little road. Often you detect a touch of pity invested in
the 'een'. You like being called a girleen, but you are not
so sure about cratureen. Nana alternates between calling
you a poor little cratur and a cratureen. In the beginning
you want to ask her why she was calling you a crater
because you can't understand what link she is making
between you and a volcano. You accept it as another
strange Irish custom until it dawns on you that cratur is a
variation of creature.

Nana pleads deafness but Kieran and Sally swear that a
fly wouldn't pass up or down the lane without her hearing
him buzz. She can hear the cars coming when the window
is open but you are consoled that, the same as you, each
one represents the same blur of sound to her. All you have
learned to recognise in the locality is the sound of Johnny
Golden's motorbike because it backfires like a gunshot.
You first hear it banging along the road above the river.
The motorbike itself is hidden away by tall trees at the edge
of the road and you actually think it's the sound of a rifle.

But there is one van that comes from the city once a
week, the sound of which, even to Nana and yourself,
stands out from all the others that purr and stutter and
rattle along the boreen. The humming of this van lifts your
heart. A van is so special that you hardly dare to believe
that it can really be the one you all want to hear trundling
up the roughly surfaced laneway and grinding to a halt at
the gable. It's like an oven on wheels with the fragrance of
baking wafting from it.

Go back to this hot August day when the window
overlooking the laneway is open. Steam lifts the lid of the
pot of bacon on the range and the smell of the meat makes
you feel queasy. (You hate to think of the bacon and where

it comes from.) You hear the faint hum of an engine approaching the laneway.

"Is that what I think I hear abroad there on the road?" Nana asks your aunt.

Auntie Jenny pauses midway on the floor with the sweeping brush and listens. Before she can say anything, Sally comes racing up the hall.

"It's Thompsons' van," she shouts. "Yahoo! Do ye hear it? Can we get buns, Mammy, can we?"

You were hoping it would be Thompsons. Your mouth is watering already. Sally races out the kitchen door, you on her heels. When you round the corner of the house, the box-like, brown, white and red van is already halfway up the lane. You can see the driver hunched over the dashboard. Everyone knows him as 'Martin Thompsons'. No one knows his real surname. Martin is a big, fat jolly man with a wobbly belly.

"He's the only man I've ever seen with a fat forehead," Uncle Con is fond of saying before advancing on speculations such as, "He must ate half the van on the run. I'm surprised there's even a currant bun left by the time he gets here."

Martin is out of the van and mopping his padded forehead with a white hanky bordered in blue.

"Man alive, the van is like a furnace today," he says. "Sally, would you do me a big favour and run in and get me a cup of water? I will give you a bun with pink icing for your troubles."

He speaks almost as if he is singing, the last words in his sentences lifting. He sounds like a Welsh chap Daddy was chums with in London.

He notices your face drop and adds, "Do you know that a bird never flew on one wing? I forget your name –

94

the little lady from London – will you please bring me a second cup to slake the thirst?"

"She's Tamara," Sally says. "Didn't I tell you last week? She could talk in London but the cat got her tongue since she came here."

"Sure, how could a man be keeping a big name like that in his head?" Martin says. "Tassara, girleen, you'll have to find that cat and get your tongue back from him."

You run to the kitchen with Sally for the water. You don't like people talking about you and trying to make you talk back, even if they mean to be kind. You won't talk – you can't talk. Not yet.

Going indoors is a relief but you are impatient to inhale that first delicious breath of bread and confectionery that's released when Martin throws open the van's double doors. You measure your steps to keep the cup of water from spilling. Sally dashes ahead, leaving a chain of splashes in the dust as she goes. Your aunt is already picking out two crusty loaves of bread with brown shiny tops when you arrive. Martin downs the two cups of water in a flash.

"Aren't you the great girls?" he says. "Go on now. Pick out what you'd like."

"I'm paying for whatever they get, Martin," your aunt says. "It's only right. Thompsons have to live too."

He puts up an argument but she's hearing none of it and he gives in saying, "Alright so, ma'am."

Martin pulls out a wooden shelf packed with snowballs, chocolate tarts, long doughnuts, sugared round doughnuts, custard slices and apple turnovers. Cream oozes from the pastries and a red stripe of jam runs the length of the long doughnut. You select a round bun soft as cotton wool and topped with a smear of pink icing, melting from the heat and dissolving into sweetness on your tongue with the first bite. Breathing in the fragrance of shelves of fresh bread, buns and cakes is nearly as good as eating them.

"Can we have a Battenberg, please Mammy, please!" Sally begs.

The Battenberg is a triangular-shaped sponge cake covered in thick chocolate with corrugated lines. Every second layer is chocolate and vanilla madeira. You look hopefully at your aunt.

"Do you think money grows on trees, Sally O'Mahony?" she says, using the full title of the name as she does when she is making an important point. "The Battenberg is only for special occasions. You'll get one for your birthday – if you're good and if you do all the jobs I ask you to do before then."

"Amn't I always good? Promise me I can I have the first and last slice with all the chocolate on them?"

"What will I do with her at all, Martin?" my aunt says, digging into her purse for some coins to add to the green pound note in her hand. The pound has a picture of a beautiful woman with a scarf on her head.

"Plenty no notice, ma'am. That's the only job."

The Battenberg is stored away in the press until Sunday when Auntie Jenny produces it as a special treat. The afternoon is so hot that your aunt brings Nana, Sally and yourself out to the grassy spot near the pine trees for a picnic. She brings out slices of the cake on a green china plate covered with a blue-and-white tea cloth. A bottle of Tanora is produced from her store in the parlour. You love Tanora. It's a red lemonade, nicer even than ginger beer and any of the fizzy drinks in London. Here fizzy drinks are called minerals. Another word that makes this place so different from home. When will you go home? Will it still be home without . . .

You settle yourselves down under the shade of the sycamore that's set in front of the row of the towering dark-green palm trees. All the trees are as still as someone playing Statues. Grasshoppers are clicking in the grass. They sound like Nana's knitting needles in top gear. You wish you could see a grasshopper but they must be invisible. Kieran is always promising to catch one for you.

Auntie Jenny tells you a story about the time some English people had a picnic on the side of the road not far from her school. It was not long after the war and she was still a little girl.

"We had no food then like you have now," she says. "Things were very scarce. We hardly ever saw a banana. When we were going home from school, we saw that the English car was gone. There was a small circle of black where they had lit a fire. Two banana skins lay in the grass. I picked one up and scraped the inside of the skin with my teeth to eat some of the banana that was left on it. I'll never forget the taste of it. That's why I want ye to appreciate that Battenberg. In our day, you'd have to live in Buckingham Palace before you'd see cake as good as that. Don't waste a single crumb of it."

After the picnic, your aunt instructs Sally and yourself to lie down, as she does, with double pages of an old copy of *The Cork Examiner* over your faces. She is always working. It's good to see her taking a rest.

"Keep your faces covered or the sun will fry them to a rasher," she says.

"We'll roast alive," Sally says, her voice muffled by her pages.

You love the smell of the warm pages and the feel of

them against your skin. Soon, you hear your aunt snoring softly. Sally whispers to you. You peek out. Sally is pointing towards her mother. The page over her face is rising and falling, keeping time with the snores.

Nana is sitting on a chair in the shade of a palm tree with a tea towel on her head. Her eyes are closed but you can't tell if she is dozing. You climbed the palm tree earlier with Sally. Your fingers are still sticky from the resin and you can smell the perfume of the tree from the fronds you rubbed between your hands. It's a fresh, tangy smell. You slide one hand slowly under the paper to breathe it in.

Sally feels your arm move and hears the paper rustle.

"Stop picking your nose," she hisses, thwacking your pages with her fist.

Your aunt wakes with a start. She reprimands both of you which isn't fair, but better that than Sally getting her dander up and threatening revenge. Gentle snores come from your aunt's direction minutes later but Nana is coming back to life. Coming back with a vengeance, as if she has been building up her energy. And you are the target. Super.

She launches into a revision course on 'Little Nellie of Holy God', the nearest thing to a saint Cork has produced. Her voice is low and gentle so as not to wake your aunt. The sound of a hurling-match commentary on the wireless in the kitchen is a faint hum. Kieran and Uncle Con have stayed indoors to listen to the match. For weeks now, the voice of the radio commentator, Micheál O'Hehir, has been the backing track to Sunday afternoons. You enjoy the drama of these games – they sound like something between a musical and an opera, and you haven't the foggiest idea of what is happening. An invisible pigeon is cooing in the branches overhead. You are drifting between sleep and wakefulness, Nana's voice weaving in and out of your consciousness. You hope you will be able to keep up with her account of Little Nellie's life if she pounces with a question.

She begins with Little Nellie's birth in Youghal by the sea, her spectacular devotion to God by the age of two, her incredible grasp of church doctrine by her fourth birthday. You are drifting again until you realise that she is diverting from the story line to address you personally.

"If that poor cratur could learn so much so quickly by the age of four, there's no call for you to be lagging behind at your age," she says. "Faith then, if it's the last thing I do, I'll get you there no matter how much lost ground we have to cover."

Uncle Con calls Nana the 'creaking door' that never falls. She is constantly predicting her own death, telling us that she will soon be 'shoving up the daisies'. She regularly has 'heart attacks' and every chest cold could be the 'nu-moanee' that could carry her to the other side.

My aunt tries to humour her. "Sure, wouldn't it be nice to see Daddy on the other side?"

"Your father wasn't always the easiest person to live with," Nana sighs.

In truth, you are fascinated by this saintly child, abandoned to the care of the Good Shepherd Sisters in Cork city when her mother died as a young woman. She adores the nuns, calls them 'mudder'. You wonder if the Good Shepherd Sisters have crooks the same as Little Bo Peep.

Sally suddenly comes to life beside you, startling you with a question.

"What would you have done if you were landed in with a rake of nuns instead of us?"

Nana glares at her but Sally probably mistakes the heat of her eyes for the sun coming out from behind a cloud. For all her bravado, Sally shares an interest in the story too.

"Nana," she mumbles through the paper, "tell us the bit about the statue dancing."

You're glad of the request because you love to imagine the scenario of the statue swirling in its gold-encrusted robes beside the sickbed of the little girl. It's the Child of Prague. You know it because there is a big statue of her – no, you mean him – on the sideboard in the parlour. Sally has told you the story of the O'Sheas across the river borrowing the statue for the wedding of Esther, the youngest daughter. The statue was put out in the garden the week before the wedding as a prayer for good weather. You think this sounds like some kind of voodoo. Sally thinks the Child of Prague was losing his touch because it poured rain for the O'Shea wedding. The mother of the bride was outraged. She left the Child of Prague out in the rain for another week, saying it served him right.

Like a lot of things on the farm, you don't understand it immediately. The Child of Prague – he that looks like a she – is supposed to hold sway over the weather. There is no supposing for Nana. She was livid at the godless O'Sheas.

"If they had prayed hard enough, he would have looked after them," she said, lovingly wiping the statue down with a canary-yellow duster on his return. "You would and all, wouldn't you, you poor childeen – out under the elements for a week. That's the last trip you'll take across the river while there's a breath in my body."

This was the statue that danced for Little Nellie. Well, not that exact statue, but the same as it. Like you, Sally was genuinely interested in what variation of a dance the statue performed, but Nana was vague on this aspect of the story.

"Maybe it was a slip jig," Uncle Con suggested during one discussion in the kitchen, but luckily the television was turned up high and his voice was low.

It's so pleasant this sunny evening with the sun warming your clothes, the smell of the hot paper, the sound of grasshoppers, of Nana's voice describing a statue dancing for Little Nellie nestling like a birdeen in soft convent pillows, 'on account of the TB, you understand'. It almost makes you forget the longing for home, for her, for Daddy.

But you're no Little Nellie, there is no dancing statue to distract you from the dull ache that connects you to the place you should be. You don't want to escape that feeling. It's like probing a hole in your tooth with your tongue. The pain you feel stops you from forgetting. To forget would be disloyal to her. You are glad of the newspaper covering your face when the hot tears slide down sideways and into your ears.

11

Tamara

You are used to her now. Long black gown, just like the ones the Arab women wear, only her face is not veiled. Face framed by the black headdress, ears tucked away tightly inside it (if she has ears), a white oblong of what looks like cardboard pressing down on her forehead and holding back her hair (if she has hair), another roundy white piece pressed to her chest like a shield. And yet another one of those crosses. This one hangs from a string of black beads. It's silver, not gory like the one in the village church which has blood dripping from the feet skewered by a big nail, spilling from the hands nailed to the timber and from the thorns pressed into the head of the suffering Jesus (Nana's words), with long hair and the bluest of eyes, a look that reminds you of a hippie on a stall in Petticoat Lane market.

Sister Dominic. A woman with a man's name. Sister Dominic, so strange, so frightening the first time she peers at you over the top of her brown glasses and fixes those stern eyes on you so that your legs turn to rubber. And then the unthinkable happens. You try to hold it back, press your thighs together but you can feel the warmth trickling down your legs. You hope nobody will notice it sliding over the brown leather of your cherished Robin sandals and pooling on the floor. Your knickers turn cold, your legs sticky. Your cheeks are flaming, hotter than the black top of the range in full throttle.

The sickly smell of pee spreads throughout the room and reaches the twitching nostrils of Sister Dominic. Sally is mortified. You know, even though you daren't turn your eyes towards her. The other girls, standing to attention for the morning prayers, are tense. You hope she will not discover it is you but she marches down the narrow passageway in the centre of the room, eyes flashing left and right until she comes to a halt at your desk.

"For heaven's sake, girl, this isn't Junior Infants!" she barks, throwing her eyes to heaven. "Am I suppposed to be a cleaning lady as well as a teacher? Not a sound out of the lot you while I'm gone."

She sweeps from the room with a swish of her robes, leaving the heavy wooden door open to the corridor and, thankfully, allowing in a waft of lavender floor polish. No one stirs, no one speaks. The silence of a September afternoon, dusty and becalmed, drifts through the open windows set high above the varnished wainscotting. Wasps are paddling hopelessly in two glass jars smeared with red jam standing on the windowsill. Others float, still and sodden.

Sister Dominic returns with an iron bucket and mop. The smell of Dettol steams from the water. She hands you the mop and you swish it around the linoleum to wash away the source of your shame. As you swish, the smell of the antiseptic makes you think of the hospital in Chelsea. But you must bring the steel shutter down again – right away. You cannot cry, you *must* not cry. You have shamed the 'bus girls' enough in front of the 'townies'. You have shamed Sally.

There is one lesson left before the school bus pulls up at the school gate. It is Irish. Could anything be worse? You have learned to parrot some of the phrases though you still struggle with the proper spelling.

Konos taw too. How are you? *Taw mey gu ma.* I am good.

The most important one you have forgotten today. Maybe not forgotten, but failed to use it on time. *Un will kad agum dull amok?* Have I permission to go out?

Sister Dominic is reading from the Irish book. As she reads, a wasp picks its way along the frame of her glasses, negotiates the bridge of her nose and continues its path above her eye. She blinks but, other than that, allows the wasp a safe passage. You don't blink. Neither does anyone else in the class. You are accustomed to wasps rambling up the nun's black sleeves that look like the surface of a volcanic island, to seeing them disappear into the ravines of those full sleeves and skirts, seemingly never to re-emerge.

"Pay no attention to the wasps and they won't harm you," Sister Dominic says.

Sister Dominic prays for you every day, prays to Saint Anthony, Patron Saint of Lost and Stolen Articles, that he may find your voice and return it to you.

You imagine a pile of objects somewhere, keys, single gloves and earrings, that slender braceleted silver watch she gave you not long before the strands of the black, shiny head of hair you loved to watch her brush began to clog the brush. No, not that, you mustn't remember that. Think instead of her voice – honeycombed with laughs, secrets and excitement.

Sister Dominic is sure that Saint Anthony will do the business. He will find your voice in that big 'Lost and

105

Found' department where God stores all the missing things. In the meantime, she has given you a copy book in which to draft your replies to her questions.

Nana is coaching you in religion so well every night that Sister Dominic has not the least suspicion that she has a 'little pagan' on her hands. For the moment at least. Who made the world? Of course you know the answer: 'God made the world.' But poor little Joseph Walsh from the Terraces must have been missing the day that response was taught. Maybe it's wishful thinking because of his name. "Saint Joseph," he replies, and is rewarded with two stinging slaps of the wooden ruler on each palm. You tell yourself to listen even closer to Nana when she teaches you about God. She promises to drum it into you. You hope she does.

12

Kieran

The cold was stinging my cheeks. The horse was dancing with impatience underneath me, steam billowing from its nostrils when it snorted. My own breath clouded in the air. It was the same for all the other riders in the field. They might as well have been kettles spouting steam. Would you ever be as aware of your own breath as on a November morning like this? Frost the previous night, a gleaming blue sky the witness to its bite. The field had been sparkling in the early morning sunlight but the horses' hooves had dulled it.

My heart lurched. I saw Kitty away from me on the big bay mare, Cherub, that was fidgeting more than my mount, Balthasar. Kitty whirled her around in a circle. She was late. She was always late but thought nothing of it, never apologised. That was Kitty. I wouldn't have left the yard before her but I had been afraid that the hunt would be gone. Anyway, Balthasar was straining to be off. What a feeling it was to be astride all sixteen hands of him, an engine more than a horse: the feeling of excitement mixed with the churning in my stomach. Balthasar was champing at the bit so much that froth bubbled at the corners of his mouth. The pure animal smell of horse rose to me. The smell of leather was on my cold hands when I cupped them in front of my face and blew into them, every scent so keen and sharp in the cool of the morning. If I could sense so much in those smells, even the crushed grass and the churned earth underfoot, what was the scent of the fox to the harriers and the beagles, baying with impatience to be released?

The slender copper bugle glinted as the master of the hunt held it to his lips at the head of the pack. My excitement sharpened as the horn sounded out across the fields. The barking of the hounds reached fever pitch as they raced ahead of the horses in a brown-and-white blur, tails in the air and noses to the ground.

I held the reins taut to slow Balthasar's pace and allow Kitty to catch up. We were approaching the ditch at the edge of the field when she cantered past me, flicking the stirrups into the mare's flanks, urging her on. The bay lifted from the ground as if on wings to mount the ditch, her back shoes kicking behind her as she disappeared down the other side. The jump wouldn't have cost Kitty a moment's thought. She hunted as she lived, in a headlong rush, no hesitation or deliberation. There wasn't a single ounce of self-doubt or questioning in Kitty's make-up, only rock-solid certainty.

Balthasar had no need of urging. The horse knew what was expected and rose like a bird beneath me. In the instant before we descended on the other side, I could see the dogs racing ahead, no longer bunched thickly together and the horses had spread across the bog as well. Kitty stood up in the stirrups and turned back to flash a smile at me. Was it the motion of the horse falling away underneath me or was it my poor heart answering that look of hers?

Balthasar broke into a canter. Kitty had slowed Cherub's pace to a trot, and I drew level with her. Up ahead, the horn was sounding again and the hounds yelping.

"They must have risen one," Kitty said. "Come on, we're in business."

Would it ever be any different? Whenever I felt I was drawing closer to Kitty, she bolted away. There was a distance between us that never seemed to close. At times, she seemed perfectly content to be with me. Time after time I fooled myself into thinking that this was the way it was going to be. But I never could fully trust myself to her because my company never proved to be enough; she always seemed eager to be off, reaching another hilltop with a different view of a valley and new possibilities lighting up for her.

I flicked Balthasar's flanks with my heels, leaned forward in his stirrups and shouted in his ears, "*Come on, boy! Show them what you're made of!*"

Ears pricked, Balthasar ignited and surged ahead. I leaned in over his neck, the thunder of hooves in my ears and the field racing past below me. I overtook a chestnut, a bay, a piebald pony with a chubby, red-faced boy on its broad back, until there were just three lengths between Cherub and me. I urged Balthasar on again. Thunder and thunder, the cold air whipping my face, the power of the horse surging. I just about registered the start of surprise in Kitty's eyes as I passed her. The ground rose ahead to become a steep slope scattered with furze. Halfway up, there was a russet flash as a fox emerged into a small patch of clear ground. The hounds were just starting on the incline. A length of boggy ground lay between me and the first knot of riders. I glanced behind. I was leading the second bunch of riders, one third of the hunt ahead of me and two-thirds behind. Kitty was gaining on me again, the white blaze on Cherub's head a dare.

Balthasar forged ahead, the soft ground suiting him. I felt fused with his energy and speed. I knew Leary's Bog like the back of my hand. An old cart track lay to the left of the

109

route the main group had taken between clumps of rushes and pools the colour of cold tea. I veered to the left and found the track after just half a dozen paces. Balthasar immediately picked up speed on the clear ground. I faintly heard a different rhythm above the general pounding of hooves. I glanced over my shoulder. Kitty had peeled away from the rest of her group to follow me. The fox had disappeared from view in a thick clump of furze on the brow of the hill. The white, black and biscuit colours of the hounds flashed between the furze bushes as they bayed their way upwards.

I had no real appetite for the kill; the thrill was in the chase. I hoped the fox hadn't gone to cover in a place the hounds could penetrate. One more bend to round and I would be tackling the higher ground myself. I had no fear of Balthasar on the terrain – the horse was as steady as a tank. I eased him back a little as we took the bend, then slackened the reins again, splashed and clattered through a rocky stream bed and up onto the soft peaty bog on the other side. Balthasar had slowed his pace, having risen out of the stream. I relaxed. I hadn't realised how tense my shoulder and neck muscles had become in the headlong flight. Balthasar cantered on, finding openings between the furze.

Suddenly, a flash of gold and scarlet came into view on my left. In the same instant, I heard an explosion of wings fluttering as a cock pheasant shot across our path. Balthasar veered wildly to the left, wrenching the reins out of my hands in the suddenness of his movement. The horse's swerve, the sight of the bird and the sensation of my body floating through the air all fused as the ground rushed up to meet me. In that fleeting glance, I saw a limestone boulder the size of a wheelbarrow below me and felt a sickening blow to my temple. Then everything blurred into darkness.

110

13

Jenny

They'll tell you that I'm exaggerating, that I'm unhinged by the shock of it all and that I'm not taking a rational view of things. Rational. What does that word mean in this upside-down world that has robbed me of my fine son and left me with tormentation? If only I had heeded the signs. There were lots of them flagging up what was coming but I didn't pay them enough attention and now I'm paying the price. If only I had said something. *If* – such a small word, and a world of consequences stored away in it.

I have always believed in signs, known things before people knew them themselves. And I believe that people and blessings are 'sent' at a given time. I believe in angels but not those cold plaster ones in blue cloaks with wings like swans that you find in the churches. My angels appear as warm-blooded human beings who land right down beside you when you're in trouble. But I am wandering here, more evidence of an unhinged mind for those wanting to build up that theory. I was talking about the signs sent to me in advance of Kieran's accident, which I ignored.

Signs of good things and of bad things are sent to me. They never come as a surprise. It's not as if they are telling

111

me something new. They're only stamping a seal on some inkling already half-formed in my heart. Something there but only half-there, submerged until the sign calls it to the surface and it takes full form.

That Sunday morning when Kieran went out to the hunt for the last time, I was wakened in the dark with an anxiety that had no cause. It pulled me directly out of my sleep. There was no strácáiling through dreams and half-sleep to wake. My eyes shot open. I was as sure as sure could be that someone had knocked at the window. I ran over because I thought a neighbour might be in trouble, but when I pulled back the curtains, I could see nothing but the dark of the night.

"Con, did you hear anything?" I asked, standing over him.

"Hear what?" he said, rolling on to his side and opening one eye to squint at the alarm clock. "Woman dear, it's only half past five and I was having the sleep of the dead till you woke me. Hear what?"

"A rap at the window. Sharp as a stone."

"Yerra, it was probably one of those starlings flying to its nest in the eaves and taking a wrong turn. Or a bat with his radar turned down. Settle, woman, will you? I have another good hour before the cows."

I got back into bed but there was no settling me. I lay there waiting for the brightening and the sounds of the pigeons and the cock crowing, the manly boyo, eager to get the day going. Kieran was the first up, no shouting at him the morning of a hunt, no need for me to head down to the bedroom with the jug of cold water as a last resort, as I had to do so many other mornings. He was eager to have the cows finished in good time for first Mass and to get away to collect that horse. It was the only morning he was out of bed before his father.

"Isn't it an awful pity we can't have the hunt every day?" Con said as he sat on the side of the bed pulling on his grey wool socks. "Maybe we'd have a better chance of making a farmer out of that lad there if he was getting up for a hunt every morning."

Normally, I'd have some answer for him. That's the way we'd go on like Darby and Joan, Con having a go at Kieran, me standing up for him. He shot me a look when I didn't reply, but said nothing more. I was puzzling over the worry inside me as I pulled on my dress over my head. Was it anything that had happened the day before? It was nothing. It would pass like all the other quare feelings that came and went. Con was right. The bang on the window was only a bird gone astray. Why did I always have to be building up things out of nothing?

The cows were milked, the girls got up and we all set off for eight o'clock Mass. We only had the Volkswagon about two years at that stage – it was still a novelty to me. The car was a great comfort, a change from getting lifts or cycling. Part of me was lonesome though for the pony and trap that I'd grown up with.

Sunday was the morning for the fry. I went to Harringtons for the rashers and the sausages and a few other messages. Tamara and Sally were delighted to find a few comics left on the counter near *The Sunday Press*.

The kitchen filled with the smell of the fry after I got to work with the spluttering frying pan when we got home. After the plates were washed, I settled into my copy of *Woman's Weekly*. The girls had their elbows on the table and their noses buried in *Bunty* and *Judy*.

Con rustled the pages of the newspaper and gave a loud sigh. "This fighting in the North is something fierce.

Where is it all going to end?"

"My heart goes out to those poor Catholic families burned out of their homes," I said.

"It makes my blood boil to see English soldiers on the street up there. And they giving out lollipops to the children, moryah. Lollipops, my arse."

I wanted to say the army was brought in to protect the Catholics but there was no arguing with Con. He was one of the West Cork breed for whom our own persecution by the Black and Tan forces in the 1920s felt as fresh as if it had only happened yesterday. I was relieved when the girls created a distraction by begging to be let follow the hunt.

"It's too dangerous and ye're too young to be running after it on foot," Con told them.

The two girls were in and out the door from 10 o'clock on, waiting for Kieran to ride up the laneway and make good his earlier promise to give them a turn in the saddle. At twenty-five to eleven exactly – I know because I looked at the clock – I saw them haring past the kitchen window and down the lane. Minutes later, the big black horse passed the kitchen window. Kieran waved in to me. The girls followed him into the yard, all excited at the prospect of him letting them have a go on the horse.

The bottle of Holy Water was on the kitchen window beside the statue of the Child of Prague and a scarlet geranium that Nana insisted we allow grow in one direction towards the light, instead of turning it around to get even growth.

"Sure why I would be tormenting a living thing by twisting it in every direction when it only wants to grow towards the light?" she would explain to visitors amused at the sight of the geranium all akilter.

Kieran had jumped off the horse and was holding it by

the head when I came out. The girls had taken their spin around the haggard and he had lined him up beside the garden wall so that they could climb down on top of it. They were all smiles but the worry was gnawing as hard as ever inside me.

Kieran caught me frowning. "Would you give over, Mam?" he said. "I only gave them a small walk around the haggard."

"It isn't the girls I'm bothered about."

"What does Nana say? 'Never trouble trouble till trouble troubles you.' You worry too much. There's no need for it."

The girls asked him for one last spin. He led the horse up past the line of whitewashed outhouses with the orange-coloured corrugated iron rooves and back down again by the barn gable.

"Down you come," he said, swinging the two of them to the ground. "We can't be tiring out Arkle here before he gets a snort of the hunt."

"And I suppose you think you're Pat Taaffe," I said, doing my best to sound light-hearted.

He leaned his foot into the stirrup and hauled himself up, the saddle complaining under his weight. I unscrewed the top of the Holy Water bottle, stood back, shook the water on Kieran and on the horse.

He blessed himself and took off, talking to the horse, "Giddy up there, boy! It's time to earn your oats." He gave one glance back over his shoulder to the three of us, saying, "See you all this evening."

I should have gone back in through the garden gate then, but my feet seemed to have a mind of their own and they carried me around the corner of the house. I watched him go down the laneway, the morning sun shining

115

through the bare November branches. Yes, that's how my fine son looked with the winter light striking his back and a whole life beckoning to him.

November 1969, will I ever forget it? Branded on my brain to my dying day is the sight of that black horse, Balthasar, stopping dead outside my kitchen window a few hours later. Riderless. The look of him, standing there, snorting, pawing the ground, steam rising from his flanks. My blood turned to ice. My legs gave underneath me, and I had to grip the side of the sink for support. Only that I know that he is one of God's creatures, an innocent in all that happened, I would have sworn that he had galloped back from the very gates of hell. He was bowing and raising his head. He was in a lather of sweat, steam spurting from his nostrils in the cold of the day. Foam flecked the corners of the bit. The reins still hung over his neck. The empty saddle.

"What in God's name is making all that noise?" Con said, putting the newspaper down and coming to the window. "Mother of God," he said when he saw the riderless horse. He turned pale.

"Something must have happened to Kieran – we have to go and find him," I said, grabbing the red comb from the windowsill and running it through my hair. The strange things you do when you are in shock.

Nana blessed herself and reached into the pocket of her apron for her rosary beads, kissing the silver crucifix. "Saints of heaven protect us," she prayed and continued to move her lips without a sound.

"He probably took a fall," Con said. "I never knew that fella not to get out of a scrape. Don't worry." There was no conviction in his words. He rubbed his forehead. "But if he did itself, why did that tramp of a horse land up to our yard? He should have headed back to Donovans' and stuck his head in the oats bin."

"He was sent," I said. "I haven't felt right in myself since the first light of day. He is the sign."

"You and your bleddy signs," he muttered. "Give over your old raiméishing."

Con knew as well as I did, believed in the signs too, and he gave up the attempt to hide how frightened he was.

Tamara and Sally ran into view in the laneway. Sally grabbed the horse by the bridle. At the same time I heard the rumble of an engine in the road.

Jerry Twomey came with the news. They sent him because his was the nearest farm to ours. Without hearing the knock on the door, without seeing the pained expression on his face standing in the middle of the kitchen, without seeing him twist his old tweed cap as if he was wringing out a dishcloth, I would have known.

"K-k-kieran . . ." he stuttered, gathering himself to go on again.

My first impulse was to save him the hardship of delving inside himself and hauling out those strangled words.

"Something has happened to Kieran," I said. "He had an accident. He fell from the horse."

I might as well have been Charles Mitchell reading out the six o'clock news. I might as well have been floating under the kitchen ceiling looking down on a strange woman mouthing those words like an actor trying out her lines for the first time.

Jerry looked at me with an expression wavering somewhere between gratitude and disbelief.

"For God's sake, Jenny, don't go putting words into the man's mouth," Con said. "Let him speak." He was hoping against hope for a different version than we were both guessing at. Who was I to fault him for that?

But Jerry's face told it all. There was hardly cause for him to open his mouth. The misfortunate man couldn't even bring himself to look into our eyes. His eyes were glued to the kitchen floor as if he was searching for a half-crown he'd dropped. His voice was hoarse when he began to speak and he had to cough to clear his throat. "Kieran has fallen off the horse down in the bog. They sent me to bring you down."

I reached again for my green coat that had been draped over the back of the chair since I had come from Mass. Mass, I thought – how long ago that seemed when we were all well and together and right with the world. Kieran used to say the coat was the same green as the moss lining the stone walls of the well. He was with me the day I bought it inside in Roches Stores. Only five years old he was that time.

"Is he alive?" Con asked, uttering the words I wouldn't allow myself to ask.

My fist flew to my mouth like a bird, pressing hard against my lips while I fought against the feeling that I was going to throw up there and then.

"He is," Jerry said. "When I left, the doctor was with him but . . ."

"God damn it, but what, Jerry?" Con said.

"There's a lot of blood. It's not looking good. I'm sorry."

Tamara and Sally burst in the door, their faces flushed from the cold and from the excitement of catching Balthasar. Or so I thought.

"Balthasar ran away again," Sally said, crying. "I tried to hold him, honest, but he kept tossing his head in the air

118

until he pulled the reins right out of my hand. He went racing down the lane and onto the road."

"Somebody else will have to take care of Balthasar," I told her. "Kieran was thrown off of him. We are going down with Jerry to see how he is. The two of you must stay here and mind the house with Nana till we come back."

"But . . ." Sally began.

Con shot her a look. As I left the kitchen, I glanced back at Tamara, her big eyes wider and deeper than I'd noticed before. The steel shutter I'd brought down on my feelings shot up and her eyes were a mirror of the terror coiled inside me. I pulled the door out behind me, pinning my eyes to the men's backs as if I would be lost to myself and everything else if I blinked.

Con didn't want me to go back to the bog when the news came but nothing could hold me back. To look at me on the outside, I was calm. I know I looked calm, acted calm. It was the shock of it, you see. How would I explain it? Some part of your mind knows that something awful has happened, but your heart freezes over, closes down to hold you together. I knew Kieran needed me more than he had ever done, and that I had to hold myself together.

God forgive me but when I saw Kitty sitting there beside him, stroking his bloodied head, and Dr O'Donnell kneeling there doing his best for my poor boy, I could have swung for her. Who did she think she was playing – some tragic Jackie Kennedy in Dallas? I should have been saying a prayer for my poor boy and he lying there with his head split open. Maybe I am wronging myself – some people tell me that out of kindness. Maybe my first thought was with Kieran, and the resentment came later. But all my thoughts were flying in every direction, like hens when the

119

murdering fox gets in.

Her and her damn horses, that's what brought us to that terrible day. That's what started the whole nightmare we have been living since. Yes, I have ugly thoughts, bitterness, but I have earned them. Could you blame any woman to feel like that after she sent her son out of a morning, all right in his world, only to have him returned to her, broken and maimed in body and spirit, so strange to her at times that it could have been a changeling delivered in his stead?

14

Sally

How many fields were there between ourselves and the bog? I did a quick count on my fingers: five of ours – Small Lough, Big Lough, Crab Apple, the Mushroom Field and the Hilly Field. How many of the Driscolls? Four at the most. And then there was the wide expanse of the bog to think of. If we ran like the wind, we could still get there before Mammy and Daddy because they were taking the long way round by the road. Jerry Twomey had insisted on driving them. Everyone knew Jerry drove like a snail. What excuse would I concoct for Nana? Maybe I'd tell her daddy was worried about one of the cows that was an early calver. I told her as much. She paused in the fingering of her rosary beads.

"It wasn't in the last cloud I came down, girleen," she said. "I know where ye're off to. On with ye. I'm not so old or doting that I'll burn the house down. Nobody will blow in that door and run off with me neither. Nothing I will say will get the thought of Kieran out of your heads, but remember there are things not fit for a child to see."

I heard her but I didn't heed her. The highest thought in my mind was Kieran. I grabbed my anorak. Tamara had already zipped up hers while Nana was talking.

"The blessings of God go with ye," she said, making the

Sign of the Cross. "I'll be praying for Kieran."

A long time afterwards, she told me that she had been praying that the ambulance would have taken Kieran away before we reached the bog. But she hadn't bargained on the fear driving us. Ditches, briars, thorns, cow dung, barred gates, drains, were nothing to us as we sprinted to close the distance between Kieran and ourselves. My lungs were the worst. At least they were the worst before I got the stitch in my side, sharp as a pincers. We were at the edge of the bog at that stage and could see a knot of people way ahead of us. Farther away towards the village, I could just about make out the green of Jerry Twomey's Land Rover crawling along the New Line road. Tamara was a small bit ahead of me but she doubled back because she thought I was struggling. God help her head. She tried to catch me by the hand but I shook her off, took a deep breath and ploughed on. The bleddy river was the worst of it. I knew it would be freezing. There was nothing for it only to jump in, the cold of the water slapping us, our wet trousers sticking to our legs. My ankle turned on a loose stone and down I went on my knees. I could have got up myself without a bother but, of course, Tamara had to lift me up. We pulled ourselves onto the opposite bank by grabbing handfuls of rushes.

We were there. The Land Rover was nearly there too. But we were first to see Kieran lying with a pile of jackets thrown over him. His hair was slick and oily on the right-hand side, but it wasn't oil. There was blood trickling out of his right ear too. I couldn't see the left. Blood had clotted under his nose. Kitty was crouched beside him, stroking his head. Her hand was all blood. Dr O'Donnell had his fingers in Kieran's mouth. I learned afterwards that he was doing this to keep the airways clear. Kieran's face was as white as flour. The blood, the paleness of him, were terrifying but worst of all was his breathing. There were these choking, rasping noises coming from his mouth, and his chest was rattling. It was the sound people made on the telly when they were finishing up. The death rattle they called it.

I was rooted to the spot with fear. Tamara started like a bird out of the crowd and tried to dash towards Kieran but a man grabbed her and held her back. I was angry with her. If anyone should be beside Kieran, it was me and I hadn't dared. Why? I was a coward.

The rumble of the Land Rover could be heard over the heads of the crowd. Then silence and the two doors banging. Mammy rushed by me, brushing my sleeve and not even seeing me. My father followed her and they both knelt down beside Kieran. The helplessness that swamped me was stamped all over my father's face. My mother shot Kitty a look and took Kieran's hand and held it, rocking ever so slightly on her knees. Her chin trembled but there were no tears.

Dr O'Donnell beckoned my father with a nod. Daddy drew closer to him and crouched low while the doctor whispered in his ear. My father spoke back to him. I couldn't hear what they were saying because of the low murmur of the men and women gathered around. All I caught was the word 'hope' coming from my scared-looking father.

Mammy was still holding Kieran's hand when the ambulance crew came across the bog. They couldn't drive right up to Kieran because the track was so bad. Kitty hung back and bit her fist. Mammy stayed beside Kieran. Settling him on the stretcher seemed to take forever. Finally, all the straps were buckled and they headed slowly towards the ambulance, the silent crowd following. Mammy climbed into the ambulance after the stretcher. The double doors closed on them. Kitty's mother was talking intently into her ear as she led her away. Kitty's arms were hanging loosely at her sides. She looked for all the world like one of the patients you'd see from the big red-brick asylum on the Lee Road, not a flicker of life in her eyes. A zombie. The ambulance, all white and red and flashing, looked as alien as a flying saucer among the withered brown and tan colours of the bog as it trundled down the track. Daddy said nothing about Tamara and myself being there. He was like a blind man in need of someone to guide him home.

The knot of people began to unravel. It was then that I noticed Balthasar tied to an ash tree growing beside a stone ditch. He must have galloped all the way back to the bog again from our farm. He was pulling up clumps of the tough grass with his yellow teeth and munching it. I ran at him, striking his face with my fists. He snorted and backed away from me in alarm. Suddenly I was swept up into my father's strong arms. I could smell the damp tweed of his jacket. My feet were so cold.

15

Sally

Timmy Donovan was spouting away in the kitchen. I'm calling him Timmy Donovan here to give him his full title for starters but he was ever and always referred to as Donovan in our house. No 'O' either for the O'Donovans, in the same way that we, the O'Mahonys, were Mahonys to the whole parish. People never bothered sticking the 'O' in.

Mammy was gone to the hospital when Donovan came to visit three days after the accident. It took him all that time to work up the courage. All the rest of us were in the house when he landed in. To give him his due, he was doing his best but you'd know by the cut of our faces that we only wanted him to clear off. He was trying to cheer us up with stories and was making a complete pig's arse of it. It was obvious he felt the accident was his fault. You could tell from the thin line of my father's lips that, in his opinion, it *was* just that. Whatever my father's feelings, he couldn't abandon the hospitality of the house and so he poured a second glass of whiskey for the visitor. Donovan was gulping it back as if it were cold tea. His nose was as red as a cherry. With every nervous swallow, Nana fixed him with a disapproving stare.

"The quietest of horses can go quare on you," he said.

"There's no accounting for what can happen. I remember the time I was out in the pony and trap with two dry auld American cousins that had blown in from Boston. I had a young bay mare at the time, safe as houses or so I thought, but there's no trust in any of them. Down by Mullane's Cross, a fox leapt out from behind the creamery stand and frightened the living daylights out of her. Off she took as if she were Nijinsky's first cousin, the ears flattened and the shoes lighting off the road. Down by the bridge, she took the bend so fast that the trap clattered off the stone wall. The Yanks were lifted clane off the seat and launched about two feet into the air. The *Apollo* wasn't in it. The only luck was that they thought it was all part of the trip. It was Connells' Hill that saved us. She was bate out by the time we got to the top of it. Do you know, I had no trust in her after that. I sold her off at Cahirimee Fair not long afterwards."

Donovan seemed at a loss when he ran out of steam. My father's dead eyes were trained on the back door. Nana took up *The Far East* missionary magazine and turned the pages so violently that I thought the little magazine would fall asunder. Mammy was due back from the hospital with the latest report on Kieran. My father had come home before her because he didn't want the neighbours left with all the work.

"No trust, no trust at all," Donovan said. "I could never understand why Kieran didn't just stick with the tractors and the machinery like yourself, Con. I was blue in the face from telling him that but I gave up in the end because he was mad for the horses."

Nana was putting it all down to the will of God. She left Balthasar off the hook, which was more than I did.

"You can't escape what's marked out for you," she said,

taking her nose out of *The Far East* and back to rural Cork. "Whether it's a fall from a tractor or from a horse, there's no turning from it. We can only pray to the Good Lord that the doctors will be able to set him to rights."

"You never spoke a truer word, ma'am," Donovan said, grateful that someone else was breaking the silence.

My father ran a hand across his unshaven jaw. His eyes were bleak. There was a grey rim inside the collar of his blue shirt. I had never seen him look so rough. He worked with oil, diesel, earth and muck, but these things were all 'clane dirt'. This look was new to me and it was quare. More than quare as well was not to have Mammy around the house.

"They will have their work cut out for them," he said. "He hasn't opened his eyes all day. I couldn't give any more time looking at him in that state."

Didn't he know not to be saying that class of stuff in front of myself and Tamara? That was another sign that he wasn't himself.

Nana closed the magazine and blessed herself. She seemed to have grown smaller. Smaller and greyer, like one of those negatives that come back with the photos from the chemist's shop.

"I swear to God, Con, I tried my best to persuade him not to take Balthasar but he begged me, said he was able to handle him," Donovan said, finding his voice again. "He persuaded me. And you know he would have been fine if the horse hadn't bolted."

"Leave it, Timmy. For Christ's sake, leave it," my father said.

The house had been full of neighbours all day – every second person arrived with sandwiches, apple tarts, shop swiss rolls, jam tarts. The teapot was constantly on the go

– a team of men milked the cows and fed the animals.

There were whispered conversations in the yard and the corners of the kitchen, men and women dropping their voices and looking over their shoulders at us. Still, the voices weren't low enough. "Might never walk again. If he pulls through at all. Jesus, Kieran'd never take being a cripple." Did they think we were deaf or half-simple?

After tea, they all drifted away. They had cows to milk and some of them had small children who were getting contrary.

Suddenly we all heard the sound we had been waiting for – the purr of an engine in the laneway. A pair of headlamps lit up the darkness outside the kitchen window, disappeared around the side of the house and then passed the window again, the engine's drone fading as it headed back to the road.

My mother blinked as she came into the full light of the kitchen. She walked over to the range and put her hands out to the red glow of the embers behind the bars.

"I'll be off now," Donovan said. "Best let ye to talk among yerselves."

No one protested.

My mother kept her back to Donovan as he sidled his way out the door.

"You could at least have saluted the man," my father said when Donovan was out of earshot.

Ignoring him, she pulled the silk scarf from her head. It was the navy-and-white one Kieran had given her for her birthday. There was the chesnut head of a horse and a bridle on it. She must have pulled it out of the drawer without thinking when she left for the hospital. The dullness of her eyes changed to sharpness when they swept over the kitchen. As well as bringing food earlier, the neighbours had set to work cleaning, polishing and chatting with Nana, who was delighted with the company.

"The fairies must have been in," she said. "Wet a cup of tea for me, Sally, like a good girl. I couldn't bring myself to eat a bite all day but I think I'll chance one of those egg sandwiches."

While I was rinsing out the tea leaves from the pot, I looked over my shoulder towards Mammy and I asked her was it true that Kieran was going to be a cripple.

"Where did you hear that?" my father barked with such temper that he scared the life out of me.

"Some woman from the village was saying it in the yard this morning."

Mammy's voice was gentle and careful but I knew I was on shaky ground. "Some people would put legs under eggs. Don't take a blind bit of notice of any old raiméis you will hear people going on with over the next couple of weeks." Her eyes swooped around the kitchen. "Where's Tamara?" she asked sharply.

Tamara had felt uncomfortable with the bustle of strangers in the house. She was taking Kieran's accident desperate bad. If you hit her a clout of a flour bag, you couldn't make her any whiter. The only bit of colour about her were her red-rimmed eyes. Usually, once it got dark, she came in from her hideaway in the haggard and threw herself down on her bed and began reading a book. But when I went upstairs to call her, the bed was empty.

"What do you mean she's not there?" my mother said in alarm. "Isn't it enough to have one calamity in the family?"

"Will you rest, Jenny," my father said. "She's probably up in some corner of the yard. Here, Sally, take the flashlamp and go out and call her."

I began to protest but Mammy gave me *that* look. She

129

told me to come back in five minutes if I hadn't found her and they'd all go out. I knew she was only looking for an excuse to get rid of me so they could talk about Kieran. The air was cool when I went out and a breeze was chasing the crisp brown leaves from the chestnut tree around the yard. That October they had fallen from the top of the tree first. Mammy said the bare top reminded her of a bald man.

I knew it would be easy to find Tamara. For the past three days she had spent every hour she could with Kieran's dog, Trouncer, in the big, wooden Ford box behind the dairy. When he wasn't hunting, Trouncer was tied to a long chain. The bale of straw he slept on had a deep, smooth hollow from the shape of his body. From the orchard ditch, I had spied on her there, sitting on the bale, stroking the heavy head of the brown-and-white harrier. How she stuck the smell of dog in there, I couldn't imagine, and I thought the whack of him would be on her clothes when she came in but it wasn't. This was her hiding-place, and this was the way she was dealing with Kieran's accident, and I wasn't going to take that from her. For my part, I had turned to Nana and her prayers. Even the rosary didn't seem boring anymore when we prayed for Kieran to be brought safely home to us.

I walked through the barn and crossed the haggard to the milking stall. I stood by the dairy step and called Tamara. I was far enough away for her to emerge from her lair without thinking that I knew where she had been.

Within seconds, the shadow was coming towards me and into the thin beam of light shining from the bicycle lamp. I felt a surprising glow of affection light inside me as we turned and fell into step on the way back to the house. Maybe it came from the relief of being able to share my worries about what was being spoken about around the kitchen table – worries of what would be told to us but, more so, what would be held back and left to take on a shadow life of its own.

"Mammy is back from the hospital and she's giving Daddy and Nana some news about Kieran," I said.

Even in the dark, I could sense Tamara stiffen beside me. Then she quickened her step and I broke into a half-run to reach the kitchen just a few steps behind her.

Tamara and myself returned to the welcome warmth of the kitchen to find my father brushing the back of his right hand roughly across his wet cheeks. I had never seen him cry before. My older sisters, Tess and Sheila, used to talk about seeing him cry just the one time when he had come from the hospital after his own father had died. He quickly turned away from us. Nana was fingering her rosary beads. Mammy was sitting bolt upright at the table like a pillar of stone. She waved Tamara and myself towards the long stool underneath the window. She told us that Kieran had broken a lot of bones but the thing the hospital was most worried about was his head. He had hit it a fierce bang off a stone when he fell from the horse.

The hospital in Cork was very good, she told us, but there were even better doctors in a hospital in Dublin where they specialised in treating people like Kieran who had been in car accidents or bad falls. He was being taken to Dublin by helicopter the following day.

"Kieran always wanted to go up in a helicopter," I said, regretting my words as soon as they were out when I saw the way my mother's lips began to quiver.

She probably used the words Central Remedial Clinic but, if she did, they went over my head. He would be away for a long time, she said. Herself and my father would have to go and see him as much as they could.

"But they're going to be able to fix him, aren't they?" I asked. "If they're going to all the trouble to take him up there in a helicopter?"

It was going to be hard, she said. So we would have to be very good. My father was cradling his head in his hands, elbows on the kitchen table.

"But he'll be home for Christmas, won't he?" I said. "They'll nearly have two months to make him better by then."

My mother shook her head gravely. "If we are to get through this, Sally, we can't be running away with ourselves. We can only do the best we can with every day God sends us. God saved Kieran from being killed. Now we have to pray to him to make him better."

Killed. The thought that Kieran have been taken away from us completely was awful. A world without Kieran. How could you imagine it? I felt as if a lump of coal was stuck in the back of my throat.

"Tamara and yourself will go back to school on Monday," Mammy said. "The two of you will have to keep up with your lessons, and help Nana when you come home if I'm away in Dublin."

She made us two steaming cups of cocoa, as if to give us a sweetness that would soften the grim story she had to tell us. I sipped it little by little, thinking of Kieran away from us in the hospital bed. I imagined him with a big bandage around his head like a soldier in a war film. But then I could see a dark red patch, as big as a side plate, and I had to bring my eyes back to the kitchen and to focus on the light of the Sacred Heart lamp.

I was so tired I put my arms on the table, rested my head on them and drifted off to sleep. I was dreaming of the old paraffin lamps we used to take to the bedrooms before the electric came. There was the warm, oily smell, and the flicker of moths around the glass globe that sheltered the yellow flame wavering inside. Kieran was in the dream. He was making shapes with his hands in the lamplight and throwing shadows on the bedroom wall: a rabbit with its two ears twitching, a bird flying away, its wings flapping.

I woke to hear Nana calling me for the rosary. For the feeling of being with Kieran to last, I would have get back into the dream. But there was no going back. Kieran needed every rosary we could send up into the heavens. I prayed the words as hard as I could for as long as I could concentrate but, in between the prayers, I was bartering with God. Make Kieran better and I will do without the Raleigh bike I want for Christmas. Make Kieran better and I will stop trying to get Tamara to talk. Make Kieran better and I will give everything in my piggy bank to the Black Babies. Make Kieran better and I will do every job I'm asked to do without grousing. Just please, please make Kieran better.

Tamara had gone up to bed before me. The down quilt was pulled up over her head but I could hear her sniffling underneath it. I patted the top of the quilt gently. She went silent. The next morning when I woke, I wished that the whole thing would be a bad dream and there would be a box of Smarties under my pillow, placed there by Kieran any night he was at a dance. I slid my hand hopefully in the space over the sheet but it was empty. Well, almost. I pulled out a note. It was a page from a copy-book, folded tight. I recognised Tamara's careful script.

A single sentence. *"Don't worry. We will believe Kieran better."*

16

Kieran

Kitty couldn't understand why we couldn't go on being friends. I should have been happy to see her walk in the ward door in Dublin late that November. Any other time, the sight of her was like a light switch for me but, that day, I would have given my eye teeth to disappear. Eye teeth, that's gas. I hadn't much else left to give, had I, the cut of me thrown in the bed?

I closed my eyes, let on to be asleep, but she just sat there. In the end, I had to open my eyes. She might have been cocked there yet like some class of a statue if I hadn't. In fairness, I gave her a chance to buy some time, to get used to the state of me, to fix her face in such a way that the flashes of pity and shock were done and dusted. My mother says Kitty has a touch of the actress about her. If she has itself, it served her well that day in the hospital. She had a smile pinned on her face, and eyes so bright you could have sold them with the brooches in Woolworths. The eyes were all soft and kind. I would have preferred to see them dancing in her head with the madness and the craic or with the temper like before, but it was hardly the occasion, was it now?

I must have grunted some sort of a hello. I might even have gone as far as telling her she shouldn't have made the

journey, though I doubt that. Words were in scarce supply
with me, those demented days, as my mother calls them.
And I could get away with it. "Poor Kieran, the shock
hasn't hit him yet. Poor Kieran. Sure, he's trying to come
to terms with it. Those black moods are something fierce.
No wonder he hasn't a kind word to throw to a dog.
There's no point in telling him to cop on. We have to cut
him some slack."

I let Kitty do the talking. I let all the visitors do the
talking. All that yapping might have cracked another fella
up but it was fine by me – it took me off the hook. I just
lay there and listened to the same old raiméis over and
over again.

"You're still the same Kieran to me," Kitty said.

That was a laugh for starters but I let it go. There was
another fella in the ward with me, a right nosey fecker,
and I wasn't going to give him the satisfaction of a scene,
though the poor bollox could have done with the
distraction. Another wreck like me, only worse, he was
after cracking his neck. Did a right good job on it, coming
off a Honda 50 on a bend. A Honda 50, could you credit
it? The shame and the disgrace of that.

"The doctors can do wonders these days," Kitty
continued with the same bright eyes but I noticed she was
twisting one of her brown leather gloves round and round
in her lap. "I heard of a fella that got the same injury as
you in a rugby match and he is managing away. He's even
training a junior team."

She got stuck into the hope talk then. I didn't even look
at her while she was talking. Couldn't bear to. I might
have wanted to put my hand out – my good hand – to
touch her. Instead, I kept it safe under the blankets, my
fingers dug into the white sheet for fear she might have

tried to catch hold of it. To keep myself from roaring at her or worse still – crying – I imagined myself building a wall, stone by stone, between us. But when she got onto the 'helping me' bit – they all usually got to that sooner or later – I couldn't take any more. It was wrong of me, I know, but there is only so much a fella can take. How many more of them did I take that rubbish from before her without a word? But coming from Kitty's mouth it was a thousand times worse.

"You know I'll always be there for you, Kieran," she said. "I'll be there to help you any way I can."

Her voice was cracking a bit then. I was afraid that she was going to get all emotional on me, start crying and throw herself across the bed or something. I made up my mind to put a sting in my words and issue her with her marching orders.

"Will you give over, Kitty?" I said, throwing my eyes to heaven. "'Tisn't as if we're in a fucken picture or something. Cop onto yourself. There's fuck all you or anyone else can do for me. You never signed up to hanging around with a cripple."

She began to protest, a bit of the fire coming out in her, but then she probably remembered that it was 'Kieran the cripple' she was dealing with and she drew in her horns. She was holding onto the notion that the 'same Kieran' was still buried somewhere in this fucked-up excuse for a body. I turned my head towards her and looked her square in the face. The heart nearly jumped out of my chest straight towards her, but I swallowed hard.

"But you know there is one favour you can do for me," I said.

She looked at me all eager, like a dog when he knows you're going for the cows.

"The best thing you can do for me now is to fuck off out of here and lave me alone," I hissed, and repeated it in case I wasn't making myself clear enough. "Lave me alone, and don't come near me again."

Kitty's tough – hard as nails in one way. I liked that about her always. But she's still a girl. They were rough words I drove at her when she perched on the edge of my bed. They hit their mark right enough. Bull's-eye. I did a right good job of it, so I did. She was tough enough to hold back the tears but not tough enough to hide the sting.

I watched her then, taking in every detail of her, the beautiful red hair all scraped back off her face save for a few stray strands that I would have loved to smooth back, the green coat catching the colour of her eyes, the brown boots laced up at the front. No bag, everything in her pockets. Bags were too 'girlie' for Kitty.

She didn't go quietly, I'll give her that.

She was up off the bed by then and reversing towards the door, her eyes wide. Another girl would have cried, but not Kitty, well, not while she was still in the room, anyway, and no nurse came running with any gossip to me afterwards.

She stood at the door for a few seconds. I thought she might make one final plea and, by Christ, I was ready and gunning for her if she did. And in case you think I am an out-and-out bollox, I was doing it more for her than for myself.

She squared her shoulders and looked me straight in the eyes. For an instant, I thought she was going to spit at me. I wouldn't have put it past her.

"Well, fuck you, Kieran Mahony, and the goat you rode into town on," she said, swirling away from me and booting out the door as if the hounds of hell were on her heels.

I might have laughed if the heart wasn't pounding like a jackhammer in my chest.

She wrote to me loads of times after that, in Dublin and back home. She was in her last year in the fancy boarding school down in Waterford at that stage. I opened the first couple of letters but they didn't sound like the real Kitty, hard and all as she was trying. I thought I got the smell of her from them, some kind of soap or perfume, and that did me no good at all. After that I used to throw the letters into the bottom of the chest of drawers. They were safer not opened anyway because Nana would have had a good read if she'd got her hands on them. I caught her red-handed with one letter. I had scrunched it up in a ball and fired it into a corner of the room. What had she done only smoothed out all the pages on the bed. She was halfway through it when I came back in from the toilet and I grabbed it from her. Was she bothered? Not a blind bit.

I was alright when no one mentioned Kitty or when I didn't see her. Boarding school was right handy for that. But sometimes my mother or Sally would come back with some report of seeing her down the village and that would send me right back into the black pit. I used to be haunted with thoughts of her, of memories of the good times we used to have out on the hunt or working in the stables. The dreams of her were the worst, and there were tons of them. Most of them I forgot, thanks be to God. In one, she was giving out stink to me for pretending to have hurt myself.

"Going on like that and you not able to walk properly, moryah," she said in the dream. "Do you take us for right thicks altogether? I had you copped all along."

Oh, the relief in the dream that I had only been letting on and that, now that Kitty had found me out, everything

139

would go back to normal. Picture yourself waking up from that. Yeah, that was a good one. Cracking, it was.

All those weeks lying in the room in Dublin were the worst because the addled mind would be running rings around you. Mind over matter. Let me tell you 'twas more matter over mind. I missed her so much. Think of a toothache, nagging, nagging, nagging. Then it stops for a while. You swear it's gone away, but doesn't it land back worse than ever. You get over these things if you can stay busy. Fat chance I had of keeping busy.

I got a quare old fright from a girl when I was only fourteen. We were in second year in school, and she was in the convent school. I dreamed the whole thing up in my head that she had a soft spot for me till she took off with one of my friends. I got over that by keeping busy. Work, work, work. My father couldn't get over the amount I was doing around the place.

But how do you keep busy when you have half a useless leg and an arm to match?

17

Jenny

"Be careful what you wish for. Isn't that right, Mam?" I was staring out of the kitchen window while I spoke to my mother but it was very little my poor eyes were taking in. All the while I was talking to her but yet it seemed as if the words were addressed to myself alone. She kept on knitting, the clicking of the grey needles a sound that kept my mind connected in some vague way to the kitchen my body was in. I wished I was a slip of a girl again, small enough to sit on her lap and feel her wrap me in her arms like she did so long ago.

"When Kieran was still in Dublin all I could think of was getting him home, taking him away from those hospital smells, away from the sickly disinfectant clogging my nose," I said. "Above all else, I wanted to get him away from the stale air, every breath of goodness leached out of it by those radiators. I wanted him back here, Mam, where the wind might blow down from the Top Field and redden that peaky face of his. I wanted him sitting here by the range with the hot coals winking at him with an honest heat. I wanted my Kieran back here at home so that he could mend and be the way he was before. I wanted the hands of the clock to rewind, the pages of the calendar to flutter backwards and all this to have been a desperate nightmare that I could wake up from. What in God's name was I thinking of, Mam, at all? What make of a fooleen did you raise? Shouldn't a grown woman know better than to expect miracles? Surely she should have learned by now that God is very selective about the prayers he chooses to answer. Sometimes I wonder would we have been better off to lave the boy up there in Dublin a couple of months longer, like the doctors wanted. I think 'tis worse he's getting since he landed home. Maybe it's my fault but he begged and begged to be taken out of there until he wore me down."

"Don't be so hard on yourself, a stór," my mother said. "Mother of God, when did it become a crime to hope for the best? If you hadn't the hope of something better waiting for Kieran here at home, you'd never have got him through these last two months up there. And if you were fooling yourself itself, amás to God, wasn't that the least you were entitled to?"

She finished the row of stitches, and dug the two needles into the big ball of bottle-green wool from which she was knitting the sleeve of a jumper.

"You were only buying yourself time until you were able to face the facts," she said. "The lonesome facts. And that's the dark valley you find yourself in now. But it won't always be dark. The sun will shine back into it again from over the shoulder of the hill. That's life. Day following night. Light following the dark."

Her words faded away into the silence of the kitchen where the Christmas decorations still hung, striving for a gaiety nobody in the house felt. Paper chains with orange, purple and red links stretched across the ceiling. The red candle in the window was half its original size, growing down towards the paper flowers it was bedded in. Tamara and Sally had put up the decorations. No one else had mind for them. I usually hated the bareness of the house when the decorations came down on the 6th of January, Women's Christmas, but now I was glad that there was only one day left. The bright colours mocked the black-and-white world I felt inside me. My heart might as well have been stuffed with wet ashes.

Neither of us spoke for a while. We sat there, locked in our own private thoughts. The big black kettle on the range had heated up and sang a steamy song under its breath. The room grew a shade darker than it should have been in the mid-afternoon.

"Look, Mam," I said suddenly, pointing to the garden where flakes of snow had begun to fall so thinly that they were barely visible at first. Slowly they grew more substantial as they slanted across the air, wide spaces separating them in the first few minutes. "Where did that come out of? There was no mention of snow in any forecast."

"I knew it was on the way," she said. "The cold always softens before the snow falls. I could feel the mildness this morning."

The snowflakes increased their hurry to the ground, thickening as they fell.

"That's the worst thing about being a mother," I said, my voice hollow. "Watching your child suffer and being powerless to do anything about it. I would do anything to put myself in his place, to take his pain on myself, but I can't."

The snow was settling on the grass, drawing a white line along bare black branches. A handful of finches and a single robin flitted between the rose bushes and the hydrangea that still held some faded flower heads. My mother took the ball of wool between her hands and held it as if the softness was a source of comfort.

"It's the same the world over, Jenny, a chroí," she said. "We bring them into this world wanting the best for them but we have no idea what's coming down the road for us or for them. Do you think I don't be wishing that it was me thrun below in the bed instead of that poor cratur? Sometimes I wonder why it is the Man Above has to send us these things to try us. If I didn't think it was a sin, I'd be asking does he know what he's doing."

I reached across the table and cut a slice from the brown cake of bread on the board. I crumbled it in my fist, allowing the crumbs fall on a blue-and-white side plate. I opened the window, admitting a cold draught of air. Quickly, I threw the crumbs on the flowerbeds outside: small earthen islands remained uncovered by the snow. My mother shivered. The birds had scattered when the window opened but they returned to search for the crumbs when I closed it.

"It's good in itself to be able to make life easier for someone," she said, watching the birds feed on the bread.

"If only I could make it easier for Kieran and for ourselves," I said. "I am praying and praying that there will be some break in the clouds. Do you know that I didn't shed one solitary tear that first day I saw him thrun down or in any of those days I spent at his bed in Cork or in the first weeks up in that Rehab place in Dublin? It was like there was a big block of ice inside me, ice frozen so solid that the fires of hell wouldn't melt it. Then, one week I came home and started tearing his room apart to give myself something to do. I picked up his duffle bag and pulled out his jersey and his togs. I sat there on his bed holding the jersey to me and crying as if the tears would never end. Poor Sally and Tamara came and stood there looking at me with their eyes opened wide with fright. I had been hiding everything from them for weeks, keeping it all locked up inside, but, that day, even the sight of them couldn't stop me. There was a black well inside me that no amount of tears could empty."

My mother hobbled across the kitchen floor, lifted the metal lid from the top of the range and threw in a block of wood. When she closed it up, she ran the dusty goose wing across the top. She sat down again and drew a deep breath.

"Do you know what ails you, girleen? You never let up, you never ever let up for one minute. You are going to drive yourself into the ground if you don't take some class of a break. And what way would we all be left if *you* collapsed on us?"

"Are you out of your mind? If I'm not here to keep an eye on Kieran, God only knows where he will end up."

"God never sends us a cross that he doesn't think we're strong enough for."

"Yerra, Mam, only five minutes ago you were wondering if the Man Above knew what he was doing," I replied, more bitterly than I'd intended. "The next minute you are on about him assessing what size of a cross he will give us, depending on what we're fit for. Has he a barn full of small, medium and large, do you think?"

As she turned away, stung, I regretted my tone. She took a deep breath and faced me again, her eyes boring into mine.

"You have two choices, my girl," she said. "You can bow down under this and let it destroy you. Or you can put your trust in God and face into it like a headwind. Face into it like a brave young soldier. And I will be right beside you – and your Con will be behind you too."

"Con," I said. "I wonder if that man feels anything. I

don't know if he has faced up to Kieran's accident. Nothing but work, work, work, morning, noon and night. The worst part is that I think he *blames* Kieran for all this. He can't even bear to look at him."

"I won't hear a word spoken about Coneen. Would you prefer to have him skiving off into the pub down the village after he goes to the creamery, like some of those amadáns in the parish? Is that what you want for yourself?"

"Sometimes I wonder whether it's his mother you are instead of mine. It's his side you are always taking instead of mine."

"Aisy, now," she said, eyes twinkling. "Isn't that just a poor old woman's insurance against being thrun into the County Home? I can count on my own daughter not to ship me out – at least I think I can – but you can't fault me surely for working on the son-in-law."

"Don't be counting on this daughter too much at all now if you keep on singing his praises like that," I said, smiling in spite of myself.

"As God is my judge, that boy has too strong a spirit to give up," she said. "Once the days lengthen, he will come on in leaps and bounds. Pray to God for courage for Kieran and patience for yourself. Give him time. As sure as bone heals, the heart will heal too, but the heart heals a hundred times more slowly."

"I will trust in what you are saying, but what is worrying me is Kieran's head," I said. "I hope and pray that it will come right."

Outside the window, the snow was falling hard and fast, the plump flakes racing each other to the ground. The birds were still foraging for stray crumbs. A robin landed on the topmost branch of the bare rose bush that climbs the barn wall.

146

18

Kieran

After I landed home my mother was on my case straight away. 'Twas enough to make me want to be back in the clinic in Dublin where she couldn't get at me. Mostly I left her spout away until she ran out of steam, but a day came when I couldn't stand another sermon. I pulled myself up on the pillows to let fly at her.

"Do you know what your problem is, Mam? Do you? You wanted us all to fit into one of those fucken *Ladybird* books you were always shoving at us. Peter and Jane, my arse. We're stuck into a hill at the end of a lane branching off a boreen in the wilds of Cork. What did you expect of us? And your 'Peter' is damaged goods now. Look at me and face up to it. I couldn't walk across this room without staggering like a drunk. Do you have any idea what the fucken tiredness is like? And you're telling me to get up, to make an effort, to pull myself together, that I'm lucky not to be a vegetable. Lucky? My God, Mam, do you call this lucky?"

She was standing at the end of the bed with the face of a martyr. "Look me in the eyes when I'm talking to you. Are you listening to me? Kieran, look at me."

I spat out my words as if they were a bad taste. "Say your piece and lave me alone."

She took a deep breath before getting into her stride. When I heard her put the 'O' before Mahony, I knew she was all set to burn the ears off me.

"Kieran O'Mahony, you might be giving up on yourself but I am not giving up on you. You're thrun down at the bottom of a hole as deep as any well but you're not going to stay there. Do you hear me? I'm not letting you if I have to torment the life out of you every single day. Inch by inch you're going to pull yourself up out of it. You are going to do it yourself. No one else can."

I began a slow clap. "Great speech, Mam. They'll be signing you up for the election campaigns yet. Did you never think of running for Cork County Council? You can blow hot air as good as any of them, fair play to you. Maybe Jack Lynch could take you out with him on the next canvas."

I was a prize bollox. I see that now. But she didn't flinch, and I had to admire her for that.

"Sarcasm doesn't suit you," she said. "You're only running for cover. You wouldn't be talking like this to me if your father was here." Her voice softened again. "Kieran, I know you're hurting inside and out but staying down here stuck in the bed isn't doing you or the rest of us any good. You're home two months now and you're throwing no shape at all. You're going to have to consider yourself and your future. This is affecting the family too, remember. It's like a dark cloud over all of us to think of you festering away down here in the bedroom. You could still have a dacent future if only you'd make some sort of a cut at getting better."

I pulled a pillow over my face. "Just go away and lave me alone, Mam. For fuck's sake, lave me alone. You haven't the first fucken notion what it's like not to be able to do the things you were used to doing. Even the sight of a hurley would make me puke now."

Next thing I knew she was pulling the pillow off me and roaring like someone possessed. "You might be suffering but that doesn't give you the excuse to use that filthy language to me. Mark my words, it won't chase me away, if that's your plan. I won't let up until you make an honest cut at the life that God has spared you for. Just tell me that you are going to make some effort."

I punched the pillow and turned my face to the wall. But she kept on coming. I shouldn't have used the F-word so often. 'Twas like a red rag to a bull.

"Alright, have it your way for now," she said. "Give up, throw in the towel. Is that what you did when you were playing a tough team and were a few points down? Fire the hurley away and walk off the pitch. Was that the way it was done? You had more fight than that in you. Right, the score is uneven now but you still have that fire in you. That fire is still there, and it will flame up if you give it a chance."

She was waiting for me to talk but she'd have a long wait on her hands. No one was going to corner me like that. I knew she was praying, wishing, hoping for one sentence, one crumb of hope, but all she was getting was silence. I just hadn't it in me. She walked over to the window, yanked the top half right down and let the icy breeze blow into the room. I had no idea how the room smelled but Sally used to pinch her nose when she came in. She'd be giving out about the smell of fags and stale sweat. Good job she'd never have to go into a hurling dressing room at half-time.

I listened to my mother's footsteps on the pine wooden floor and then clicking along the lino in the hallway, every

149

creak of the floor and thud of the doors familiar to me. I
twisted round and took the packet of Carroll's and a box
of matches from the chair beside the bed. Lifting out this
useless left leg with my two hands, I flinched at how thin
and lifeless it felt. I moved along the wall to the straight-
backed chair by the window and dropped down into it.
Here I was, the twelve and a half stone of muscle and sinew,
the senior county championship medal winner, reduced to
an eight-stone bag of bones with a wheezing chest.

Shivering in the cold breeze, I put a fag in my mouth,
took a match from the box and went to strike it with my
right hand. The box slipped to the floor.

"Goddammit," I said, sliding the box closer to the chair
with my right foot, bending down and straining to pick it
up. Suddenly I could sense someone in front of me. I
looked up as Tamara swooped low like a swallow and
handed me the box.

"Don't worry, Tamara, I won't rat on you. Do you
know what they call that in the court? Aiding and
abetting." I pointed to the window. "Close that bleddy
thing. I think Mam wants to freeze me out of the room
and up to the range."

Tamara climbed up on the sill and pulled the window
back up, struggling with the metal clasp to hold it in place.

"I suppose the walls have ears. Did you hear me
chewing the head off Mam a while ago? I'm not proud of
myself but sometimes I think I'm going to crack up. Come
on, strike a match there for me. I could murder a fag after
all that."

Tamara smiled at last. She lit the cigarette for me. I
leaned back, inhaled as deep as I could and blew out the
smoke slowly.

"The fag is the only thing that relaxes me, the only

pleasure left to a freak like me. You're the best company for me these days, Tamara. No lectures from you. I don't think you would have a go at me even if you could. No lectures except maybe from those dark eyes of yours. Deep as any pool in the elbow of the river."

Tamara waved a hand in front of her face to get rid of the smoke drifting across the room. She signed an 'O' in the air with her index finger. On cue, I started blowing rings of smoke. I looked at my watch.

"Milking time must be nearly over," I said bitterly. "At least I'm spared that. Thank heavens for small blessings."

My eyes settled on the picture on the wall to the left of Tamara's head. It was a photo printed in 'De Paper', alias *The Cork Examiner,* after the County Club Championship. That was the game I brought the team over the line with a winning point. 'Twas the game that finished the drought in the parish: our first win in thirty-seven years. Put that wan in the history books.

"See that, Tamara," I said. "The best time of my life. But all that is gone now. Gone. And it's never coming back. Get used to that, Kieran, old stock. Victory and defeat. That's what sport is all about. Rising and falling, but this is one I'm never going to rise up out of. They've brought all the team to me for the pep talks. Christ, they couldn't even look me in the eye, the pity reeking from them. Pakie, the trainer, took the best shot at it, fair dues to him. Offered me the chance to come back coaching the young lads. I wanted to laugh in his face. Do you know what he said to me? 'At least you're not in a wheelchair, Kieran boy. You have to think of those worse off than you. Think of that poor rugby player inside in the city that broke his neck in a scrum and can't even twitch to get a fly off his nose.' That was very consoling alright."

I took a scallop shell overflowing with butts from under the chair and stubbed out the cigarette. I took another one from the pack and Tamara lit it for me automatically.

"Can you imagine me at a training session?" I said. "Wouldn't I look nice dragging myself up and down the sideline, wobbling like an auld fella with a stroke or some drunk on the wrong side of a dozen pints?" I thumped my left leg. "It wouldn't be fair on the youngsters to put up with that. Anyway, I couldn't bear to look at the pitch I used to fly over. And have some smart scuts laughing out of the corners of their mouths at me."

When I stopped to take a deep drag of the fag, my eyes met hers. She looked so worried, the poor cratur, that I knew I should change tack, but when I talked about the torture I was putting up with – and that wasn't often – it was like sticking a needle in a boil and watching all the green pus spurt out.

"It's alright, Tamara. I can hear myself: the bitterness, the poor-auld-me whining. I know I'll have to let up at some point but not yet. In fairness to Pakie, he took everything I spewed at him and he still came back for more. Every single week, he sat with me. 'Lob them all at me, boy,' he'd say. 'High ones and low ones. You know me, they cracked my head open with belts of the hurley and I was still in there in the thick of it. You're down, laid low, but I know you,' the hell he did, 'you're made of sterner stuff. You'll be back out there, not like you were before, but you have something left to give.'"

The room was a cloud of smoke now and Tamara was beginning to look sick. I'd have to stop soon. Her eyes were watering from the smoke. I was only halfway down the fag but I stubbed it out.

"Go on away out before I poison you. One casualty is enough in the house."

Tamara stood up and took a few steps towards the bedroom door. She gestured to me to follow. I shook my head. She begged me with her eyes. Tempted, I half-rose out of the chair, but slumped back again.

"No, Tamara, I'm going to dig into the stinking burrow a little while longer. If there's any crowd lining up to make speeches at me, I want some fella who will give me the go-ahead to be an awkward bollox for as long as I need to be, to be complaining on the sidelines till I'm good and ready to get back out on the pitch."

Tamara left the room, with a backward glance.

I made my way back to the bed, dragged the eiderdown over my head and blocked out the daylight.

Two of the lads, Mattie Cotter and Joe Golden, had pulled the short straw a fortnight after I had come home and were the very first of the club to be sent to visit me. What a job they got, the poor feckers. I can imagine how it had gone some evening in the dressing room after training.

"Now, listen, lads, someone has to go up. 'Tisn't as if he's after growing two heads or losing a leg or anything. He's the same Kieran," voice drops a degree or so at this lie, you can imagine, "Are ye a team or what? A team sticks together through thick and thin." Except maybe when a fella has gone a bit dulally after a belt in the head.

Mattie and Joe volunteered in the end. They landed in all shy and awkward, eyes twisting every which way except towards me. My mother brought them in, so delighted and grateful you'd swear they were first prize in a raffle. I thought I was going to get sick. I was so sorry for the poor feckers – it felt as if I should be consoling them instead of the other way round. So I put on the big act, the funny-ha-ha lark, gave an Oscar performance, pulled every fecking trick out of the book until they loosened up and looked at me instead of the floor.

"Exhibit A, lads, as good as dead as a dodo," I said for openers, catching up my useless left arm with my right hand. "They tell me I'll get some use back in it if I exercise it. But, to tell you the truth, I couldn't really be arsed. There's plenty of time. Haven't I my whole wonderful life stretching ahead of me?" Then I pointed to the left leg and hit it a slap on the thigh. "This auld fella is half on strike too but I can do a bit of a walk. Only problem is that I look as if I've had about twenty pints."

I levered myself up out of the chair and walked to the end of the bed.

"What do you think of that, lads? Is that like the Hucklebuck or what?"

But the big joke wasn't coming off. I fecked up, didn't I, couldn't finish the course. I decided to extend my ramble towards the door and was motoring away up the final furlong when my foot caught in the mat that Mam had put in that morning to make the room look 'nice' and I fell face forward on the floor.

Roll the camera to the two faces of the lads and cut to pity in the script. There were the lads all concerned like, rushing to pick me up but, of course, being the brave lad that I am, I shrugged them off, roaring 'No!' A fine loud 'No!' repeated about three times. Ever try to lever yourself up off the floor with a half-dead arm and a leg that's not much better? No leverage, boy. There I was wriggling like an eel on the riverbank, all action but going nowhere. Mattie and Joe came over again and made an attempt to grab me, in fairness to them. I told them where to go with themselves. Nothing would have pleased me more than if they'd shagged off and left me there on the floor. I told them to eff off out of my sight, which was a bit rich given that I was at eye level with the mat. What did the pair of flutes do only gather their courage, the bauld Mattie first and Joe coming up on the inside behind him.

"Fuck off yourself," Mattie says. "You were always a mad bollox. Happy to see you haven't lost it, whatever else you're missing. Joe, come over here with me and catch one side of this auld sack of potatoes."

But they weren't going to have it that easy. "I'm warning ye. Lave me alone and fuck off out of my sight. Are ye thick or what? I'm the one that's supposed to have the brain damage. Don't think ye're getting in on the act."

"Yerra, shut the fuck up!" Joe said, gathering his courage. "Do you think we're going to let you thrun down there? It wouldn't be safe trying to step over you getting to the door. You might hit us a flake and where would we be then with an injury coming up to the next game? Anyway, Packie'd box our ears if he heard we'd walked out and left you like that."

Before I knew it, I was landed back up in the chair.

"There you go, sound as a bell, boy," Mattie said.

I took out a fag and demanded a light to steady my nerves. I offered them the pack and they took one each. The room began to fog up. None of us said anything for a few minutes. We just sat there dragging away for all we were worth. The lads were acting all tough like but I guessed they were shook up too. Not your normal visiting session.

"Take that auld puss off you," Mattie said at last. "It's bad enough to be sent up here without having to look at that. You're as cheerful as a cut cat."

"Nobody's asking ye to stay. Don't tell me 'tis how ye need directions to the exit."

Silence fell again. All we wanted now was for Mam to come fussing in with a tray of tea and ham sandwiches. Strange that she hadn't landed in already. More than likely she was out in the hall with her ears pricked. How she managed to hold herself back when she heard all the commotion, God only knows.

Mattie exhaled a jet of smoke and started in on me again. "Tell us about the nurses up there. Any goers, or are they all sergeant-majors ordering you around? Did you get the shift? A feel even. I'd murder for a bit in those uniforms. Jesus Christ, nurses," he shifted in his chair, "the thought of them! With their hearts going out to you, you must have been on a roll, boy."

Joe threw his eyes to heaven. "Will you give over, you mad animal. No self-respecting nurse would let you within a mile of her. Unless you were unconscious, and there wouldn't even be a guarantee of safety then."

I looked at the two of them, the funny men, and in that moment my guard came down. For an instant, the old times were back again. We were having the craic. I forgot the leg, the headaches, the tiredness, the tubes, the useless struggle to walk properly, the well-meaning sermons that all translated into the one message: 'Pick yourself up and get on with it.' I managed a smile, just a small one. I didn't want them to think they were winning – not just yet.

"That's more like it, you old bollox," Mattie said. "You're a piece of work alright but you know you're dealing with two mighty men. We take no shit, Joe boy, do we? Never did nor never will, Mr O'Mahony, even if you start using that old gammy leg and arm as excuses. Don't mind the head. There's no points for that. You were always a bit touched in the head. Amn't I right, Joe boy?"

"Right as rain, whatever is right about rain," Joe replied.

I asked them what they had expected before they came up to see me. The question cut through the chat like a knife. Joe looked towards Mattie, the spokesman up to now, but Mattie passed the ball back to him. Mattie was always the man for a neat pass at a key point in the game.

"This one is all yours, Joe," he said.

"Do you want the truth or what?" Joe asked me.

"Sock it to me, baby."

"Well, to tell you the God's honest truth, we were afraid you were gone mental, like. After the bang on the head and everything like, you know what I mean."

"Well, I am a bit mental in some ways but not mad enough or bad enough to cart me up to the madhouse on the Lee Road."

The mood had dropped again. I wasn't in the form for baring my soul any further. Anyway, hadn't they put up with enough from me? It was time to lighten it up a bit.

"Ye were asking me about the nurses, weren't ye, and we got sidetracked along the way."

They relaxed immediately. Good old funnyman Kieran to the rescue. I gave it wellie.

"Well, there was this big, tall blonde one, thin as a whip but with knockers this size," I said, giving an approximation of an oversized turnip with my hands. "This night, she was leaning in over me fixing the bed when didn't the buttons pop and a big creamy one with a red cherry at the tip come bursting out, nearly knocking the eye out of my head. As if I didn't have enough injuries to be going with by then. Then the next thing I knew, wasn't she climbing up on top of me? And by God, it

157

didn't look as if she was out to take my blood pressure, even though it was shooting pretty high by then, I can tell you."

"Go away to fuck," Mattie said.

"That was the highest notion on my brain, but then I woke up," I said.

The three of us roared laughing. I prayed to God my mother wasn't outside in the hall listening. If she was, I knew for certain who my next visitor would be – the parish priest. To hear my confession. Sure I could always say my brain was affected.

There was some small talk about this and that after the laughing stopped. The two boys left to go back to the world of the classroom, the dressing room, the pitch, the village, the pub, the dance hall, and living breathing girls instead of makey-up nurses. I sat there smoking and wondering why it had all been taken away from me and how I would finish up.

'Twas good to get the visit over and done with though. Nothing was as hard again as facing them that first day. Fair play to them, they played a blinder. And so they did every time they met me. I tell you I wouldn't like to have been in their shoes. Not by a long shot. Shoes, another funny story. I wouldn't be wearing out much shoe leather at the rate I was walking. Slouching around the bedroom didn't amount to much punishment for leather soles.

19

Sally

It was April. In two weeks, it would be six months since the accident happened. Of all of us, Mammy seemed to have taken it the worst. Half the time she seemed as if she was putting on an act. She was flying off the handle at the smallest thing. I had to watch myself for fear I would set her off. I'm telling you it was hard going.

"I'm demented," she said one evening under her breath.

The word set off an echo in my head. *Demented, demented.*

Tamara and myself tiptoed around her. Any fine day we were out of the house and away from the feeling that stiffened the rooms like Robin starch. Winter still had a bitter hoult on April, even though its time was up. Like this one evening when the brightness should have lasted way past six but the rain clouds were darkening the garden and the kitchen light was switched on early. Outside the window the branches of the lilac tree were tearing over and back like mad things. The kitchen was warm and the kettle was singing. Tamara had her nose buried in another *Nancy Drew* mystery. Of course Nana was delighted with her. Her little scholar. Made a change from 'the little pagan', I suppose. There was no end to the books she brought home from the library: *Nancy Drew*,

The Hardy Boys, Just William, The Famous Five, Treasure Island and *Uncle Tom's Cabin.* She loved Mammy's copies of the *Reader's Digest* too. She tried to read the Walter Macken novels, but they were too hard for her. The digests weren't too bad, especially the jokes at the end of the pages. I introduced her to Pudsy Ryan in *The Far East.* He's gas out but Tamara couldn't understand why someone with such bad spellings could be allowed into a magazine. I did make an attempt to read a few books when the weather was bad. I had a go at *Black Beauty* and *White Fang.* I liked them. Any fine day that came along I much preferred to be out in the fields, even more so after Kieran came home and Mammy's nerves were at her. But Tamara was different. She coped by losing herself in books. I was jealous of her in a way. There was no magic carpet to take me away.

"Would you not go down the hall again to him and try to get him to come up here to the kitchen?" Mammy said.

My father sighed and put down the paper with a crackle of the pages. He had come in out of the shed early in the evening. Work was escape. Normally, we didn't see him till very late but he had a terrible hacking cough, worst when he spoke. Good job he was a man of few words. I don't know why Mammy kept sending him down to Kieran. I don't know why he kept going. Sometimes I stood outside the bedroom door and listened. There would be only one voice – Daddy's. He would talk away as if Kieran was going to answer any second now. And when he didn't, he would supply the answer himself.

"That bleddy carburettor is doing my head in. It looks perfect from the outside but when it comes to firing, there's nothing at all. I have pulled it apart and put it back together a dozen times but it's still besting me."

Silence from the bed. My brother was some flipping tulip. Not a word out of him.

Kieran did leave his bedroom. He left it in the dead of night when we were all in bed. He woke me sometimes. I would hear him shuffle up the hall, keeping to the wall, just the faintest sound of him dragging his leg over the lino if you listened really hard. I crept downstairs one night and followed him.

The kitchen was dim, save for the red glow of the Sacred Heart lamp. He was standing over the teapot on the range. I slipped behind the table and onto the long stool. He was making tea, spooning the black leaves out of the old orange Cow and Gate milk-powder tin into the pot. My heart was in my mouth as he lifted the heavy black kettle with his right arm. It trembled. Some of the water spattered onto the surface of the range and hissed.

"Do you want a cup?" he asked, without turning around. His voice was hoarse. The hoarseness of someone speaking after a silence of hours. He coughed a little, to clear his throat.

You couldn't imagine how delighted I was to hear him ask me that. I slid off the stool and took a cup off the hook on the dresser. The hen was pecking away on the clock face, up and down, up and down to an endless supply of grain that would never run out, no matter how many hours passed.

Kieran poured the tea into the blue cup. "Do you think I'm gone mental, Sally girl?"

I blushed to the roots of my hair. My face was so red, a drop of water would have sizzled on it. I was thinking of the conversations between my mother and father, times when they had forgotten Tamara and myself were in the back of the car or times when we were larking about in the hay beside the milking stall. "Will he ever be right again? Is there more damage to his brain than they thought? I don't like that stare in those beautiful green eyes of his. I can't bear to look in them."

Kieran held out his mug. "Get me a drop of milk, will you? What's the matter? Cat got your tongue? I thought it was only Tamara had her tongue tied. There's some excuse for me, you know. I got my brain shook like a baby's rattler inside my skull. I suppose that would class me as at least half-mental. What do you think yourself, Doctor Sally?"

He sank back into the chair and bored his eyes into me. I brought the milk from the table. He swirled the tea round in the cup.

"If Nana is so good at reading the tea leaves, it's a wonder she didn't predict this coming down the road to me. Remember the pictures she could see when the leaves stuck at the side of the cup – a castle, a clown, a pile of gold coins."

"Don't you remember?" I said.

"Remember what?" His eyes were sharp.

My stomach tightened. Something told me I should not go on.

"Nothing."

"What do you mean, nothing?" His voice was quare out.

"Well, there was this day when Nan was looking at the tea leaves and she saw a horse."

He fixed me with a stare. I knew he didn't remember. I was glad he didn't.

"Don't mind her old mumbo jumbo," he said.

"You're different," I said, pouring some milk into his tea, watching the thick cream separate into tiny globules.

"You changed. We all wish you'd spend more time here in the kitchen and talk to us instead of being stuck on your own all the time."

His eyes pierced mine with a cruel stare. He mocked me. "*We all wish you'd come out of the room and talk to us. You're different.* How the hell you think I'd be after having half my skull smashed in? Different. Of course I'm fucken different. Would you like to be parading yourself in front of pitying eyes with one leg trailing after you like a dead piece of wood and an arm swinging useless by your side?"

I dropped the jug with the fright. The amber and brown rings shattered on the floor and the milk ran through the cracks. The crash was as loud a gunshot. We looked at each other, waiting for the silent house to rouse. Poor old Sam had slept right through the smashing of the jug. The miracle of deafness. No such luck with my father.

"Who's that down there in the kitchen?" he shouted down the stairs.

"It's only me," I said. "I came down for a drink of milk and dropped the jug."

"You have my sleep broken on me," he said. "Get back up to bed."

"I will in a minute," I said, bending to pick up the pieces.

Kieran was running his right hand through his hair. He pushed back the fringe, revealing the jagged red scar at his temple. It reminded me of Frankenstein, but we couldn't even joke about it.

"I'm sorry, Sally," he whispered. "Don't mind me. I'm not fit company for anyone. Now can't you see why I don't want to come out of that room? I don't want to inflict myself on ye."

I was blubbering. Furiously I rubbed my pyjama sleeve across my nose. I knelt down on the floor to pick up the smallest bits of the jug, so glad that my hair was falling across my face like a curtain. Part of me wished he had broken his bleddy neck when he fell, putting himself out of his misery and saving us all from having to endure his moods.

"I don't blame you if you hate me," he said. It was as if he had seen right into my head. "I hate me too – what's left of me, that is."

The words melted away the bitterness that was clenching my gut but the tears were still falling. I got up and put the last fragments of the jug on the table. I wiped the milk up with a stale-smelling floorcloth. A wave of tiredness crashed over me.

"It's alright," I started but my voice was choked with sobs.

I made for the hall door but Kieran called me back in a fierce whisper, *"Don't go. Just sit here for a while. You don't have to say anything."*

Sitting in the kitchen with him was the last thing I wanted to do. I wanted to go back to my room and bury my head in the pillow and cry for him, for myself, for the whole shagging lot of us. But I couldn't go. I got into the armchair at the other side of the range and pulled my legs under me. I rubbed my nose again on the pyjama sleeve. My father's snores floated down the stairs, rising and falling until he stirred this way or that and the sound stopped – for a while. At least he wasn't going to come down and check on us.

Sam was still dozing on the hearthstone. Her chest was whistling and wheezing like a set of bagpipes. When she growled, it came not from her throat but from somewhere deep down in her chest. We watched her. Her paws flexed and fluttered as they always did when she was dreaming of a time when she was young. She gave her chesty growl.

"Bet she's way off down the Hilly Field chasing rabbits right up to the door of their burrows," Kieran said. "There's none of the auld arthritis pinching her bones. At least she has that in her dreams. She can run like the wind like she used to. All that stiffness is way ahead of her, hasn't come near her yet. Dream on, Sammy girl."

Was he talking about the dog or himself? My head was hurting with pity for them, but pity was the last thing he wanted.

"Bring the bottle of whiskey up from the parlour," he said. "Be as quiet as a mouse so no one will hear."

His voice reminded of the one the tinker women used when they came to the door looking for Mammy to give them some food to put in the basket under their shawl.

"Mammy will kill me. You know she never takes the whiskey out except for visitors or at Christmas."

He started begging again. I could tell it was an act.

"It's only one glass. A splash of the cratur in hot water to make me sleep. She'll never know the difference. We can top the bottle up with the smallest dropeen of cold tea. Yerra go on, Sal, go on.' He had dropped the Sally in his desperation to persuade me. 'You don't know what it's like to lie there on your back, not being able to sleep, thoughts racing around your bleddy brain like toy cars on a Scalextric track, thinking of the minute when you went falling, falling down, never to rise up again as the same person."

Somewhere between those words, the false, pity-me-please tone disappeared from his voice to be replaced by a lonesomeness. The feeling that he was out to trick me to get the whiskey was gone and his despair won me over. I slipped from the chair and tiptoed down the hall to the parlour. I twisted the wooden knob. The sharp click set my heart pounding but no one stirred. I don't know why but the mahogany sideboard reminded me of a coffin in the shadows. The pair of white stuffed owls sitting in their glass dome on the sideboard surface were no doubt judging me with their glassy eyes. The brass key was in the cabinet door, reminding me of the big sin I was about to commit against Mammy. It was an unwritten law in our house that no one opened the drinks press but my mother, who doled out a glass of whiskey to the vet or the parish priest, a hot whiskey for 'medicinal purposes' to anyone suffering from a cold, a glass of sherry to special visitors or a couple of bottles of porter to friends who called for games of Thirty-One over Christmas. She was so trusting that the key was never hidden. I felt as Judas must have felt when he fingered the cold and shiny pieces of silver, but my version was the goldie liquid inside the bottle of Paddy whiskey with the map of Ireland on the label. Half-full, its last outing had been on Saint Stephen's Day when a glass was given to the vet who had delivered the shorthorn heifer of a fine bull calf after a troublesome birth. Offered one glass, he had tossed it back and put out the glass for a second and a third. He would have kept going if my father was the one to give out the measures, but Mammy knew his weakness and retreated to the parlour with the bottle while he was still standing there with the arm outstretched.

The bottle was cool to the touch. My fingers clasped it so tightly around the neck that I thought it would shatter.

Kiean had the sickening face back on him when I walked into the kitchen but, as soon as he saw the bottle, his eyes turned cold. I knew then that I was a right eejit and that he had tricked me. I was so sorry I had brought up the bottle.

"Fill half a glass from the kettle and put in a teaspoon of sugar," he said.

I followed his orders. Then he supervised me as I poured the whiskey into the glass.

He signalled me to keep pouring until the glass was almost full to overflowing.

I then attempted to take the bottle away.

"Bring it here!" he barked.

His voice had risen but I was afraid to tell him to quieten down.

He cupped the glass with his hands. His left hand was unsteady and some of the whiskey slopped on to the floor.

"Jesus Christ, can you do anything right?" he said.

I wanted to tell him that he was the one who told me to fill the glass so much but I was afraid to. While he lifted the glass shakily to his lips, I took the bottle from the table and headed towards the hall.

"Where do you think you're going?" he said. "Bring that back here."

I hesitated.

"Put the bottle down there," he said, pointing to his feet.

I did as I was told.

He raised the glass a second time and swallowed half of the whiskey in one gulp. I began to panic. What if somebody got up and came into the kitchen? What if it was Mammy and she saw the bottle? He leaned back against the chair, closed his eyes and smacked his lips. I never dared look at the scar while he was aware of me but, now, with his eyes closed, it was like a magnet tugging my eyes to the ugly red line zig-zagging its way across his left temple and up along his forehead, disappearing into his hairline. As if he sensed my eyes probing its passage, his eyes shot open.

"What are you looking at?" he asked coldly. "Is it how you didn't have your fill of looking at me since I came home? You and all the rest of them."

He stretched out his damaged arm towards me, holding the glass in his good hand, the left. He could see my puzzlement. It was only when he spoke that I realised he was pretending to ask for money. "How much is it worth to you? Isn't it obvious? You have to pay for admission to the freak show."

He put the glass to his mouth again and dispatched the second half, wiping the sleeve of his jumper across his lips. He demanded another glass – his bad hand wasn't steady enough to hold the bottle to pour – but I stood my ground. The whole thing was getting out of control.

He began to whimper like a new-born pup. "I'm sorry, Sal. I don't know what got into me. Just this glass and I'll go back to bed. It will make me sleep like a log. Just one more glass. That will do the trick."

But then he flashed me one honest look. It was my Kieran, the old Kieran come back to me. He had convinced himself that this was true.

"Just one more glass, please, and I'll have that sleep I need so badly."

He believed himself and I believed him too. I wanted to hold on to the real Kieran even if it was only for a few seconds, even if I ran the risk of my thieving being found out.

The clock struck five: just one hour to the house coming back to life. Kieran drank the second glass more slowly.

168

The desperate look was gone from his eyes. I relaxed a bit. Maybe this was what he needed. It was 'medicinal'. Surely my mother would understand that if she found out. He was calmer. I bent to pick up the bottle. It was dangerously below the halfway mark. Cold tea wasn't going to fix this. Dread was worming around the pit of my stomach.

"Not so fast," he said, whipping the bottle up off the floor with his good hand.

Anger flashed through me. "It's me that'll get the blame," I said, making an attempt to grab the bottle.

But he held onto it with a grip stronger than I could have believed. I pulled again, quickly and with greater force, and the bottle slipped from his fingers. I fell backwards on the floor and the bottle went clattering across the tiles. It didn't break but the whiskey spilled all over the place.

"*Fuck off!*" he said venomously.

I could hear the stairs creaking. Then my mother appeared in the doorway, an old grey cardigan pulled over her blue nightdress. She was blinking in the light, unsure if she could believe what she was witnessing. Tamara was at her heels. My father was calling from the bedroom.

"What's going on down there, Jenny?"

"Fuck off!" Kieran told me again. "It's all your fault."

I backed away in horror, the tears streaming down my face.

My mother glanced from me to Kieran, to the bottle and the whiskey running into the crevices between the tiles, the sickly smell of it rising all around us.

"What are you using that filthy, dirty language to Sally for?" she said. "I won't have that kind of language used in this house, do you hear me, Kieran?"

"Yerra fuck off yourself," he said, half-rising from the chair but falling back again.

"By the almighty God, you'll pay for that, my boy," she said, grabbing the sweeping brush that was leaning against the green press. She brought it down full force on his shoulders.

He put up his good arm and grabbed the head of the brush. They tussled. With one violent jerk, my mother pulled it towards her. Kieran held onto it and she pulled him towards her. He fell forward and ended up sprawling on the tiles, sobbing with rage. A jet of cowdung green snot shot from his nose and hung there.

My mother roared and bellowed as she belted him with the brush. "*I can take no more of this, you ungrateful pup! I curse the day you were ever born! Do you think you are the only one suffering here? You have our lives turned upside down just because you wanted to go careering around the countryside on a horse, and all you can think of is yourself. Poor Kieran stuck in his bed all day and coming out at night. Think of someone else for a change. By God, my brave boyo, I'll make you sorry for what you are doing to us!*"

It was desperate. She kept belting him and belting him with the brush while he put his arms around his head, trying to defend himself. He squirmed and jerked on the floor like a worm on a hook. Suddenly there was a piercing scream, a scream so loud that Mammy stood frozen with the brush in mid-air.

"*Leave him alone! Stop it! Stop it! Kieran! Kieran!*" It was Tamara, howling as she ran across to the table and grabbed the bread knife. She stood over Kieran, fire sparking in her eyes and burning into my mother's face. "*Don't touch him again or else!*" she shouted, waving the knife at my mother. *"I hate you, I hate you!"*

My father made his entrance in the middle of this scene, his eyes roaming in disbelief from Mammy, wild-eyed and still wielding the brush, to the warrior Tamara clutching the bread knife. You should have seen the hurt look in his eyes when he saw Kieran, who was making use of the break in the drama to drag himself across the floor. I could only think of the time that one of the hens was sick and the others attacked it, pecking it until it collapsed on the caked henhouse floor in a flutter of wings.

"What kind of an asylum is this?" my father said. "Are ye all gone clane mad or what? Tamara, girl, give me that thing for the love and honour of God."

"Promise me no one will hurt Kieran again," she said. "Promise me."

Tamara was talking! Given everything that was going on, this historic development wasn't ringing all the bells it should have rung. I had waited so long for this moment, tried so hard to make it happen and yet here I was without a blind bit of excitement. For one thing, her accent was throwing me. She was talking with a flipping English accent, and a posh English accent at that. What did I expect, a sing-song Cork accent? Don't ask me but I had built up another voice entirely in my head.

Kieran looked up at her, his streaked face and his red eyes stamped with the same shock as us all.

"It's alright, Tamara, peteen," Daddy said soothingly. "Leave it, will you, like a good girl."

"I'm alright, Tamara," Kieran said, breathing fast. "Give it to him. Don't worry about me. It's all over."

My father took the knife from her and placed it back on the breadboard. He moved in slow motion and I had this strange feeling that we were all on the surface of the moon, a long, long way off from anywhere familar. Was I dreaming? My father leaned down to lift up Kieran but he shrugged him off. He crawled across to the sink and pulled himself up. Leaning against it, he looked as if he would slide back down at any second but none of us dared give him a hand.

My mother was in bits. Her chest was heaving. She was after coming back to her senses and, from the cut of her, 'twasn't a place you'd be going on your holidays to.

"Oh my God, Kieran, I am so sorry. I don't know what came over me. I'm so sorry. I didn't mean what I said. Not a word of it. Say something, please. Don't turn away."

Kieran looked straight towards the hall door, as if he were calling up every ounce of energy in his body to get there. He leaned his shoulder against the wall, advancing with the awkward gache he hated anyone to see. My mother fell to her knees, rocking and keening. Miraculously the whiskey bottle hadn't shattered when it fell but the whiskey was all over the floor. My father told me to mop it up. I was sick to my stomach after everything that happened but I was also relieved that nobody guessed at my part in it.

Nana had slept through the entire drama. She was positively disgusted when she discovered, later in the morning, that Tamara had found her tongue without her being there to witness the wonder. For her, it was the same as a mother being out of the room when the baby took its first step. We were all ducking and dodging her questions about the exact circumstances in which the miracle had happened. If Nana suspected any of the violence that had gone on in the kitchen, she chose to ignore it.

"Don't go trying to turn the child into a performing canary," my father said that first evening.

Nana was fierce insulted. "Can I help it if I can't get over the sound of her, the little songbird?"

Her highest notion was to teach Tamara to sing 'The Boys of Kilmichael' now that she had learned that, not alone could she speak, she could sing as well.

Tamara's words came in torrents as if she was making up for all the lost months of silence. I began to think of the saying, 'Be careful what you wish for'.

"But why didn't you talk all along?" I asked her a few days later. We were all trying to put as much distance as we could between ourselves and that disturbing night in the kitchen.

Tamara shrugged. "I can't really explain it. Maybe being silent was the only way I could keep safe. If I stayed inside myself, nobody could hurt me or get to me. I don't really know. "

"Are you glad you can talk?" I asked. "You're not afraid that you will shut up again?"

"Don't worry. I shan't stop," she said. "Nana has her prize canary, and I shan't disappoint her."

"You know she is claiming your 'cure' as one of Little Nellie's miracles?"

"Maybe I'm glad that Little Nellie took me on," she smiled. "Even if it means I will have to recite lots more catechism."

"We'll have to get Little Nellie to storm heaven and earth for Kieran next," I said.

Neither of us smiled.

20

Sally

Going on a bit of a mission. That's all my father would say. Mammy threw her eyes to heaven. All evening she had been trying to winkle it out of him but he was haulding tough. He told Tamara and myself to be up at the crack of dawn if we wanted to come, but we hadn't a notion where he was taking us.

"What business have you dragging those two slips of girls out of their beds at that hour of the morning?" Mammy said. "Tomorrow is supposed to be as raw as today, according to the weather forecast. They'll catch their deaths."

She was kneading dough in the big biscuit-coloured bowl. I thought it would fly out over the edges at the rate her hands were working the soft mass flecked with freckles of brown flour.

"Yerra, wouldn't an outing be good for them, Jenny?" he said. "Good to get them out of the house. Maybe you might come yourself."

My mother caught a tin mug with holes on the lid and shook a dusting of flour on the kitchen table.

Nana opened her mouth to make some pronouncement from her throne but the cross way my mother tipped the mound of dough out of the bowl stopped her in her tracks.

175

"What are you thinking about, Con? How can I go anywhere with the amount of work that's to be done around here?"

She jerked her head in the direction of the hall leading to Kieran's bedroom. "How can I leave him here on his own?"

"Alight, alright," he said. "I won't open my mouth again."

I was wide awake long before he came into the bedroom to call Tamara and myself. He must have been out at dawn to milk the cows in order to get away so early. It was ten days since the drama in the kitchen and none of us had quite got over the shock of it. I was glad to have a whole day away from home stretching ahead of me. I'd knock a bit of craic out of trying to get Tamara to cultivate a Cork accent.

The first thing she had asked for was to phone her daddy in London. We had no phone at home, so an arrangement was made to bring her to the doctor's house every Friday evening at nine to make the call. Mammy drilled her not to be giving too much information away in case 'Herself' operating the telephone exchange in the post office was listening in for nuggets of family information to fatten on. Up to this, Uncle Jack had sent a letter every couple of weeks, asking how Tamara was faring and putting in a crisp English twenty-pound note towards her keep every time. Now that she could speak to him on the phone, Tamara was missing him more.

We still hadn't a clue where we were going when, after about two hours driving in the Land Rover and trailer Daddy had borrowed from Jerry Twomey, we ended up in a traffic jam at the edge of a town I had never seen before. The jeep crawled on for about a quarter of a mile until

Daddy saw a car and a horsebox pulling out and he took the parking space. By then, I had guessed we were going to a fair. After we had parked the car and walked a couple of hundred yards, there was no doubting it. Horses, ponies and donkeys lined both sides of the street. Mares with long-legged foals leaning close to their bellies and flanks, some of them suckling from the udders so small and neat compared to those of our cows. Horses stood, their heads hanging and their big bodies still as statues. Spirited horses dancing and striking the tarred road with their front hooves. A Clydesdale with the hoof below its hairy hoof tipped back, resting. Piles of horse manure, some untouched and shining like glossy chestnuts, but more mashed into the road and flecked with oats. Horses of all sizes and colours: chestnut, bay, white, grey, piebald, white stars and blazes on some. Fancy horses with manes plaited, tinkers' horses with manes spiked, most of them still in their winter coats. There was a smell of horse piss and dung every couple of steps. I pinched my nose and Tamara copied me.

Daddy issued instructions. "Stay close to me, keep away from back legs, watch out for cars squeezing through the crowd."

There was no way I wanted to get lost in a place that was full of excitement and life but, at the same time, stinking. I like the smell of a horse in a stable or out in the open air but, to be honest, the fair was a bit much. We filed through the crowd with me gripping the hem of Daddy's grey tweed jacket.

Soon I heard his voice call out, "Look at him! That's him. He's the one."

I had to push through the circle of men he had joined, to see what he was getting so excited about. Tamara

177

followed me. A red-haired boy was holding a grey horse on the end of a rope. But grey was too plain a word for him. He was the grey of a rainy sky – silver fading through to the lead of fishing weights, and white patches coming and going through the grey like a line of clouds. He was the most beautiful creature you could ever imagine: milky grey eyelashes, navy eyes, blond highlights in his grey mane, his legs the same mixture of dappled cloud. I can tell you all this because I admired him for months and years afterwards. But even on that first day I looked on him as a kind of sky horse. My father used to say he felt he radiated luck from the moment he clapped eyes on him as a two-year-old.

Tamara, of course, drew from the store of big words that had been gathering dust for too many months. "He is splendid," she said. "Splendid." It was a posh word but, I had to agree, a perfect word for this creature.

The three of us were carried away by the discovery, but he was, after all, no Pegasus but a horse for sale at a fair. Tamara and myself were thrilled to be given the rope to hold onto him while the youngster ran off to find his father who had taken a break in one of the pubs. We stroked the animal's fine face while we waited.

"How do you know he's the one?" I asked my father.

"How do you know there's rain in the wind?" he replied. "I just felt it when he came before me." He struck his chest. "I felt it here. You only have to look at him. Look at the way he's put together. The eyes. You can see the intelligence shining out of them." He patted the horse's neck. "You're a good one, sure and certain. All I hope now is that I can afford you."

This side of my father was new to me. He had sworn that he would never let another horse darken the gate after

178

Kieran's accident. I didn't dare question him about his change of heart.

The owner returned. He was a stout man with sandy hair and a rosy face. He walked with a bad limp and leaned heavily on an ashplant. My father had already found out by chatting with some of the other horse traders nearby that he was a horse dealer from Kenmare. A mad stallion had dashed him against a stable door years before and smashed his hip.

The bargaining began for the horse that we learned was a half-bred, a type of horse bred from a thoroughbred and an Irish draught. What intrigued me most was that the owner hadn't given him a name. He did tell my father, though, that he was bred from a stallion called 'Stormy Lad'.

"I'll give you seventy quid for him," my father said.

The other man snorted like a horse. "Are you joking me, man? By the time I pay for the diesel and the tyre wear to get me here, you're lavin' me with nothin'."

Backwards and forwards they argued until my father had risen to ninety pounds. "That's my best offer," he said, turning to walk away. "Come on, girls. This gentleman must think the Cork farmers are made of money."

Sally and myself traded looks. We were already in love with the horse and to think that my father was going to leave him there! How were we to know that horse trading was all about acting?

"Arrah, man dear, you're not going to lave a fine horse like this at the side of the street," the owner said. "Surely ye have a few extra pound notes under the mattress up there in the fine fields of Cork."

My father sighed. "There's no doubt about it but

'twould be aisier to be dalin' with the divil himself than a Kerryman. Come on, I'll rise to a few extra quid so, I suppose."

After what seemed like ages, they met halfway and agreed on £100. The Kenmare man spat on his palm and they shook hands. I knew about this practice, but Tamara wrinkled her nose. My father took a roll of notes from his jacket pocket and carefully peeled off ten of them. I had never seen that amount of money before. You could have set teacups on my eyes, they had grown so wide. One hundred pounds. My God, did my mother know what he was spending? Obviously she didn't. And she had been badgering him for months to make a start on that bathroom for us. Every house in the parish had one added on at that stage. Mammy already had a plan worked out for an extension for our bathroom and was saving hard for it.

My father was still handing over the money when we heard shouts and the crowd suddenly scattered.

"*Watch out! Keep back! Mind the childer!*" came the cries.

A giant of a coal-black horse came charging down the road with the rider, a fair-haired young fella looking not more than Kieran's age, leaning well back on the reins. The horse had a perfect white star on his forehead. Its coat glistened and you could smell the sweat as it passed. The boy's legs were stretched forwards. He had no saddle. As fast as he passed us, I could see his blue eyes, chips of the sky. I have never forgotten them or him. Horses were neighing all round us with excitement but the crowd closed in again and they calmed down in minutes.

The bargaining was finished, the money handed over, but the man reached into his pocket to find another note.

"That's for luck," he said, handing my father back a

fiver. But they still weren't finished. My father sifted through a fistful of silver and copper coins until he found a half-crown. It was only when he was handing it to the red-haired boy that I noticed that the boy had tears in his eyes. I was sorry for him. Our gain was his loss. He was losing his horse, and such a fine beast. He wiped a grimy hand across his cheek, leaving a trail behind him.

"Here, garsún," my father said, pressing the half-crown into his palm, "a small silver horse instead of your fine grey horse. He's going to a good home. He'll want for nothing, and maybe your daddy will buy you something else to bring home with you."

The boy whispered thanks as his fist closed around the silver coin. He turned his face to his father, hopefully.

"Bad cess to you for a farmer," the man laughed. "I'm just after offloading one basht and there you go trying to saddle me with another. Come on, Maurice, we'll give a walk around the fair till we find something for you," he said. His eyes softened when he looked at the boy. "You'd never know what sort of a bargain we might spot."

My father left Sally and myself lead the horse down the street. I felt so proud holding the rope. People were looking at our horse admiringly. The crowd had grown larger if anything in the hour or so since we'd arrived, and it was slow progress through the street. We caught up with a boy and his father who had just bought a donkey foal and were separating it from its mother. The mink-brown little furry animal was digging in its heels. The boy got behind it and pushed. The donkey mare began to bellow.

Tamara glanced away quickly towards the other side of the street, but not so quickly that I didn't notice the tears in her eyes.

"What's the matter?" I asked.

She shook her head fiercely, the tears sliding down her cheeks.

"Why are you crying?" I asked her more softly.

"It's this fair," she said. "It's all about people losing things. The boy lost the horse we took. That mother donkey is being separated from her foal. It's not fair on the animals. It's called a fair but it's anything but fair."

She didn't say it but I guessed that all the goings-on of the fair reminded her of losing her own mother. Even though she had been speaking for almost two weeks, she had still not mentioned her mother. Mammy gave her plenty of chances to talk about her but she always clammed up. Mammy warned me not to be going asking Tamara awkward questions about her mother when she clearly didn't want to talk about her, and, for once in my life, I did hold my tongue. When I saw her crying in the fair, I was glad I had taken my mother's advice.

Our grey horse walked up the ramp of the horsebox without a problem. "Do you see that?" my father said. "Meek as a mouse. There's a lot of work done with him already."

He brought us to a café for burgers and chips. A real treat! The onions on the burger tasted lovely. We had bottles of red lemonade to wash them down. My father was in such a good mood that he bought us two choc ices. He was spouting non-stop about horses. I couldn't get over the talk out of him. And he hadn't seen the inside of a pub all day.

"Uncle Con, I find it astonishing that you know so much about horses," Tamara said. "All I've heard you talk about since I arrived at the farm is tractors." She had taken the words out of my mouth.

"We always had horses at home when I was growing up

but, when the tractors came in, the mechanic broke out in me," he said. "I still had a fierce interest in horses but there was no call to go talking about them."

On the way home in the Land Rover, I decided to take full advantage of his flow of talk because I suspected it would dry up once he was back home. I asked him to tell us some stories about horses. He began by telling us about a horse called Gladstone his father had once sold at a fair in a town twenty-five miles from their farm. Two days later didn't they wake up to find the horse munching grass in a field beside their house – he had found his own way home in the dead of night. My father wanted to let Gladstone stay and to give the money back to the new owner, but his father took the horse away again. I didn't like that story too much so I asked him for another one. This was the one he had for us, a better one.

"Horses have fierce nature. Mortal nature altogether when it comes to their young. There's a man living at the foot of a mountain in the Black Valley that has the proof of it. He told me this story once about a chestnut mare he kept for driving up and down the Gap of Dunloe. She was a good horse, steady as they come. One spring, she had a foal, a nate little lad with three white socks and a white blaze on his forehead. She nursed him in an emerald-green square of a field on the shore of the Upper Lake.

The foal was going on three or four months – a hardy, long-legged cratur, when the farmer took the mare over to the far side of the lake to draw out a bit of timber. He was taking a break for a sup of tae around one o'clock and he left the mare grazing on a patch of grass in a small clearing when, all of a sudden, she threw up the head and pricked up her ears. To this day, he isn't sure but he reckons she heard the foal calling way off at the far side of the lake.

183

He heard nothing, so he couldn't swear to it.

The next thing he knew she was off down to the shore like a flash of lightning. She plunged into the water and took off. And 'pon my soul, we're not talking about a small lake either. You wouldn't realise the width of it until you were out in the middle of it. All my man was afraid of was that the rope tied to the bridle might snag on something and drown her. But she held going and never stopped till she landed on the other side. When he went back over himself, the foal was nuzzling into her and she was grazing away as if she never saw a bite before. 'Twas the swim gave her the appetite, I suppose."

The car was warm and, even though it was bright, we fell asleep. Daddy wanted to be home for the cows. "There's no holiday from cows." That was his favourite saying.

Mammy was out to meet us. My father was so excited that he almost looked young to me, strangely like Kieran. My mother watched him unload the horse. You should have seen the face of her! She was far from young-looking that evening. She eyed the animal grimly. There were words and explanations bubbling up my throat but I figured it was safer to stay silent. Tamara caught my mood and did the same. Mammy looked from my father to the horse, her face so tight you'd swear she had a pain in her stomach.

"In the name of all that's good and holy, where do you think you are going with that horse, Con O'Mahony?" she said, her hands twisting.

When I heard the 'O'Mahony' out of her, I knew my father was in serious trouble.

"He's a present for Kieran," he said.

Tamara looked at me. I was afraid of what was going to

come next. The excitement of the day was disappearing.

"For Kieran!" my mother gasped. "Man dear, have you taken leave of your senses?" Her voice was low and tired as if all the life has suddenly been sucked out of her. I'd have preferred to see her spitting fire and temper.

My father pulled himself up and squared his shoulders.

"Trust me, Jenny," he said. "What I am trying to do is bring Kieran to his senses. It's the last roll of the dice but what else can we do?"

She shook her head and crossed the haggard. I wanted to run after her to tell her that everything was going to work out OK but I couldn't. I followed Daddy and Tamara through the yard with the horse.

He led the horse through the small garden gate, past the kitchen door and between the flowerbeds where green shoots were bringing the garden to life again after the winter. It was half past four and the sun was shining. Weren't these all good signs? I wanted things to work out to reward my father for taking the gamble on the horse. He stopped the horse in front of the middle window, Kieran's window. The curtains were drawn. They were the curtains he'd had since he was a boy – images of cowboys and wagons but no Indians. My father tapped on the window.

"*Kieran! Kieran!*" he called.

No answer. The horse snorted. He'd spied a clump of grass growing in one of the flowerbeds. He pulled his head, loosened the rope and began to ate like there was no tomorrow. My father banged on the window. Still no answer.

"Go in there, Sally, and open the window," he said.

"You know Kieran," I said. "He might ..."

Before I knew it, my feet had taken off as if they had a

185

life of their own. I was jumping over the flowerbeds edged with whitewashed stones. I ran through the kitchen barely seeing the surprised looks of my mother and Nana. I ran down the hall through the parlour and into Kieran's room. It was dark and stuffy and stinking of fags. The mound in the bed that was Kieran was as still as a rock under the blankets. Still until I yanked the curtains open. He pulled himself up, squinting at the light, face pale, jaw stubbled.

"What the hell are you at?" he said.

I tugged at the window catch and pulled down the top half of the window. It shot down so fast I thought it was going to break. The noise of it scared the horse. He looked so funny the way he was staring at me with his mouth full of grass. Maybe that's why I burst out laughing. It was either that or the nerves.

Daddy led the horse over to the open window and handed in the rope to me. I pulled the grey head closer to me, the beautiful face framed in the space like a painting. I could smell his breath. I hoped the lovely smell of horse and the fresh air would fill that stuffy room. No one was saying anything. We were all waiting for Kieran's reaction. He was sitting up in the bed, staring at the horse. I thought of something my father used to say, "The lunatics are taking over the asylum." I couldn't stop laughing again. I dug my nails into my arms until they made red marks. Kieran slid back down into the bed and pulled the quilt over his head.

The excitement of the morning had drained away. My father's eyes were tired. He took the rope from me and pulled the horse's head towards him. He led him through the garden and out of sight. My brother's world had shrunk back to a window with nothing to frame only the whitewashed barn wall and the bare rosebush growing towards the slates.

21

Nana

The peelings of the cooking apples were already browning in the bowl. The two lassies were supposed to be taking them out to the poor cratur of a horse but, of course, there was no account of them. Jenny was on the missing list too: gone into the city for her day out. I'll do it myself, said the little red hen. The bit of a walk would do me good. There was no sense in giving the day long hatching over the range.

I tipped the peelings out of the bowl and into a small saucepan and headed out the kitchen door. I was stiff from sitting down. God be with the days when I'd fly out that door without a second thought. Age is a desperate thing altogether. As soon as I turned the corner of the house, I could see the silvery head leaning out over the barred gate. The poor lad whinnied when he saw me coming. No doubt he was looking forward to a bit of company and some choice bits to ate.

There he was without a Christian to talk to him. An old peata he was but a robber too, murdering every sop of grass and every scrap I brought him and not a use in the wide, earthly world for him. What in God's name possessed Con to bring him home to Kieran? Talk about adding salt to the wound. And he such a sensible man most of the time. I felt sorry for the horse: as fine an animal as ever grazed a field and he bone idle.

Did you know that horses were able to speak in days gone by but lost the gift of speech somewhere along the line? I make out they can still understand human speech. My auld pal nosed the pot and sucked up the peelings with his big lips.

I crooned into his face and scratched behind his ears when he bowed his big head. "None of it is your fault, cratur, is it? You're the most dacentest animal in God's creation, a fine cut of a horse that would be happy to be out earning your keep. Instead, you're standing here at the gate with nothing better to be doing than swishing your tail to keep away the flies and listening to the raiméising of an auld crone like myself."

The horse was whisking its long grey tail. Whenever a fly landed on his body, his skin wrinkled like water under a breeze. I was away in a world of my own until I felt someone at my elbow and my heart jumped.

"Tamara, what did I tell you about creeping up on people like that? You're a regular steal-upon-birds. You frightened the life out of me."

"I beg your pardon, Nana," the girleen said in her posh accent. "You both looked so charming together that I didn't want to spoil the picture by speaking."

The two of us stood there admiring the horse. Tamara, her eyes as soft as butter, was clane in love with him.

"You're ating him with your eyes, girleen, and 'tis well you might with the beauty of him. He could have been cut out of the moon. But beauty never boiled the pot, you know. I have to give it to your uncle that he was acting for the best, but what was he thinking of? Your poor aunt's head is addled enough with the state of Kieran, without drawing this extra trouble on the house. We must put our thinking caps on to see how we can lift the sadness that's weighing Kieran down. We'll have to storm heaven and earth. Things can't keep going on like this or it will be the ruination of us all. But I won't let it come to that, as God is my judge."

I told Tamara that I was starting the novena to Our Lady of Perpetual Succour to make another gallant attempt to get Kieran up out of his blasted room.

"Our Lady of Sucker?" she said, as puzzled as if she was working out a sum. "I'm sure that not's very polite to call her a sucker. A sucker is a very bad word, isn't it? American gangsters are saying it all the time on the TV."

I smiled when I finally got the drift of what my granddaughter was saying. I explained that 'succour' meant help, and that they would all be enlisted to say the novena to get that help.

"Every single one of us will have to do it, especially you, Tamara, peteen," I said. "And that reminds me. You will have to be baptised. We must get on to your father about that."

You should have seen the hopeful little facesheen of the child at the mention of her father. What in the name and honour of God was taking him so long to come over and see her? It was high time the old troubles were forgotten. But there is no accounting for men and the way their minds work. Thank God it wasn't from my side that Jack was bringing that stubbornness.

22

Kieran

Maybe you'll get what I'm talking about, maybe you won't. Even before I begin, I'm afraid I will end up sounding like one of those prieshteens fresh out of Maynooth and telling stories to get a message across in their sermons. What harm if I do? There isn't much more that can be thrun at me by now.

There was a carnival that came to the village every August. We didn't call it a carnival, though. It was 'the merries' to us. The merries had wooden swing boats and merry-go-rounds and the like. One year, this shark of a fellow brought a small casino with it, looking to clean out the simple country folk, I imagine. It wasn't a very complicated operation, a wooden roulette wheel and a few one-armed bandits. But there was this big red-and-yellow electronic gadget that caught my attention. There was a class of a circular shelf piled high with coins in the middle of it, and the shelf slid forwards and backwards. Maybe it wasn't circular but plain straight across – I can't remember too well, but I am clear on the basic workings. You fed your coins in through a slot, they slid down a shoot and, depending on whether the shelf was in or out when they landed, you could be lucky. If they landed in the clear part at the back, they acted as leverage to press the shining heap forward to a sheer drop that the very first coins hung out over. Piles and piles of coins could slide down that chute with no effect other than to join that pile but if you were the lucky one, your coin could tip the whole overhang over the edge and out into your sweaty palms. Of course, there were fellas, frustrated with the lack of progress: fellas that gave the machine a hefty shoulder when the carnival man's back was turned. Helping it along like.

Now here comes the part where I might sound a bit like a prieshteen. When I was hiding out in that hole of a bedroom of mine all those months, people were feeding their tuppence ha'pennies of wisdom into me left, right and centre to see if they could knock a budge out of me. Some of them came with heavier tactics, the shoulder if you like, but I was stubborn. My poor old father thought he'd cracked it when he arrived with the horse. He had in a way. He sowed the seed, but that seed didn't put its nose up for about another month. And it was all down to Tamara. Don't go telling this to my lovely Sally but Tamara delivered the bright shining coin that tipped all the others down the pay-out chute and set me on the road back to myself.

It was the middle of May, the loveliest time of the year here on the farm and I was still choking in a fog of Carroll's smoke and under a black poor-old-me cloud pressing down on me. A fox's burrow would have smelled better than my room the day Tamara came in and sat at the edge of my bed, sobbing with this tale of woe.

"Uncle Con is going to sell the horse. He bought him for you and he says it was a mistake because you have no interest. He says he can't be throwing good money after bad, feeding an animal that is no use to anyone on the farm."

192

I'm after neatening her words up, but all this and more that I can't record because I don't remember it came rushing out in a torrent of gulps and sobs. She was talking about 'the horse'. The horse still hadn't a name more than a month after it had arrived to the farm where every cow and horse and donkey and dog that ever came up the lane had been 'christened'. The girls told me they had picked all sorts of names but my father wouldn't allow any.

"It's Kieran's horse," he said. "It's the name Kieran will pick or no name."

But of course the bould Kieran was down the room with the curtains perpetually closed.

"It's not fair," Tamara said. "I'm like that poor donkey mother whose baby was taken away at the fair. She just lost the one thing, but *everything* is being taken away from me. The worst was when the cancer took Mummy away. They told me she was very sick but that she was getting the treatment and that she would be OK. But then one evening Daddy came to the babysitter with his eyes all red and …"

She couldn't go on for a while. Her shoulders were shaking and she was breathless from the sobs. To look at Tamara, you could have been forgiven for imagining that she was a pushover, but there was steel behind that timid face. She took out a handkerchief out, blew her nose delicately and sat there until she pulled herself together.

In a matter-of-fact tone that surprised me, she told me all about her mother's sickness, the hair on the pillow, the slice of cold toast with the perfect crescent of a single bite taken from it, the wig, the morphine pump.

"Then when I came over here and I missed Mummy and Daddy and home so much, I don't know if I lost my voice or whether I stored it away on purpose. You had the accident and I lost you in a kind of a way."

She blushed when she mentioned me and I knew she didn't want to be laying blame at my door for my quareness since the accident.

"Daddy says he will come and get me soon if I want," she said. "But I don't know what I want. I want Daddy so much, but if he takes me back to London I am going to lose you and Sally, Auntie Jenny, Uncle Con and Nana. Now, this morning, I heard Uncle Con saying he is going to send the horse away to another fair, and I hate fairs." She wailed like a banshee. "Why is everything being taken away from me? Why? What did I do? I'm not so bad, am I, Kieran?"

I hated the walking stick. I never used it. Sticks were for auld fellas. There were lots of reasons I stayed in the room, the stick being one of them. I couldn't bear to think of people watching me limping around. Even when I went up to the kitchen at night, I moved along the walls for support.

"Do me a favour, Tamara. Go down on your hands and knees and look under the bed. Don't mind the dust and the cobwebs and the odd spider you might see – you've faced worse and survived – and pull out that stick for me."

The request distracted her. By now she was hiccoughing anyway. She dabbed her eyes with the sopping handkerchief and rooted under the bed.

I wiped the dust off the stick with the bedspread and got out of bed in my awkward way. From the way Tamara was looking at me, I imagine that she thought this was another sign of madness.

"Come on. We're going to have a look at that horse of mine. Call Sally too. We'll need help to dream up some class of a name for him."

The eyes were popping out of Mammy and Nana's eyes

as we passed through the kitchen. Nana blessed herself and muttered something about Little Nellie. I nodded as if this was the most natural sight in the world. My legs were as weak and wobbly as those of a newborn calf but I held my back straight, leaned heavily on the stick and motored on.

Back in the bedroom, I had vowed that I would save the horse for Tamara's sake but when I looked into those navy eyes set in the fine head resting on the gate, I was under the spell myself. While I was standing there surveying him, Sally came sprinting across the yard, shouting with all the excitement and welcome normally reserved for returned Yanks. I had taken my first shaky steps across the yard. They would always be shaky, I knew, but I would get rid of that stick. That was my first goal. Better to look drunk than auld in my book.

I stood there with the two girls admiring the horse. It was a lively, cloudy day, with the sun coming and going. When it came out, the sun was warm on my shoulders. I felt alive in a way I hadn't felt for months. But the fresh air also made me feel dirty. I had lived in the same old jeans and tops since I'd come out of hospital. I would ask Mammy to burn them.

Daddy was the next to arrive. Mammy must have gone looking for him in the haggard and told him. Being the man he is, he walked down to the gate as if it was the most natural thing in the world to see me there. He said nothing but shook my hand and held it for those extra seconds that said everything.

The girls were prattling on about naming the horse. Sally was talking about Sky from the sky horse.

Tamara suggested Moonbeam. "Nana said to me that he is like something that was cut out of the moon," she said.

"They are lovely names, girls, but since he is going to be my horse, I think I'm going to have to find a name of my own for him," I told them, preventing a new risk of World War Three.

There was such hope and excitement in their eyes that I knew I couldn't let them down. I'd have to throw my whole heart into getting fit. They were only two slips of girls but, even then, I knew they'd drive me on. They took me on as their special project, flanking me on my walks, sharing my exercise routine and sharing in the care of the horse.

Training Apollo and growing in strength went hand in hand. Yes, Apollo, that was the name that came to me that first week. Correction, the name that was 'given' to me for him, as Mammy liked to point out. A black horse had carried me to the dark side of the moon. A silver horse was going to carry me home again.

23

Sally

In the corner of the parlour was a black sea trunk bound
with bands of thin metal. It was a very big trunk – about
the size of three tea chests lashed together though not near
as tall as a tea chest. Daddy brought it with him when he
married into the farm. It belonged to his father who had
emigrated to Boston in the 1930s without a pot to piss in,
or so the family history goes. He came back with the
trunk, a ball of dollars, a wife from Dunmanway and a
lifelong distrust of hospitals. Between himself and my
grandmother, a maid for a Jewish family who owned a big
department store in Rochester, they earned enough in the
ten years in New York state to buy a mountainy farm
outside Bandon and a rake of shining white enamel pots
with blue rims to go under every bed. Daddy told us the
hospital thing was down to what his father saw when he
was working as a hospital porter: this deduction came out
of Daddy's own head because his father wasn't inclined to
talk much, a trait that came down in the genes. I don't
remember Daddy's mother and father because he was the
youngest in the family and they died before I was born.
But we have an oval-framed picture of them looking very
serious. I think it was taken on their wedding day, a bit of
a puzzle in itself with the sad old faces on them. But that's

a topic I wouldn't start Nana on.

Mammy called the trunk his 'treasure chest'. She always used a mocking tone when she said that, a tone that I'd get a clip across the ear for. The trunk was strictly out of bounds, even to her. That wouldn't have made a blind bit of difference to me only that there was a brass lock securing it. Many's the search I carried out for that key but I never found it. Daddy kept anything important to do with the farm locked away in the trunk. I knew about the ledgers and the blue metal cash box I saw appearing and disappearing at certain times of the year: Christmas, fair days, harvest time. But it was a huge trunk and I often wondered what treasures it contained. Maybe there was a set of silver candlesticks or a fancy tablecloth embroidered with gold thread that the Jewish family had given my grandmother when she was setting sail for Ireland again, some old photographs of my grandparents as a handsome pair emerging from a crowd on a sunny Boston street, or a gabhál of dollars they had stashed away for a rainy day in a false bottom which no one, not even Daddy, knew about. There could have been anything in there with the dollars, a few diamonds that my grandmother might have got from the Jewish son who could have been madly in love with the 'Irish maid', who wouldn't have been the least bit suitable. 'Tis true for Daddy: I do have an 'over-worked imagination' at times. If I have in itself, doesn't it keep me from getting bored? Anyway, what I made up in my head about that trunk was far more exciting than what Daddy fished out of its depths for us. The revelation took place the Sunday after the day that Kieran first went out to have a look at Apollo.

Tamara and myself were delighted that Kieran was talking to everyone again and coming up to the kitchen, but I used to catch Mammy looking at him when he was staring off into the distance with a little-boy-lost look about him. And Tamara told me she had overheard Mammy and Nana whispering together late one night in the kitchen: I imagine they had forgotten that Tamara had got her tongue back from the cat and thought they could safely talk in front of her without a story being carried. Mammy said she was afraid it was too good to be true, that he'd throw a strop again and that they'd be back to square one. I don't know what Daddy was thinking but that was nothing new. Mammy used to say she could read every book in the library if she had the time but, if she had all the time of some rich fella's wife with a fleet of servants at her beck and call, she'd never get the knack of reading the man she was living with: whether she meant he was a book written in another language or a closed book, I don't know. The result was the same anyway: you couldn't make him out. But I'm rambling away from my story again and I must dive back into the bottom of that musty chest, a mystery object that would have far better stories than me if only it could talk.

That Sunday afternoon the weather was still so warm that we had cold bacon and tomatoes at dinner time. Well, as usual, Tamara had the tomatoes and something else I don't remember, probably loads of bread, because she wouldn't touch the meat. I do remember we had lovely juicy Pamela pears out of the tin with cream floating around on top of the syrup. Kieran was kind of quiet, but not too bad. I was watching Mammy watching him. Then Daddy nudged Kieran with his elbow, stood up and tilted his head towards the door going into the hall, a signal to follow him down to the parlour. Tamara and myself were sitting on the long stool inside the table. I dropped down under the table, as fast as a rabbit disappearing into a burrow, and shot out the other side. Tamara was at the far side of the stool and in the middle of the kitchen floor nearly as fast as me.

"Where do you think you two nosey parkers are going?" my mother called out, but we were already in the hallway. I could hear my mother's voice receding behind me.

"I said it before and I'll say it again: she's a bad influence on Tamara. Tamara will be as bould as her before she's finished." The way she went on, you'd swear I was some sort of criminal from Cork jail.

Daddy was bending over the trunk, turning the key in the lock. Kieran pulled out one of the high-backed chairs from under the parlour table and sat down. He was always looking for the chance to take the weight off his legs. Daddy raised the lid and leaned it against the wall. The inside was lined with peacock-blue paper mottled with spots of mould. I came right up beside Daddy to peer in but he waved me back with his hand. Kieran smirked at me and I stuck my tongue out at him. Tamara and myself stood on either side of Kieran's chair, waiting for the submerged treasure to come up into the afternoon light of the parlour. I'd be waiting yet. Daddy was poking around from one corner of the chest to the next until he surfaced with a twist of yellowing newspaper. I was up on my tippy-toes to see if I could get a glint of anything more promising but no such luck – mo léir, as Nana would say.

"Here, Sally," he said, handing me the paper bundle. "Catch that and put it up on the table."

My fingers were itching to pull back the pages but I wouldn't chance it. Daddy's head and shoulders had disappeared again. This time he came back up with a soft brown-paper parcel tied with string, about the size of a high Thompson's loaf. This looked more promising.

My father stood up again, his knees cracking as he did, and locked the trunk. No chance of him forgetting that. He pulled out a chair, sat down opposite Kieran and began to unfold the newspaper parcel first. As he did, Tamara took the pages and smoothed them out. They were ancient pages from *The Cork Examiner* of March 1947. As the last page was untwisted we were rewarded with a glint alright, a dull silver but not any type of precious object I was hoping for. It was a horse's bit but no ordinary one, a very complicated-looking contraption that Daddy was about to enlighten us about.

"This is a special bit," he said. "It's known as a key bit or a training bit. Watch me now and see how it works." He held it up. "The bar is running between the two rings, and it's rigid, not like an ordinary bit that's split in the middle."

Then he pointed to a small circular plate and demonstrated how it could move up and down the bar. The three pieces of metal attached to the bar were keys, he explained.

"The keys work by having the horse sucking them," he said. "According as he does this, he starts frothing and then he's getting a mouth."

"But sure he has a mouth," I said. "What do you mean?"

"Any horseman would know what I'd mean by a mouth," he said. "By moving the keys, he gets a mouth. There is such a thing as mouthing a horse. The tissue in the horse's mouth gets more pliable. If a horse wasn't mouthed, you couldn't control him. If you pull the reins to the one side, he'll come with you when he's mouthed. You have to lunge him with a long rope and go round in a ring. That's called lunging. You must lunge him to the left and the right. That means you would go left around a ring and then go right. Lunge for ten or fifteen minutes to the left, then the same thing to the right. After about seven days doing this, the horse is mouthed."

It was all getting too technical for me but I stayed silent in the hope that it would become clear eventually. It was strange to hear my father spouting so many words about something that wasn't some class of an engine or a machine.

I got a sense that someone was behind me. I turned and saw my mother leaning against the parlour door, arms folded. Her lips were pursed in a thin line. No one else noticed her. My father was still spouting away about the bit. Kieran was listening intently. He had moved off into a world of his own – again.

Tamara was frowning. I could guess what was coming.

"But that looks very hard," she said, eyes brimming. "It will hurt Apollo. He's not used to anything like that. It might even cut him."

I wouldn't have been surprised if she had lodged an official complaint about the treatment of the animals on the farm some day and the cruelty crowd would land out from the city and up the lane, taking us by surprise in a van we didn't know the sound of, releasing all the calves from the shed and reuniting them with the cows, ordering that none of the bullocks or the sheep should be brought to the mart, giving the hens free run of the fields, banning the killing and castration of the pigs, outlawing the wringing of the hens' necks, and not letting a bite of meat pass our lips.

"It doesn't cut the horse's mouth," Daddy told her. "It's

not supposed to. It'd be sore alright. It takes about seven or eight days to mouth one. You'd see the sign of the bit at the side of his mouth."

Daddy continued to address Kieran, who was nodding. "It's very important to keep the straps even because if you have one strap too tight, he'd be weaker on one side. And then if you want to get a horse with a bow neck, to improve his neck you cross the straps over his neck to give him a bow neck. It makes him more stylish. It's the way he'd hold himself."

Tamara was flushing at the mention of a bow neck but I kicked her under the table. A moderately firm kick – I didn't want her screeching. These instructions were for Kieran, not for us, I thought. Little did I realise what was coming down the line.

Daddy put the training bit down on the table. "You see now that's only one part of the gear. You have to have a bridle and two single straps coming back on either side from the rings on the bit. There's a thing like a thick belt or a hoosen around his girth with a buckle on each side. The straps have to be attached to the buckles. You start with them loose and, as you're training the horse, you tighten them up a hole each day. But we'll cross that bridge when we come to it."

Daddy drew the brown-paper parcel towards him. It didn't look too promising and, not to put a tooth in it, I was savage bored at this stage. A part of me had come out in sympathy with Tamara. Apollo was happy out as he was. He was spending all day every day munching juicy green grass to his heart's content. All this talk of putting that hard, cold bit in his mouth and lunging and mouthing and frothing didn't sound great to me. The only thing keeping me in the parlour was the curiosity of finding out what was in the parcel.

As well as that, Mammy was manning the parlour door like Saint Peter at the Pearly Gates. She had a grim class of a puss on her and I didn't want to chance passing her. I wasn't too hopeful of there being anything wildly exciting in the parcel and, as it turned out, I was dead right. Maybe Mammy's knack of predicting things was breaking out in me. Daddy's big hands with their blunt nails and oil in the cracks of his skin looked awkward as he struggled to open the knot. (One time, I saw him hold a pen between his fingers, and it might as well have been Skippy the Kangaroo holding it, the sight was strange.) In the end, he lost his patience and snapped the brittle twine. Out of the nest of paper, he lifted a horse's head collar, so old that it looked as if the leather would break between his hands.

"It's dry alright, but nothing a dropeen of oil won't fix," he said.

Daddy was a great believer in the power of the dropeen to bring an old clapped-out piece of machinery to life again. A dropeen of Dettol to sort out a cut in animal or human. Or if it was drink, a tosheen. A tosheen of whiskey to cure a cold. Better the dropeen or the tosheen than any hard-earned money to be shelled out to garage owner, doctor or vet.

He handed the manky old collar across the table to Kieran as if it was made from gold itself. I was of the opinion that he was losing his marbles. From the look on Mammy's face, she was of the one mind as me.

"That belonged to my own father," Daddy said. "That and the bit. He was a great horseman. He tried to teach me everything he knew but, once I got into tractors, the horses went out the door for me. After he died, all the horse stuff was left hanging in the turf shed. I don't know what my brother did with it, if anything. Maybe it just rotted away out there. Don't ask me why I took these when I left home. A souvenir of him maybe or maybe some part of me never let go of the horses. Like the bog maybe. You can take the man from the horse but you can't take the horse from the man."

The few stories that my father came out with – usually after a couple of bottles of stout at Christmas or at harvest-time – were as familiar and well-worn as a pair of bate-out slippers to me by now, but this was a new story, one I had never heard him tell before. It was strange to hear him come up with a new story and to talk for so long. Between Tamara and now this, I don't think I'd have batted an eye if the cat herself opened her pinky little mouth and started giving guff about the small bit of milk given to her.

"This is what you'll start with," Daddy said to Kieran, who was eyeing the head collar with an understandable lack of enthusiasm. "Get him used to wearing this. You'll walk him round the place like a dog for a few weeks till he gets used to the feel of it. After that, we'll think about trying the bit."

Kieran was still fingering the head collar. His brow was creased.

"Yerra, I'm not sure if I'm up to this yet," he said. "It's my own fault that I didn't stick with the exercises when I came out of the hospital. I'm only started building up the muscles again. The tiredness is still a bastard," he turned around sharply when he heard Mammy's intake of breath, "alright, the tiredness is something fierce. This is a big job to be taking on when you consider the cut of me."

"What do I keep telling ye all? Mind over matter?" Daddy said. "Rome wasn't built in a day. And it wasn't

205

one man built it on his own. You'll have help."

Kieran straightened up in the chair. "Well, there's no harm in giving it a shot, I suppose. It might help me build up the muscles."

"Now you're sucking diesel, boy," Daddy said. "One step at the time."

My mother cleared her throat. We all turrned to her. Her eyes were boring into Daddy, flintier than any steel bit in the shed.

"A word," she said, retreating towards the kitchen.

He sighed and followed her, for all the world like Sam the dog. He closed the parlour door firmly behind him. We didn't dare follow, but I wheedled an account of some of the argument out of Nana, our war correspondent, in her bedroom that night.

"The holy all of it was that she 'read' your father for drawing too much pressure on Kieran," she said, "by encouraging him to think he would be able to take on the training of the horse. Your father stood there like an auld dog with his head bowed while she ranted and raved. 'Don't just stand there like a martyr with your eyes closed,' she told him. Where I got her, don't ask me. There's one thing sure: 'twasn't from my side she brought the temper. She was on fire, I tell you. On and on she went to beat the band."

Nana obviously had access to extensive genetic analysis of the Cashman (hers) and the O'Mahony (Daddy's) lines of the family. Any tendency towards drunkenness, extravagance, laziness, stupidity or, God between us and all harm, mental instability, could be traced with certainty to the O'Mahonys. Meanwhile, her tribe, the Cashmans, had had sobriety, thrift, industry, brains, sanity and saintliness encoded in their genes for generations.

"But she pushed him too far this time," Nana told me. "And she mouthing off like a red divil. Even a quiet, dacent man like your father has a limit. 'God blast and carry you, woman, can't you see I'm doing my level best to do a good thing?' he told her. 'Will you let that much to me or is that too much to ask you? Do you take me for a complete stump of a fool altogether?'"

If I know Daddy, the 'eff word' was probably sprinkled all over the shop, but Nana gave her own version. Mammy flew off the handle every so often, usually when she was tired, and she'd been tired a lot since Kieran's accident. It took a lot to make Daddy blow his gasket but when he did once in a blue moon – usually when some repair job went against him – the air turned blue with the 'eff word' and other words that I suspected were of his own invention.

But whatever about blue air, the storm in the kitchen cleared the air to some degree. Mammy and Daddy settled into an uneasy truce as 'Mission Apollo' took shape.

Daddy knew that Kieran hadn't a hope of working Apollo through his paces on his own. 'Team Apollo' was assembled, starting with Tamara and myself for stage one. Tamara was a reluctant recruit to begin with but Kieran explained that it had to be done to keep Apollo on the farm. Every animal needed to earn his or her keep.

"If we can knock Apollo into a good show jumper or a winner in the point-to-point races, then he could have valuable foals," Kieran said. But, as the words were coming out of his mouth, I realised he had taken the wrong tack.

"But then the foals will be taken away from the mares that Apollo makes them with," Tamara said. "I shan't help you. That would be dreadful."

"Will you ever learn anything?" I said to Tamara.

"What do you think would happen if not a single animal left the farm? Where would we find space for them? They'd be ating themselves and us. We haven't the space of the African bush you see on the telly. Anyway, aren't all the African animals ating one another?"

I thought it was a mighty argument – the African animals came into my head only as I was talking – but Tamara didn't say anything, just bit her lip.

"I'll do it for Kieran," she said finally. "If it helps him to get well again, it will be worth it."

24

Kieran

Some bleddy astronaut I'd make, wobbling along. Wobbling so much that people who don't know me think I'm drunk. Deaf, too, probably. I heard the likes of: "Isn't he a disgrace to whoever reared him? He's a holy show, staggering around the place at this hour of the day, footless." Too right, footless. But not from the gargle. That's what a belt in the head will do for you. The hardness of a rock lying there in the ground, waiting all its life for the big moment when it gets to connect with the eggshell otherwise known as the skull and rearranges all the wiring inside ever so neatly. That's right, missus, have a go at it some time yourself and see how well you'll manoeuvre in those pointy shoes of yours.

Damn right I take the remarks to heart. What do you think I have inside in my chest – a skelp of that auld boulder that waited a couple of million years to have a crack at me? A chip off the old block – that's what I'd need in here not to mind them. But I'm getting there. Turning it into a laugh. That's what you need to do. Nobody loves a grump.

Wibble wobble. Christ, if they only knew the effort it took to get out of the wheelchair, to stand up again, to throw away the stick. Like a baby, learning everything over and over again. But the children will steady up; their legs will strengthen, they'll walk and they'll run. Whereas I'll just keep on shaking. But do you know what? I'm a great fecken man to get this far. I'm proud of myself and I plough on.

So Tamara gets to asking me if I'd like to be an astronaut. I'm still not used to that voice of hers, so prim, so proper. So English.

"What do you think, Kieran? If they make lots more rockets and they want to send more men to the moon, would you like to go?"

We were sitting on the ditch in the top field, a bed of last year's crispy ferns cushioning our behinds. The new barley had risen well over a foot but it was still green. It was so good to feel the warm breeze on my face. In the hospital I swore I'd welcome any breeze or wind, hot or cold, even flinging hailstones in my face: anything instead of the suffocating wards.

Astronaut. I savoured the word as if it were a piece of Hadji Bey Turkish Delight from MacCurtain Street. "I suppose that would be the job alright. No gravity. I'd be bouncing around the place as good as the rest of them."

Tamara sat bolt upright. "That would be splendid. You would have no problem walking. You wouldn't be getting so tired."

I smiled to myself at her pronunciation. It could be the Queen herself talking. But I wouldn't tease her. She'd been through enough.

"The tiredness is a fecker alright," I agreed. "I can get over the quare looks people throw me when I'm walking, but the tiredness is the man that pulls me down."

"I know it's going to take years," she continued gravely. "Maybe they'll have holidays on the moon by the time

210

Sally and I are twenty. We could all go together. That would be smashing."

"There's a small bit of a complication, though," I smiled. "You see, I've been to the moon already. I've been way over to the dark side, the place so dark you can't see your hand in front of your face, and I'm in no hurry back there."

"But you're back with us again," she said. "Apollo brought you back to us."

Apollo, my saviour and my tormentor. He was the reason I got out of bed in the morning. He was the reason I sank totally wrecked at night into the sleep of the dead. He was the craft that carried me to a hope beyond this mí-ádh of a body I was left with.

25

Tamara

I should have learned by now that anything is possible on this farm where the life of every poor creature is valued in pounds, shillings and pence, and where everything must 'earn its keep'. Only for the crisp pound notes that Daddy posts over in those envelopes with the Queen's head on the stamps, I shudder to think what would become of me. This is a joke – of a sort. Perhaps you may ask then why I'm so horrified when I hear Kieran and Uncle Con discussing plans to have Apollo shot. It is such a ghastly conversation that I feel positively ill. I feel as if I am back in that time when I couldn't talk. I am speechless about what I'm hearing.

"I think it's high time Apollo was shot," my uncle says.

"I was thinking that myself," Kieran says. "We should get him shot and then send him away out on the road."

"We'll bring him down so next week to have the job done," my uncle says. "There's no point in wasting time. The sooner he's shot, the better."

"I hope he won't rear up or anything," Kieran says. "He mightn't take too kindly to the noise and everything."

"I think he'll go quietly enough, not like other blackguards that lose the head and lash out," his father says. "You will have to prepare him, though. I'd start straight away if I was you."

I remember a discussion Mummy and Daddy were having once. They were reading a murder story in the newspaper and they were talking about psychopaths. Daddy thought I was too young to get an explanation but Mummy insisted. So I may not know exactly what a spring harrow is but I do know all about psychopaths.

A pair of psychopaths are leaning on the bar gate and looking out into the field where Apollo is grazing away unconcernedly, unaware that his life is about to be ended. The lump in my throat is so hard I think I'll choke. How can they speak so casually about taking the life of an innocent living creature? It is just typical of this beastly place. I need to ring Daddy and get him to fetch me immediately. Uncle Con must have decided not to pay for any more oats. I have come to understand his thinking. But Kieran? How can Kieran agree so easily with him? I thought he loved Apollo. Then I thought he loved Kitty too. Maybe Apollo has outlived his usefulness, like Kitty did. I just can't understand it. It's so wrong.

Sally is only a few feet away. She doesn't bat an eyelid. They are all monsters. I shan't let them get away with it.

"You shan't do it, you shan't, I won't let you!" I sob. "How can you be so cruel?"

The three of them stare at me, astonished at my outburst. Of course they are surprised. Dispatching animals is a way of life for them. They are an utter holy show.

"What's the matter with you, girleen?" Uncle Con says. He looks so concerned – the hypocrite.

"You know what I mean," I say. "What were you talking about just now? Don't pretend you didn't say it. I heard every word."

They look genuinely worried about me. Perhaps they

think I am, in their words, 'losing my marbles'. But they aren't going to get away with horse murder if I can help it. I face up to them defiantly. I have to put up with the murder of chickens, and pigs and turkeys, of calves being stolen from their mothers, but this is a step too far.

"What did we say to make you cry?" Kieran said.

Oh, he was such an actor, pretending that he didn't know.

"You are such a rotter, rotters all of you! I heard you saying that you are having Apollo shot."

"But sure every horse has to be shot sooner or later, peteen," my uncle said gently. "It would be cruel not to do it."

Oh, the beast, trying to make it sound so reasonable.

Sally's expression is as shocked as the two horse killers but, suddenly, she breaks into a broad smile.

Yes, Sally, dear cousin, this is a smiling matter, is it? No doubt you will have some of your usual funny remarks to make – at my expense.

"I have it, I have it!" she says excitedly. "She thinks you're going to *shoot* Apollo. That's what's wrong with her. Tell her you're not."

The faces of Kieran and Uncle Con dissolve into smiles. My uncle stretches out a hand to touch my shoulder, but I shrink away from him.

"God bless your poor heart, cratureen," he says. "I said *shot*. We are taking the horse to be *shot*."

I look at him in bewilderment amd outrage.

Sally is speaking now in that slow and superior manner she used when I arrived on the farm first. "He is saying *shod*, Tamara, because that's the word for getting shoes put on a horse," she says. "*Shod*," she repeats loudly as if I have a hearing difficulty.

Kieran breaks in eagerly. "Apollo is getting his first shoes – like a child gets his first shoes. He is getting *shod*. How in God's name did you think I'd have Apollo shot?"

The penny drops. Relief floods through me. *Shod*. Of course. I know what 'shod' means! I am so happy that I only imagined the death sentence. It's the relief of waking up from a terrible nightmare.

I stammer an apology. But nobody is really listening to me because Uncle Con is already starting on a plan of action.

"Dinnie will never go near a colteen unless you pick up the hooves every day and tap them like," Uncle Con says. "Come over to auld Poll and I'll show you."

Apollo looks up, anticipating a treat. He isn't disappointed. Kieran gives him a ginger-nut biscuit. My uncle runs his hand down Apollo's front leg on the inside.

He grips a fistful of the hair just above the hoof, tugs at the hoof while coaxing Apollo saying, "Atta boy, Poll". He taps the hoof firmly five or six times before repeating the process on the other leg.

"Now, girls, do ye think ye could have a go at that?" he says. "Let the two of ye not knock me down in the rush."

He makes it all seem so simple. When Sally and I try, Apollo seems to glue his hoof to the field. I'm sent into the house for an apple. Kieran slices it with his penknife. Every time Apollo lifts the hoof, we give him a slice.

We continue through the week right up to Saturday evening when Kieran and Uncle Con say he's ready to go to the blacksmith, Dinnie McCarthy, down in the forge at the edge of the village. The forge has a big wide opening in the shape of a horseshoe. Every time I pass it, the blacksmith seems to be leaning against the wall chatting to some old men. I don't think I have ever seen a horse there. Apollo has an appointment for Monday evening.

"Wait till we're home from school, please," Sally says.

"I don't know if we should bring ye," Uncle Con says. "Tamara mightn't know what to make of it with the red-hot shoes and the smoke and everything."

"Well, she can stay at home so and I can go," Sally says.

I *do* want to see Apollo get his new shoes. But maybe Uncle Con is right and I'll get upset. The forge looks like a dark cave. That makes me curious to go inside.

"There's a very easy way to sort this out," my aunt says.

We are in the kitchen. She reaches into one of the presses and produces her sewing basket. She rummages among the coloured spools of thread and finds a little scissors.

"Come here to me, Tamara, and stretch out your hands," she says.

I'm embarrassed because there are black rims under my nails. Sally and I were picking potatoes and I didn't have time to scrub my hands properly afterwards.

"Is it the Queen that died?" my aunt asks. I don't know what she means. "You must be in mourning with all the black."

She takes one hand, then the next, snipping off any extra-long nail rims.

"Did that hurt a lot?" she asks when she's finished.

I shake my head.

"You just remember when you're down in the forge that no matter what you see Dinnie McCarthy do, Apollo's hooves are just like your nails. He will feel nothing. Are you still sure you want to go down there?"

I'm not sure at all but I don't want to back out now because I like to think of myself as Apollo's Guardian Angel.

Dinnie McCarthy is a short man with a big tummy. The

wisps of gingery hair draped across his bald head are sparse but there are furry tufts of hair growing out of his nose and his ears. He is whistling when we arrive.

"Oh, you never told me you were bringing the two young ladies," Dinnie says, two merry blue eyes dancing in his creased face. He slaps his big leather apron with his grimy hands. "I would have scrubbed myself up if I'd known. Girls, girls, go into the house and ask the film star to give ye a drop of lemonade and a bit of cake."

The 'film star' turns out to be a thin, grey-haired woman with glasses so thick you can scarcely see her eyes. She gives us a glass of Tanora and a slice of madeira cake each. While we're eating, she asks me dozens of questions about London. When she turns to the dresser for more Tanora, Sally shakes her head at me and puts her finger to her lips.

"That was lovely, Mrs McCarthy – thanks very much," she says. "We'd better get back out to the forge because Tamara never saw a horse being shod before."

The forge is dim. A coal fire is smouldering on a raised stone platform thingy at the back.

"Can we have a go on the bellows, please?" Sally asks.

"Work away, girleen," Dinnie says. "Only don't go blowing the fire to the high heavens."

Sally pulls down on a long handle by the fire. As if by magic, the ashes stir and the fire reddens. She explains how the bellows blow air under the coals.

"Here, have a turn," she says.

I take my turn at the magic handle but I pull down too strongly and a flash of flames and ashes rise.

"Aisy, aisy. I'm not made of money," Dinnie says. "Coal is far from chape."

When I see him assembling the big metal tools to work

on Apollo's hooves, I should be worried but, strangely, I trust this small, whistling man. So does Apollo I should think by the way he stands so still.

"Aren't you the darling colteen?" Dinnie says, as he picks up the left hoof. "Stand up there now, good man."

He takes a metal bar with little bumps on it and rubs the hoof until grey shavings shower the ground. Sally tells me the bar is called a rasp. He uses a knife next and cuts a little more off. I think of Mummy doing her nails at home in Earls Court. I don't know how that bright image has flown into the forge like a bird. It makes me sad: sad and guilty. Thinking about Mummy shouldn't feel bad but, just now, I make myself think about Apollo to make the hurt go away.

"This is the scariest part, but remember what Mammy said about your nails," Sally says.

Two elderly men have arrived at the forge door to observe the shoeing. The tall one has his hands in his pockets, the smaller one is leaning on a stick.

Kieran turns to Sally and myself.

"The TDs are starting to land," he says. "The Dáil will be in session soon. That's the name for our parliament, Tamara. Dinnie's forge is a kind of a Westminster – all the local wisemen come here to debate the big happenings in the world."

The tall man asks Uncle Con what his plans are for Apollo.

"Ask the man here, Johnny," my uncle says, pointing to Kieran. "He's the gaffer."

"I'm training him to be a hunter," Kieran says. "Or, if I'm lucky, a show jumper. You put a good few of them through your hands in your time. What do you make of him?"

Johnny makes a circuit around Apollo and returns to

219

his spot by the forge door. He scratches his chin thoughtfully.

"He's a fine cut of a basht," he says. "Of course I'd have to see him jump to give a right opinion but from the make-up of him, I'd say you have a right flier on your hands. Start looking out for a Tommy Wade for the saddle. Who knows he might end up in the RDS having a cut at the Aga Khan some summer."

"That's praise indeed," Uncle Con says. "I saw something in him too the very first day I clapped eyes on him."

"Thanks a million," Kieran says. "It means a lot to hear that."

Sally has told me all about the Aga Khan Cup at the Dublin Horse Show. Watching it on the telly is a big part of her summer. She is full of praise of the Irish horses who score clear rounds. The dream of Apollo taking part is born right there in the forge.

Kieran is beaming from ear to ear. I feel so happy for him. Apollo is a star in the making.

Mr McCarthy has been standing over the fire while the men are chatting. He allows Sally and me to work the bellows as much as we like because he wants the coals red hot. He has buried a horseshoe in the centre of the fire. It comes out glowing red, no trace of the silver colour left.

Kieran steps to one side of Apollo's head, holding the bridle and stroking his neck. Uncle Con is on the other side.

I guess what's coming next. I take a deep breath and turn my eyes on Apollo's face. I shan't look down. I *can't* look down.

I hear the sizzle, the hiss. A cloud of grey smoke rises so densely that the men stand back. It's not a nice smokey smell like the smell you get from leaves or turf or wood. It's sharp and it makes me think of Christmas when my auntie was singeing the feathers left on the poor plucked turkey. I'm coughing. I don't know how Mr McCarthy stays in the middle of it.

"It's not very agreeable, girls, is it?" Uncle Con says. "Blacksmiths were killed with the heartburn from having their heads stuck in the middle of the smoke so often."

Apollo is snorting, but he stands still, Kieran and Uncle Con stroking his neck.

Mr McCarthy takes the shoe away to the other side of the forge and dips it into a deep bucket of water. More hissing, but this time it's steam rising and not smoke.

"Any of you young ladies got warts on your fingers?" Mr McCarthy says. "Just dunk your hands into that bucket of water. There's a cure in it for all sorts of things."

Kieran reads the horror on my face and laughs. "It's true," he says. "It's an old cure for all sorts of ailments. People bring their tin cans and jam crocks to take away some of the water. But they have to steal the water, moryah. Dinnie has to turn his back when they are taking it."

What strange things people do when they're unwell. It must be something like the holy water Nana gets in the church, except that's so clean.

Mr McCarthy is back at the anvil and he's hammering the horseshoe like crazy. Apollo is pawing the ground with his right hoof and snorting. The noise is frightening him. He calms down when the hammering stops. Mr McCarthy carries the shoe over, tries it against the hoof for size and brings it back to the anvil to hammer it a little more. Then he comes back and taps it into Apollo's hoof. I watch this time, shuddering with every blow. It is so difficult to

221

believe that the nails aren't hurting Apollo. One shoe on now, so the whole process begins again for the second one. I know Apollo is only getting front shoes today – that's how it goes with a colteen, apparently. They're light shoes, not like the heavier ones he'll get later when all four shoes will go on. I will be an expert on horses before I go home to London. I like learning these things, but I think I've had enough for one day.

Uncle Con pays Mr McCarthy and all the men stand around chatting. No one seems to be in a hurry. I do like this about Cork. Even when you're in the city, people seem to move more slowly than they do in London.

"I suppose myself and my kind are like the big elk that were roaming around Ireland in the days gone by," Mr McCarthy says. "There won't be sight or sound of us in another couple of years."

"More's the pity," my uncle says. "The smith is a noble trade. Sure you nearly know as much about horses as the vet himself, and maybe more besides."

"Well, if I do itself, it's because it was handed down to me. Four generations of us working here out of the forge. The tractor is a grand invention, I'll grant you that, but it started pushing us out and we'll all die away yet."

"Ah, but the horse never died, and he'll never die, Dinnie," my uncle said. "The work horse might have had his day but there will be always the racehorse and the hunt."

"Only for the few hunters around here and in the neighbouring parish, and only for the pet ponies in some families, I'd be closing the gate and selling the anvil for scrap."

He looks very sad when he says this. I don't know much about the forge but even I feel sorry.

222

The man called Johnny straightens himself up. "Will ye give over this lonesome talk and come away for a pint," he says. "If Kieran here has a winner on his hands – and I feel it in my water that he has – he might be keeping you in work for another few years, Dinnie boy. Hang up d'auld apron and we'll have a deorum to celebrate this fine basht's new shoes and raise a glass to him."

"Right you are so," Mr McCarthy said, brightening. "We never died a winter yet. We'll keep a hauld on the old place for another while. Sure, the parish would be falling apart only that I'm here to fix the gates and the railings, the ploughs, the harrows and the scuffers."

"That's the man," my uncle said. "I knew the fight couldn't have gone out of you that easily. Come on across the road, Kieran. Ye'll be alright to walk away home with Apollo, won't ye, girls?"

It was strange hearing Apollo's new shoes clinking on the road as we walked home. The evening light was slanting through the trees, and midges were flickering in the heat the day still held.

"I really hope that Johnny fella is right," Sally says. "What do you think, Poll boy, have you got it in you?"

I think of Mummy again but this time in a happy way, as if she's with me. I hear her saying, 'You can if you think you can.'

"I do believe he has," I say. "We just have to keep helping him."

"Wouldn't it be class?" Sally says. "I can see us all getting our pictures took with Apollo and Kieran and a big cup. He'd have to give us a cut of the prize money, of course, after all our help."

The road home seems so short as she plans out our glory days. I let her build up the dream in every detail. I

believe in it too. It will happen – it *must* happen – but I
don't see myself in the pictures. I imagine Sally's excited
voice at the other end of a phone, words spilling out about
Apollo. There is no plan, no decision, no word from
Daddy but somehow I know this. Maybe I'm like Auntie
Jenny with a sixth sense. Where will I be then? I wish I
knew. I am here walking this road but somehow I am
missing them all already.

26

Tamara

Kieran is sitting in an old car seat in the centre of the earthen circle beaten into the field by Apollo's hooves. The seat came from a Volkswagon car in the scrapyard at the edge of the village. There is a kitchen chair beside it. At the start of every training session, Kieran sits in the wooden chair because it is higher and he is always up and down around the place. When he gets tired, he sinks into the car seat. When it is time to go back to the house, I catch one of his arms and Sally catches the other to pull him up. We laugh and joke and sometimes we pretend to fall back on the grass as he gets up. We take no notice of having to help him any more, though it was awkward in the beginning. Kieran is such a good sport. He says things like, 'Come on, ye useless pair of nurses! What am I paying ye for? Get the old angishore up.' If you care to know, 'angishore' is the word for a miserable person. I am looking forward to trying it out back in Earls Court. Whenever I'm back there.

Daddy keeps changing the month he is supposed to come and fetch me. I tell him I could go back by myself but he says, no, he wants to come over to thank everyone personally for taking such good care of me.

I have spread a white plastic Gouldings 10-10-20 bag

225

on the ground beside Kieran's chair. I am lying back, relieved to have a rest from walking the field. The sky, blue at last, is decorated with white clouds as fluffy as candyfloss at a funfair on the edge of the Thames. The sun is warm on my face – in between the passage of the clouds. It's the last week in June and the heat is so welcome after a neverending springtime of cold, rain and grey skies without a chink of blue or light. I close my eyes and try to doze.

Kieran is coughing. He has been coughing for weeks now but I never get used to the dreadfully bad spasms when he sounds as if he is coughing from the very bottom of his lungs. I hear the rattle of a box of matches. I open one eye and tilt my head. He is tapping a ciggie on the red-and-white Carroll's box. They all call them fags over here, except for Nana, who prefers 'coffin nails'.

"Them coffin nails will be the death of him if he doesn't give them up," she keeps saying.

Sally shouts across the arena to Kieran. "I'm jaded. We've been walking him since we came from school."

"Hauld going for another ten minutes," he answers. "Yourself and Tamara have a great week put down, fair play to ye. He's motoring well. I've asked Donovan to come up this evening to chance the training bit on him and to try a bit of lunging. He's a mouse with the two of ye, and he should be ready for the next step of his career. Donovan should be here soon."

My tummy tightens. I knew this day would come but as long as it was weeks away or even days away, it was alright. It isn't fair of Kieran to spring it on us like this. Yes, Apollo is his horse but we are training him too. I never complained about mucking out the stable in April when there were days too wet to leave him outside. I liked it actually. I liked seeing the floor so clean with fresh barley straw shaken all over it, the clean bucket of water in the corner, an armful of hay and half a sweet can of oats spilled into a trough. Yes, our Apollo is as spoiled as a baby. But if Mr. Donovan is coming now to meddle with him, I don't know if I can bear to watch.

Sally is completing another circle. She calls to Kieran again. "Can you or Tamara take another turn because the legs are going to fall off me, and I'm starved with the hunger?"

My cousin can be a proper angishore at times. She knows that Kieran is too tired at the end of the day to do any more walking.

I jump to my feet. I am not too bothered because the sun has gone behind a cloud again and it's pretty chilly.

"It's nearly half five," Kieran says, glancing at his watch. "Donovan said he'd be here half an hour ago."

He hesitates. Where there is hesitation, there is hope. How did that come into my head? It sounds like something Mummy used to say. The sun is well-lost behind a cloud, and there is a procession of them waiting to keep it hidden. My tummy is rumbling. Lunchtime was so long ago. All I had was a banana sandwich washed down with milk stored in a small Power's bottle and tasting faintly of whiskey. I prefer the flavour of whiskey on the milk to the taste of brown sauce I get when my aunt fills a YR bottle with milk for me.

"We'll give it five more minutes," Kieran says.

Sally gives a dramatic sigh. My heart goes behind a cloud of its own.

"OK, you take over," he says to me.

My reluctance melts away when Apollo whickers as he sees me walk towards him. I cup his nose in the palm of my hand – it's so soft. He's a lucky creature. He knows nothing but kindness from us. On we go round and round again. It's so late that Mr. Donovan can't possibly be coming. I think of Uncle Con's motto, 'Mind over matter'. I pull in closer to Apollo and inhale his warm, horsey smell.

I don't realise that Mr. Donovan is here until the car door slams and I catch the glint of the maroon-coloured Sunbeam Wolsey between the bars of the gate he is opening. He has a long, thin stick under his arm. As he comes closer, I see that it's a whip. Apollo pricks up his ears, looking in his direction with nostrils flared. He has no idea what is going to happen to him. I feel ill. I should walk him back to where Kieran is now being helped up by Mr. Donovan and Sally, but my feet won't move. I stroke Apollo's face and rub the backs of his ears. Mr. Donovan takes the bridle from Kieran who reaches into his jacket pocket and pulls out the training bit. I had often dreamed of taking it and throwing it down the well but they would have bought another. Mr. Donovan examines the bit and attaches one end of it to one of the bridle rings.

"Sally," Kieran says, pointing to the coarse brown potato bag beside his chair, "open the bag there and take out the crupper – the big leather band – and the two short leather straps."

As Mr. Donovan walks ahead of Kieran and Sally to where I'm standing, Apollo flattens his ears and snorts. I have seen him do this once before when a neighbour's dog got into the field and barked at him. Flattened ears are a sign that he is angry. Kieran notices too.

"Manners, boy," he says to him. "It's not like you to be showing a flash of temper."

"Human or beast is nothing without the odd show of

temper," Mr. Donovan says. "Even Our Lord himself lashed out in the temple – he did, faith."

He doesn't even say hello to me. He is so interested in Apollo that he doesn't notice me. I catch a sour whiff of whiskey off his breath, and I don't imagine he has been sipping from a Power's bottle filled with milk. Maybe the breeze carried it to Apollo and that's the explanation for the flat ears. He walks around Apollo, scrutinising him through narrowed eyes.

"Fair play to you, Kieran boy, he's in fine shape," he says. "No want of feeding there. He's a grand cut of a beast. Fat as a snail."

He stretches out his hand to take the rope from me. I grip it for a second longer than I should but he doesn't acknowledge this midge. Why should he? He has a job to do. I should go now. I don't want to see what happens next. It's not my fault but I feel like a traitor. I have handed Apollo over. If I had clapped my hands and shouted when I saw that beastly Mr. Donovan arrive, Apollo would have galloped away down the field, his tail flying behind him. It would have taken them too long to catch him again and so he couldn't have done his dirty work this evening. But I know if it's not today, it will be tomorrow. I should leave the field now. I don't want to see this, but the least I can do for Apollo is to stay.

Sally catches my coat sleeve and pulls me a few steps away from Kieran.

"This is awful," I say.

"I know, but there's nothing we can do." Sally's freckles stand out against the whiteness of her face.

So this is it. This is the beginning of what they call the 'mouthing' or the 'lunging'; all steps in the business of 'breaking a horse'. Breaking the spirit of our poor, trusting

229

Apollo, who has known nothing worse than a head collar up to now.

"Do you want to come in home?" Sally asks.

I shake my head.

She stands closer to me. "Don't go losing your voice on me. I couldn't go through that again."

I want to smile but I can't. My head is aching and my tummy is queasy.

Mr. Donovan takes the rope off the head collar and loops it around Apollo's neck. The horse is uneasy, moving from foot to foot.

"*Whoa, boy, whoa!*" he says. "Nice and easy does it."

He wants us to hold the rope while he puts the bridle on but we don't move. Kieran catches the rope instead. This is another worry. Mr. Donovan takes the head collar off and attempts to put on the bridle, but Apollo keeps tossing his head skywards and backing away from him. This is strange behaviour for him but Uncle Con has told me that horses can smell the nature of people.

"Blood on a butcher, harriers on the hunter, the kindness of a woman, even cruelty has its own particular smell," my uncle said.

What does Apollo smell now? Sour whiskey or something worse?

Kieran can't hold him. He looks as if he is going to fall but he steadies himself.

"Hold up there, stand, will you, stand!" Mr. Donovan says to Apollo, more sharply now, the coaxing tone gone. "Stand, you rip!"

"Take it aisy," Kieran says, but Mr Donovan ignores him.

He gives one more push and succeeds in getting the bridle up over Apollo's ears. Fast as lightning, he secures it with a strap behind the horse's neck. He has a grip now. He works the training bit against his mouth and his clenched teeth. The horse is frightened. He tries to pull away but Donovan – he doesn't deserve to be called Mister – is strong and is used to horses. He keeps clattering the bit against Apollo's teeth until he works it into his mouth and fastens the second side. Apollo is constantly tossing his head and shaking it.

My nails are dug so far into my palms that I feel they will draw blood. Sally's brow is creased in a fierce frown.

"Hand me the crupper," he says to Kieran. "Quick, quick, we haven't got all day!"

Kieran gives him the crupper and tries to soothe Apollo. The horse stops shaking his head but he's still snorting. The crupper thing is in place, running over his back and under his belly. Donovan runs two short straps from it to the rings in the bit.

"Shouldn't they be a bit looser?" Kieran asks, testing one with his hand.

"Is it me or you that's doing this?" Donovan says.

Kieran frowned at him. "You'll have to to loosen the straps by a hole or two."

"Where is the lunge line?" Donovan asks me. "Wake up, wake up!"

I tip the canvas bag over and a length of thin rope spills out. Donovan picks it up and ties it to one of the bridle rings.

"Stand back, the three of ye now, if ye don't want yer brains driven out with a lash of his legs," he says.

We retreat a safe distance away.

Apollo is shaking his head. His tongue is working furiously in his mouth as he tries to get rid of the bit. Suddenly he rises on his back legs, front legs thrashing wildly. Donovan only laughs.

"Now, that's what I call spirit," he says. "We'll see how much of that is left in two or three weeks' time."

I can't restrain myself any more. "*You're a cruel man. Positively beastly. I should just love it if he kicks your brains out!*"

Kieran and Sally are as surprised as I am at my outburst. But Donovan doesn't give a fig. He is standing in the middle of the circle with a long rope to guide Apollo. I could compare him to a ringmaster but this is no circus. He flicks the whip at Apollo's rump and sends him running round and round the circle in one direction. I feel wretched looking at him. I don't know how long we stand there watching him as he makes Apollo run circles at the end of the long strap. Apollo is foaming at the mouth. He looks like one of those dogs you see on TV – the crazy dogs with rabies. Every time Donovan allows Apollo to slow, I think his torment is over but he is only changing the strap to the right or the left side of the bridle to put equal pressure on the two sides of Apollo's mouth.

Only the dimming of the light at dusk brings it to a finish. Donovan's forehead is shining and there is a ghastly smell of perspiration coming from him – as if he has raw onions under his armpits. He leads Apollo to the gate and ties him to a concrete post. The second he walks away, Sally and I fly to Apollo as if on wings. Donovan goes over to Kieran and they stand, heads close together, smoking and talking. The smell of the cigarettes blows towards us on the wind that has grown from the breeze. Only for the fresh air I'd throw up, I feel so ill at the sight of Apollo. His skin is slick and shiny with sweat. With every blast of the wind, his skin ripples like water. He is shaking his head and snorting. And the horrid yellow froth is bubbling in the corners of his mouth. I expect I should see blood on the bit but at least the poor creature is spared that.

"It's OK, Apollo, peteen, we're here now," Sally is crooning to him on one side. "You're alright, peteen, don't worry."

I'm at the other side of his head, stroking his cheek. I whisper to him fiercely, "I shan't let this happen to you again. I promise you faithfully I shan't."

I hear the sound of the tractor rumbling in the yard. It comes to a halt beside the car with the engine running. I am blinking in the glare. Uncle Con jumps off and comes striding through the gate. He catches Apollo by the bridle, runs his hand along his steaming back and wipes it on his navy boilersuit. Donovan is walking towards him at the same time.

"Jesus Christ, man, what do you think you are doing with the horse?" my uncle says. "Do you see the sweat pouring off him?"

"Sure, that's only normal when they're not used to the lunging," Donovan replies. "You have to go hard on them for the first session to knock some of the teaspach out of them."

"It's alright if he doesn't catch pneumonia out of it," my uncle says. "That's an east wind wherever the hell it's after coming out of. He'll have to be kept inside tonight. He should have been covered as soon as ye were finished."

Donovan throws his hands in the air and begins to protest but my uncle is already leading Apollo through the gate and towards the stable with Sally and myself following him. I am so happy to see Donovan get a telling-off. I should just love it if he followed us and got some more of the same medicine but we hear his car starting and the engine grows fainter as he drives down the lane.

My uncle takes down a brush from a space where a stone is missing from the wall, and begins to brush Apollo from ears to tail with long, firm strokes.

"Run up the haggard, the two of ye, and bring down a bucket of water as quick as ye can carry it," he tells us.

Sally picks up the iron bucket that has fallen on its side on the straw and we dash out, almost knocking down Kieran who is on his way in. There is an awfully lost look on his face.

It's getting dark now and the harsh electric light is spilling out towards us when we take long, steady strides back down again, the water bucket between us. The light is not the only thing spilling out. We can hear the raised voices of my uncle and Kieran. I grip the cold metal handle tighter. Another argument. There hasn't been one in weeks and I was hoping there would be no more.

"For feck's sake, they're at it again," Sally hisses. "That bleddy Kieran is a nutcase, pure and simple."

I'm too tired to protest, too nervous at the thought of what we'll hear in the stable. The air is cold inside and Apollo is still steaming – the beautiful warm smell of his body hits me in a wave.

We rest the bucket on the stone threshold. He turns and whickers when he hears the metal strike the stone. Sally picks it up and, leaning to one side with the weight of it, struggles the last few paces. Apollo sinks his head into the bucket and raises it again, water streaming down from his mouth, when the bucket is half-empty.

Kieran and my uncle have fallen silent on our return, but the ceasefire is temporary.

"Who else did you want me to get to start the lunging?" Kieran begins. "I didn't want to be bothering you, with all the milking to be done and the work in the shed afterwards. And, anyway, I'm not sure what to make of your new interest in horses."

Kieran is full of temper. His voice is loud. But Daddy refuses to be drawn in. His voice is low and steady every time he answers.

"Didn't I explain to you I grew up with horses? But you have to move with the times, and any fool could see the tractor was the coming thing. I'm not saying you were wrong to get Donovan. I'm only saying he went too hard on him for the first evening. I suppose he wasn't to know it was going to turn cold."

"That's the same as blaming me," Kieran says. "If you want me to train the horse, you have to let me do it myself. You can't be breathing down my fucken neck the whole time. Either I'm in charge of the horse or I'm not. How can I ask Donovan to do anything again?"

"There's plenty more around the place to help you besides him. I can explain the basics to you myself. We're not talking about putting a man on the moon."

"That's the same as saying you don't want him around the place but you're not man enough to come out and state it baldly."

"Aren't those lads you played hurley with only dying to give you a hand? I was talking to them after Mass last Sunday."

"You were discussing me with them, were you? That's nice. That's just lovely."

My uncle is brushing Apollo with long, leisurely strokes while he speaks. Kieran is brushing him too with a handful of hay balled tight in his fist, but his strokes are short and vigorous, like the division of his sentences.

"I will look after this horse the way I want. Or I won't fucken look after him at all. Take him to Puck Fair and flog him to some tinker if you're not happy with that."

The sobs erupt, big heaving sobs that take my breath away. My tears are as hot as candle grease on my cheeks. Sally is trying to pull me out the stable door but I shan't budge. She looks so upset that I want to stop but I can't.

"Jesus Christ, that's all I want now," Kieran says, flinging away the fistful of hay.

I am crying on one level but, on another, I notice how gently the hay falls and how weak an expression it is of Kieran's temper.

"There's no call for any of this, Kieran," my uncle says. "Go away and sleep on it, boy. It will look different in the morning."

"Sleep on it," Kieran replies bitterly. "The same old line. You haven't a blind notion what kind of a world I wake to every morning since this happened to me."

I am wishing that he'll walk away, that any one of them will leave the stable. Kieran opens his mouth as if he is going to speak again but thinks better of it. He limps out of the lighted stable into the night.

"Ye might get another half-bucket of water and one of oats from the barn, girls," my uncle says.

On the way up the haggard again, Sally tells me to pull myself together but not in these words exactly.

"Cop onto yourself, Tamara," she says. "It's just another storm, and it will blow over."

Maybe it will, maybe it won't. The only certainty I have is that life on this farm is as changeable as the Irish weather.

27

Kieran

My mother says some things are meant to happen. "What's for you won't pass you," she says, though she'd have loved to see Kitty passing me at the rate of ninety. Sometimes you'd be a way better off if what was for you did pass you at the pace of a scalded cat or a pedigree greyhound fresh out of the trap. Sometimes no bread is way better than half a loaf, but I was so low at the time that I would have settled for a scattering of crumbs, as I did that first summer when I was throwing some shape at clawing my way back to being halfway normal. And, if the truth be known, I thrived on those crumbs when I had them, and would put my two hands up for them without thinking twice if I could have that last summer with Kitty Donovan back again.

I was finding it hard going with Apollo that first summer even though I had all the help from the hurling lads and from Sally and Tamara. It was the end of July and Kitty had been home a few weeks. I knew because I heard Sally and my mother talking about her when they got back from first Mass of a Sunday. I was still using the excuse of my leg for not going to Mass. This explanation was wearing a bit thin by then but Mammy and Nana had given up picking at me. I wasn't very inclined to go singing the praises of a God who had dealt me this hand of cards. When the priest came to visit 'the sick' – me now lumped in with all the auld ones as 'the sick' – I played along for the sake of a quiet life. I had enough on my plate without Nana, fresh from her success with Tamara, trying to save my mortal soul. No, sirree, that was not for me.

I wasn't stirring out that much. The odd weekend I went to the pub in the village with the lads but I drank too much when I did go out. I looked drunk enough without taking a drop of the hard stuff and I knew it didn't suit me anyway. After the lads brought me home covered in puke three or four times, the father put a stop to my gallop. Part of me was still hoping that I'd bump into Kitty somewhere around the place. There was another fella inside of me, telling me to have a bit of sense for myself. "Never trouble trouble till trouble troubles you" – that was one of Nana's sayings.

Trouble came to find me in the end. I was down the Bog Road with Sally and Tamara. We were getting Apollo used to being on the road, and it was nice and quiet down there. My father had dropped me off in the car before he went milking, and the girls led Apollo through the fields and out the gap at the bottom of the Hilly Field. It was evening time. The weather had been misting on and off all day but by then it had dried up but the rain made everything smell so good, especially the woodbine climbing up along the briars and the trees in the ditches. It was Sally's turn to trot Apollo ahead of her, holding the long reins. Apollo was so used to the routine at that stage that a baby could have held him, but I wanted to have him one hundred per cent right, especially on the road. Tamara was rooting around in the ditch. Her feet were soaking because a small stream was running along below the road, and she had slipped into it. You couldn't see it with all the briars but you could hear the chatter of it in the hollow spaces it was making its way through. After a while she came back to me and held out her palm. It was full of tiny wild strawberries.

"Here, Kieran, taste a few," she said. "They're gorgeous."

"Where are you going with your gorgeous?" I said. "I think they're splendid."

"Do you not want me getting the Cork accent, boy?"

In the few short months that Tamara had begun talking again more and more of our own words were creeping into her speech and she often lapsed into the sing-song Cork accent.

"Penny for your thoughts," she said, alerting me to the fact that I had drifted off into my own world without even noticing.

"You won't buy my thoughts as chape as that. I think you'd have to take the bread knife to the arse of Sally's piggy bank."

I wouldn't tell her I had travelled back to the day we picked the wild raspberries in the Top Field. I was thinking how fit and well this poor amadán was back then, little knowing that Nana's all-merciful God was up there in the clouds, biding his time to take careful aim and peg a spanner into the works. Yeah, it's a gas bleddy thing when it gets going – this will of God.

Sally had turned Apollo around just before the small stone bridge and was heading back up the straight stretch of road, running behind to keep up with the trotting horse. Just the look of Apollo was enough to get me back on track. All that horse was short of doing was speaking, he was so smart. And he was cracked about me, I knew. I had only to cough or to speak crossing the yard and he was whickering and making his way over to the gate. When they drew level with me, Sally pulled him up.

"Whoa, Poll! Stand there. Stand now, boy," she said breathlessly.

"Good man, Poll," I said, taking half a ginger-nut biscuit from my pocket and feeding it to him. His lips twitched over my outstretched palm and his strong teeth crunched it. Then he dropped his head and started pulling tufts of rough grass that were growing from the middle of the road. The three of us stood around him, our silver lad. The few pounds spent on the oats were worth it all when you saw the shine on his coat. I ran my hand down along his front leg and picked up his hoof. The shoes were lasting well, and he was used to them by now. I leaned against him, transferring all my weight onto my good leg so the bad one wouldn't give underneath me; I had been walking the road far longer than I should have been.

Tamara was gearing up to take a turn up and down the road when we heard the tinkle of a bell coming from the direction of the river. A bike had crested the hump in the middle of the bridge and was heading towards us. The evening sun was glaring and I had to shade my eyes to see who it was.

The brakes screeched when Kitty pulled up. Apollo threw up his head and snorted but Tamara kept a tight grip on the reins.

Sally scowled at Kitty. "He could have bolted."

"I'm sorry," Kitty said. "I forgot the noise they make."

Sally raised her eyes to heaven before following Tamara down the road with Apollo.

"He's a fine colt," Kitty said, watching them go.

"He is," I agreed, thankful to have at least two words

to say to her. How could I have ended up so awkward with Kitty? I couldn't think of anything else to say.

"He is that and all," I added.

The little stream might as well have been Niagara Falls, the way it sounded so loud in the silence that hung between us on the boreen. I was frightened out of my life that she would take my quietness as a sign that I was mad at her and that she'd hold me to the words I had thrown at her in Dublin and cycle away again. I was frightened out of my life too that she would stay and that we would continue stiff and awkward, so different from the jokey way we used to have of going on.

"How's the training going?" she said, after a while.

"Yerra, grand out," I said.

Some of the tension left my body but my head was beginning to pound. If I moved, she'd see the stupid auld shaky way I had of walking. I didn't know how much longer I could stand there without the bad leg giving way.

"I heard ye put the run on Himself," she said. "Something about lunging the colt too hard."

"My auld fella lost the rag with him, and your auld fella took the hump."

"Ye were as well off. You couldn't rely on him. You know the way." She raised her hand and mimicked someone throwing a glass off the head.

The girls had stopped at the bridge, and were leading Apollo down to the water for a drink. If they'd only come back up, I could lean against him again, give myself a chance. I couldn't stay standing there much longer.

Kitty began to put a foot on the pedal. I was relieved, disappointed. Jesus, I didn't know what to feel. I didn't know whether I was coming or going. I could hardly believe that she was there in front of me after so long.

241

"I'd better get going," she said, adding with a smile, "before Sally comes back up and clears me. Good luck with the horse. You have a good one there."

"Thanks," I muttered, my heart sinking.

I watched her pedal away down the road until, a good few yards from me, she wheeled around again and turned back towards me. Circling me without stopping, she called out, "I could always give ye a hand with the training!"

"Fine so," I said before I knew it. When she rounded the bend, I made for the stone ditch with the zig-zag shaking motion that now passes as walking for me. I sank down on the middle flagstone. The sweat was cold on my back.

28

Sally

"What in the name of God does he want to go drawing that wan around the place for again?"

Mammy was operating with her 'cross voice'. Her words were booming through the kitchen door as clearly as if they were coming from the radio with the knob turned up to the last. I pricked up my ears as I came through the garden gate and stopped outside the door, my cheek pressed against the warm stone. Keep your ears open and your mouth shut. There is a lot to be said for it, except I was still trying to get the hang of the second half of that nugget of wisdom that Nana had passed down.

It was the beginning of August, and Kitty had made her first appearance in the field to help Kieran and ourselves train Apollo. As if we needed her doing her sergeant major act around the place, giving us orders. I mean trying to give me orders. Tamara was an easy target but I'd bring her round yet.

The worst of it was that Apollo was acting as if he was mad about her, nuzzling her palms for those fancy sugar lumps she was after bringing for him. I told Kieran they would be bad for the horse's teeth but I might as well have been a fly buzzing past him for all the notice he took of me.

"Won't she be a help with the colt?" Daddy was saying. "Another pair of hands."

Daddy would have brought in Hitler if he thought he'd get a day's work out of him – on the chape.

"I know where these hands will end up if she upsets Kieran – wrapped around that scrawny neck of hers," Mammy said. "You know how easy it is to throw him off track."

Jeecus creepers, she was fairly boiling. No way was I going to stand on her corns while she was in that flipping mood.

Nana was throwing her tuppence into the debate but her voice was low and I had to strain my ears. Speak up, Nana, won't you?

"The girl might keep him on track," Nana said. "Doesn't the poor boy need a bit of distraction? She might do him good."

"If I thought she would, I'd put up with her," Mammy said. "I'm just afraid that she'll knock him *off* the bleddy track and we'll all be back at square one with him. And she'll go waltzing off to her fancy friends and her fancy life, leaving us to deal with the mess."

"You wouldn't know till afterwards," Daddy said. "Give it a chance."

"Do I have any other choice?"

You have, I wanted to shout – *just tell her to clear off!* You are the one who could do it. Daddy and Kieran are only a pair of cissies. Take her to one side without Kieran knowing and tell her that you can't take the risk with his head the way it is after the accident. Make her feel guilty. Come on, Mammy, we were doing fine without her.

"Trust in God and offer it up for the Holy Souls in Purgatory," Nana said.

244

Oh, Nana, will you let her be! Go away and say another decade of the rosary or something. Sometimes I think you really are starting to dote.

"There must be acres of empty space in Purgatory with the amount of offering up I've been doing since Kieran got sick," Mammy said.

The heat was gone out of her voice. It looked like we were stuck with the lovely Kitty. I had been sent in from the field for a sweet gallon – one of the tin ones that boiled sweets came in — filled with tea and a few cuts of curranty cake. The servant girl, no less. Kieran had forgotten to bring the ginger-nut biscuits for Apollo, and I had to bring them too. I didn't mind coming in because I was going to puke if I had to take any more of Kitty organising the jumps. We could have started them without her, anyway, but Kieran, the half-wit, was making out that she was doing us a huge favour. He was like a dog – a pure 'Shep' – as far as she was concerned, so eager to follow her ladyship's every command.

I ran into the kitchen, trying to look as if I had just landed in from the field but I wasn't going to make it to the stage in the Opera House any day soon.

"I know that face, Sally O'Mahony," Mammy said. "What are you up to? Out with it."

"Nothing," I said, all innocent, and creating a diversion by listing all the things they wanted in the field.

"I'll carry them out with you, but then I want Tamara and yourself to go down the garden and dig a pot of spuds and pick out a good head of cabbage. I have a nice bit of bacon for the dinner."

"Tamara will love that," I said. "She'll be crying for the poor piggie."

Mammy shot me a look but said nothing. The cups

245

were out in the field already. She made a big pot of sweet tea and poured it into the sweet gallon. Then she filled a whiskey bottle with milk and stuffed the neck with a twist of paper torn from *The Cork Examiner*.

Mammy was like a different woman when she started talking about Kitty as we were crossing the yard with the supplies. Don't talk about Kitty and her acting like she was the boss – there was an actress lost in Mammy as well, if you asked me. But nobody ever asked me anything. That was the problem. The Amazing Invisible Sally.

"Isn't it great that Kitty is giving ye a hand with Apollo?" Mammy said, testing me. "Things were slowing up a bit there for a while, weren't they?"

"We were doing grand," I said, accelerating my pace so sharply that the tea sloshed around the gallon.

She kept up the big act out in the field, and she all questions to Kitty about setting up the bars to get Apollo started on the jumping.

"We're going to start with just one pole in three places," Kitty said. "We'll walk him over a few of them for a few days, over and back."

'Twas very fast she was coming out with her flipping 'we'. Who the divil did she mean? Or maybe it was the 'royal we' that Mammy mentioned when anyone was putting on airs and graces.

Just then, I felt that Kieran's eyes were on me. I turned my head. I was right.

"What do ye think, girls?" he asked. "Since ye're my two chief cooks and bottlewashers, ye may as well as get yer spake in about the plan."

Kieran shot up a couple of notches in my estimation. 'Queen Kitty' looked a bit put out. I reckoned she wasn't stopped too often in the middle of her gallop.

"Oh, I thought we agreed that this was what you wanted to do next," she said.

The weasel Kieran, I bet he did and all, but he was just trying to cover his tracks to keep in with myself and Tamara. Well, he was after putting the bit back between my teeth and I was going to run with it. Or so I thought, until Tamara, the dark horse, shot out ahead of me with her polite English way of talking. She was red up to the gills but she was sure of what she was on about when she got going.

"I beg your pardon, Kitty, but I have been doing a spot of reading from a book I borrowed from the library – the *Encyclopaedia of the Horse*. And I was discussing it with Uncle Con. If you wouldn't mind awfully, I suggest that we start getting Apollo accustomed to weight on his back and move gradually on to the saddle."

Atta girl, Tamara, the killer punch cloaked inside a kid glove. I'd have gone straight for the target and ended up on my arse. And she wasn't finished yet.

"I think we can all make a jolly good effort if we work as a team," she said. "I propose Kieran as the captain since he owns Apollo."

As crafty as a fox cub. Would you credit it? Now, Kitty girl, doesn't that cool your cocoa? Mammy got a fit of laughing and tried to disguise it by taking out her hankie and spluttering into it. Kitty was snookered for now. At least we had won the first battle but there was a war stretching ahead of us until we had made a hunter out of Apollo.

"I second that proposal," Kitty said. "All that makes perfect sense to me."

She would say that, wouldn't she? Perfect sense, my arse. She'd be cracking the whip again if she got half a chance.

"I'm honoured to take the position, although I get the feeling I'm being gipped because it was mine to begin with," Kieran said. "Where did you come up with this team-spirit lark, Tamara? I didn't think you were a hurler."

"Don't be silly, Kieran. I told you I played hockey. How could you forget? Scout's honour, I was a dreadful hockey player but I learned heaps. Our coach, Miss Edwards, always said, 'Gels, gels, what you learn on the pitch will serve you well in life'."

I thought Tamara's voice was posh till I heard her aping that Miss Edwards. You'd swear the Queen herself was talking.

That was how August began. Apart from getting used to having Kitty on 'the team', it was like being in heaven. School was as far away as the moon. Well, that's what it felt like to me. Most of our time was taken up with Apollo, and that was good because you could see him learning things and because I could escape other jobs – not having to clean out the stinky henhouse was the best. It was good too because Kieran was happy when he saw that Apollo was turning out so well. Some of the men from the hunt used to call by and say things like, 'That's a nate horse, Kieran boy. He'll make a nice few pounds for you yet.' 'Twas all about the money to some people.

I loved being out in the field with Kieran and Tamara, and Kitty was alright as long as you let her know she could keep her notions to herself and not be bothering the rest of us with them.

Things were different, though. Kieran didn't want to come down to the river anymore with myself and Tamara. Poor Sam could just about make it but you had to keep an eye on her all the time. I'd swear she was doting because she was always wandering off and getting lost if you weren't watching her. Mammy said that old dogs went away to hide in a wood or a clump of furze when they wanted to die. I couldn't stand the thought of Sam disappearing like that, so I never left her stray too far.

I could fish myself, well sort of, but it wasn't the same without Kieran. Him not being able to walk was one thing but the worst thing was that I knew he'd rather be with Kitty. That was one battle I couldn't win. I wouldn't go forgetting about everyone else just because some stupid boy came along. When I was complaining about him to Nana, she only smiled as if she knew some big secret.

"What's the big joke?" I asked.

"You'll be the same one day when some nice young lad like that Finbarr Driscoll from across the ditch comes calling."

She had me there. I had caught Finbarr giving me special looks the time they were all over to help with bringing in the hay. I pretended not to notice but it was kind of nice. He is a year older than me and has black curly hair and grey eyes. He is always in good form and whistling. He can whistle like a blackbird. He made a point of sitting beside me on the stool at dinnertime and walked up to the meadow with me afterwards.

Kitty can drive a tractor like a man; you should see her with a load of bales up behind. I'd say she'd chance a combine if she was left up on one. She can drive cars too. I was dying for a go on the tractor but Daddy wouldn't hear of it. Kitty used to get a loan of her aunt's green Mini Minor a couple of evenings a week to go off on drives with Kieran. They'd take off down the lane and the Mini lifting off the road, much to Mammy's delight, let me add. Do you think we'd be asked to come? Not on your Nellie.

Not that Mammy'd lave us. Tamara was better about the whole thing than I was. She used to try and talk sense into me.

"See how happy he is when he is with Kitty," she said. "Would you rather see him wretched?"

"What do you take me for? Of course I wouldn't. It's just that I'm sick to the back teeth of all that lovey-dovey stuff."

"It could make me feel positively ill too if I allowed it," she said. "But this too shall pass."

"What's up with you? This too shall pass. You sound like a flipping priest."

Then she told me that she'd heard Kitty's mother saying Kitty was hoping to get accepted for nursing in London, and that she'd be going over to a place called Kent in September if she was. If that was the case, I'd have to start a novena with Nana for Kitty's career success. And a second one for Kieran's survival of her departure. For one dazzling minute, I imagined the three of us going back to the way we were before the accident. But the distance between that place and where we had landed came home to me with a whack, leaving me lonesome.

29

Kieran

Kitty was a desperate driver. Shoe down to the last and let Saint Christopher take care of oncoming traffic. The bends were the worst. There was no talking to her, only lave her off and hope for the best. But, God, I don't know if I'll ever find the equal of how I felt on those evenings that summer heading out and away with her: away from everything and everyone and, best of all, away from myself, from the worry of my weak arm and my weak leg. I couldn't wait till I heard the sound of the green Mini booting it up the lane, cats, dogs and even the odd stray duck scattering before her.

"You're like a hen with an egg," Mammy said to me while I was waiting one evening. "Would you not sit down and content yourself until she lands? Rest yourself."

She was right, of course, but, bad leg or no bad leg, I had a path worn from the table to the kitchen window, pacing like one of those caged bashts you'd see on a school tour to Dublin Zoo. It was a hot evening and there was a bluebottle buzzing around the kitchen. The sound of him didn't improve my mood. I suppose Kitty had become my drug. When I was with her, all my doubts about us melted away. We were so good together. If any few days passed without seeing her, I got anxious. What if she took up with someone else? What if her feelings for me changed? I knew it was all in my mind. But the mind can be worse than any horse when it bolts. I was at my worst when I was waiting for her and she was late. I was a different man entirely when I was out with Apollo. Those were my best times.

I knew my mother could see the roller coaster that I was on with Kitty. And I didn't want her to think badly of my girl. Like she was surely thinking when she saw me so agitated that evening I was pacing the floor. To pacify her, I poured myself a cup of tea from the pot. It was made a while and it was like tar, a taste of metal filings from it. Not that I'm in the habit of chewing metal filings – yet. But a person in my state would be fit to try anything.

"Here, have another slice of this," Mammy said, knifing thick cuts of butter onto a slice of ginger bread she'd baked that afternoon. Her ginger bread was the best thing that came out of the oven. She was killed from baking it those days. Anything to fatten me up, and to improve my form.

I'd have gone down to the gate but there was a bit of a drizzle and Mammy was afraid I might melt. No matter how many times I warned her to lave me manage on my own, she'd be back smothering me before I knew it. I hated myself for losing my patience with her but, God forgive me, she acted so thick half the time. She hadn't a fucken clue how mad the fussing made me. The hurt look in her eyes then if I lashed out – Jesus Christ, that was worse than anything. *Get away, get away. Would I ever get away?* That's all I could ever think of on the bad days when I felt like a fucken bluebottle bating himself against a window with the sun shining through and tormenting him and not a chance in hell of getting out and every chance of landing on his back on the dusty windowsill with his legs paddling in the air.

Settle, Kieran, settle. I had to tell myself that. I had to talk myself down, to keep from going out of my fucked-up mind. I opened the window and lave the poor fly out and watch him taking off for the blue sky at the rate of a jet. My day would come too.

Kitty was never on time. I knew that but it was no help to the impatience rattling inside me. I wanted to be out on the road with her, the ditches flying past us, the radio blaring, the wind whooshing through her beautiful red hair. Out there on the road I could forget. I could forget for as long as I was with her.

Kitty didn't believe in wearing a watch. What crazy notion did she get to go applying for nursing where her days would be ruled by the clock? She'd have to wear one of those brooch watches pinned to the front of her uniform. I used to be codding her about the nurse's uniform. At least, I could get that laugh out of it. I couldn't understand Kitty and nursing, only that her mother had been a nurse before Donovan had swept her off her feet, God help us, and set her up in the big house by the river where the new wife and his own mother were ating the heads off each other till the old woman passed away.

Anyway, it would probably never happen. By the time she was called for interview, if she ever was, she'd have changed her mind if I knew Kitty. Horses were her life and she was way into Project Apollo. Besides, I couldn't imagine Kitty passing any hospital interview. I supposed they'd have interviews, wouldn't they? But then again, with that hair tied up and a sensible puss on her, they mightn't sniff out the mad streak. Or maybe they'd want someone a bit on the cracked side. Sure, didn't I know from experience, from bitter experience let me add, that some of the best nurses in Dublin were clane mad, off their heads when they weren't on duty. One of them told me that they used have to put every alarm clock in the flat into saucepans to make sure they'd wake up in time for work after a night out. There they'd be facing into a day's work in that sunshine valley of a place with only two or three hours' sleep behind them and their eyes like Pandas from the mascara and the carousing into the small hours. Weren't they better off, when you think of what they had to put up with?

"How are you feeling this evening, Kieran, you handsome cut of a lad," a wan called Deirdre would ask me, her finger on my pulse, and the cheeky look in her eyes making me think what lad I'd like her hand to be on.

"Will you go away, Deirdre girl. A fat lot you care about me. All you're dreaming of is horsing back double vodkas in Harcourt Street tonight and getting off with a big guard with a langer as long as his baton."

That's what I was thinking but no way in the world would I come out with a statement like that. I'd be up for a big stabber of an injection in my bony arse if I went on with that kind of dirty talk. And proper order.

A man . . . . stall the digger and let me explain that I was calling myself a man, even though I was somewhere in the halfway territory between boy and man. A man capable of talk like that would never be backward about coming forward when he was spending every second evening driving into the summer dusk with a beautiful almost-a-woman girl, you might think. Think again. The lads were giving me fierce stick.

"Did you shift her yet? Don't go all quiet on us. We don't want a blow-by-blow account. Just give us some notion. I don't believe you. Jeecus, you must have copped some feel at this stage? What do you mean talking? Sure you could be talking to us any night of the week. Wake up, boy, you're not going to be going the road with her till Christmas. Pull the choke out, boy. Steady up, I didn't mean that. Or maybe I did. You shouldn't look a gift horse in the mouth. Or a fine filly for that matter. Fucken hell, Kieran, lighten up. You only live once. Alright, alright, I will mind my own business. Unless we do a stake-out. Can't you take a joke? Good job you can't run too fast."

They were cheeky scuts, rising me with all their nosy questions, but they weren't asking much more than I was asking myself when the red heat of my mind and my body kept me awake at night. Kitty and myself had been driving out two and three nights a week, and nothing had happened. Nothing like that anyway. I wanted to kiss her. Loads of times I came within a hair's breadth of leaning across to her but I stopped because I didn't know was that what she wanted. I'd have been gutted if she had pulled away from me. If she did pull away and got all awkward with me, the summer would have been ruined on us. I couldn't chance it.

So, up the lane she came that evening half an hour late. My mother threw her eyes to heaven as I headed for the door, all my agitation gone west at the sight of the car and a big foolish smile plastered across my face.

Off we went, and the green Mini lifting around the bends. She could have gone two hundred miles an hour and it wouldn't have been half fast enough for me. More than once, we could have been sent to meet our Maker. I wouldn't have minded if I had Kitty shooting off into the light with me.

Around a bend we came not long after leaving the house and met a tractor nearly nose to nose with us. I caught the wheel and jerked hard to the left. Kitty screeched like a banshee as we swerved but, fair play to her, she straightened up again.

"Mother of fuck, we might have been going to heaven

together," I said.

"Or hell," she grinned, eyes not leaving the road and knuckles white against the black steering wheel.

We parked in our favourite spot overlooking the huge dam built on the River Lee to generate electricity for Cork city downstream. The Lee backed up into a long lake above the dam. That's what we were looking down on. Kitty had taken one of my fags – she didn't often smoke – and we had the car windows open, puffing the smoke out into the evening air. The cigarette ends were glowing like the setting sun. I finished mine before her.

"Here," she said. "Half is plenty for me. Ample sufficiency, as my mother says."

When I reached out to take the fag from her, she flicked it out the window. She clasped my hand and pulled me towards her and kissed me. I kissed her back – you can be sure I did. Her mouth tasted of the fags. It tasted of more. Her lips were as soft as I had imagined them to be. The longer we kissed, the hungrier our mouths became, searching for each other. The water falling from the dam was humming in the distance. I felt as if I was sinking into an underwater world, like the farms with their houses and outhouses, roads and bridges, all flooded when the dam was built. We kissed and we kissed. I didn't want to rise to the surface. When we pulled apart, we were both silent. Kitty stretched across and lay with her head and shoulders in my lap. I buried my fingers in her hair and stroked her head and face.

"Do you think I'm an awful wan to go kissing you like that?"

"*Shhh*. I wanted to kiss you all summer but I was afraid."

"Afraid of what? That I might bite the head off you?"

256

"I thought that maybe . . ."

"Go on. Don't think about it, just say it."

"I thought that maybe you were just being nice to me because you felt sorry for me."

"Did that feel like a 'I'm sorry for your troubles' kinda kissing? Did it feel as if I was expressing my sympathy, like?"

"Well, if it was, sympathise away all you like."

"Christ, that handbrake was digging into my side," she said, groaning as she sat back up in the driver's seat. "Come on, we'll get out."

I took her hand in mine. It was so cold. I held it up between my neck and my shirt collar to warm it.

"Cold hands – sign of a warm heart," she said.

"Mine are always like a furnace. Where does that lave my heart?"

"Oh, it's a swinging brick, without a doubt."

"Well, you'd better duck so, because it's coming straight for you," I said, stopping dead on the road and kissing her.

"The shyness wasn't long wearing off you," she said, as we broke away.

The road was climbing gently. I knew she was slowing her pace to suit mine. That was picking at me but what could I do? At the top of the incline, we came to a bar gate opening into a field sloping down towards the water. We slipped in through a gap between the gate and a concrete pillar. The day had been clear and sunny but the sky had turned as grey as saucepans since the light had faded. There was a big rock at the edge of the field, and we sat there looking down to the water. Well, we were looking at it when we eventually took a break from the kissing session.

"My father was telling us that the people from the

farms used to come up here to light fires in the evenings when the flooding started," Kitty said. "Did you hear that story?"

"If I did, I was only half-listening. My grandmother tells so many stories that my ears are switched off half the time."

"I don't know how long it took but, bit by bit, the water rose and rose until the fields and the houses and everything were covered," she said. "And they were up here sitting around their fires. It must have been awful to watch your farm going under, even if there was compensation."

She was lost in the story. She hadn't a clue that my mind was off on another track. I was thinking that the drowned houses weren't too different from my lost self, all weighed down by muck and sludge under the surface: this new self was more wading than walking, dragging the weight of my lost self behind it. Lovely thoughts to be having, and the girl of my dreams sitting beside me, lovely to the world altogether. Good job Kitty couldn't read my mind.

I wanted to put my arm around her but I was still so slow to make a move. The breeze rose, and she shivered and snuggled into me. It was now or never. I reached my arm across her shoulder and pulled her closer. I stroked her back. She rubbed her cheek against my arm. The breeze carried the distant roar of the water.

"We stopped near the entrance to the dam coming from the city with my father when we were small," Kitty said. "He filled a small bottle of water from a drain running alongside the road. He said it was electric water and threw some at us. We were all screaming."

"The smallest thing would frighten the life out of you when you're small," I said. "They took me to a circus in Macroom. They thought they were doing a great thing. I roared and bawled when I saw the clowns."

Kitty picked up a daisy and idly turned the stem between her finger and thumb. A tractor rumbled off in the distance. The only pity was that the clouds were growing darker by the minute and the odd cold star was winking. The night was well on its way and we'd have to strike for home.

"Look at the trees," Kitty said, pointing away down to the row of shadows at the edge of the water. "Don't they look like the shapes we used to cut out of paper when we were at school?"

Just then, a bee bumbled along over the grass. He was arguing to himself as he went, like a fella who had stayed too late in the pub.

"That fella is out a bit late," I said. "He'll get a clip across the ear when he gets back to the hive. Like us, if we don't get a move on."

"Do we have to? It's so nice being here – just the two of us."

"Mammy will think we're after ploughing into a ditch," I said. "There will be a search party out for us. She worries about me all the time. You'd swear I was eight instead of nineteen."

"You can't blame her, I suppose. I feel guilty some evenings when I think of how she must feel seeing you heading out with this kamikaze pilot."

"Better you than the lads dragging me off to the pub. I suppose that's what she thinks – the lesser of two evils."

"Are you calling me evil, Kieran O'Mahony? Let me show you evil."

She pushed against me and sent me falling down into the grass, her following and stretching out on top of me. She started kissing me again, a slow lazy kiss. I buried my hands in her hair, sifted through it and moved them down her back, down, down, and she didn't stop me. Oh the feel of her arse through the thin dress! I kissed her back harder. I knew I'd have to pull the brakes but not yet, oh please not yet.

All of a sudden we heard a bang and the mad flutter of wings somewhere at the other side of the field. Kitty rolled down onto the field and held onto me as if she was going to drown.

"Jesus, we'll be shot dead," she said.

"It's probably one of the Lynchs out shooting foxes," I said. "We'll hauld tough and try and make out what direction they're going in."

Two more shots rang out. They sounded no nearer. Kitty was lying so close to me, you'd swear her heart was a bird trapped inside her dress. My own heart wasn't much better at the rate it was hammering. If any of the Lynchs walked up to us, I'd be mortified to be caught courting in the field. Better mortified than dead, though.

Ten long minutes dragged past before we judged it safe to move. Given the state of my leg, I could hardly say we made a run for it but we got out of the field fairly lively and booted down the road towards the car. Whether it was the relief or what, we were wake with the laughing once we sat back into the Mini. I could hardly ever pass that stretch of the road after that without smiling to myself.

From that evening on, we kissed our way through the rest of the summer. I learned to kiss and I learned a lot more besides. The lads were delighted that I was finally 'shifting'. So was I. Everything comes down to practice, doesn't it? Kitty and myself weren't total novices to start out but we put in a lot of practice. When we weren't busy with kissing and the like, we were talking. We talked about everything under the sun. We talked a lot about horses.

"If you could wish for anything in the world, what would it be?" Kitty said, adding gently, "Beside the obvious."

The obvious was code for getting rid of the gammy leg and being the same as I was before.

"That's not much of a wish so, is it?' I said. 'Go on. What's your wish?"

"I asked you first."

I thought for a while. I couldn't very well tell her that I wished that summer would go on forever, and that she would never go away. Of all the things we talked about, there was one big question we shied away from: what would become of 'us' at the end of the summer.

"I'd like to be another Vincent O'Brien," I said. "I wouldn't care if the horse was good at racing or showjumping as long it was a class horse."

That sounded daft so I explained I knew I would never come anywhere near Vincent O'Brien as a horse trainer but if I could even go a tiny way towards being as successful as him, that would be good enough for me.

"Himself had the eye to pick out Apollo, and he's turning out great," I said. "I think I might have the same eye to spot a winner, even if it was a colt that didn't have any big names behind him. 'Twould be even better if he came out of nowhere. That would be my wish for now. To find good colts and to train them. I hope Apollo will put me on the road to that."

"You need the eye and you need a way with horses," she said. "I think you have those gifts, but you'll need buckets of luck to go with them. The luck is hard to engineer. All you need is one or two lucky breaks and the horses and the money will follow."

"Well, Apollo is lucky to start with, isn't he?" I said. I

felt she was making it sound too hard, as hard as aiming for the moon.

"He is. You're right. He's looking very good, but he needs to make his mark as a hunter for starters. He won't do that without a good rider."

My stomach felt as if it was in freefall. I was banking on Kitty riding him out for me in the first season at least. She said nothing. That silence was enough.

The weekend afterwards she said too much. She was going to Kent to start the nursing course. She had known for about a month but she didn't want to spoil the end of the summer for us. We were down by the riverbank when she broke the news. Her gaze was away from me and across the water when she first began to speak.

"It's for the best because we're still too young to be getting serious about each other." She paused, turned her head and drilled her eyes into mine. "Your condition doesn't make a blind bit of difference to me. You know that, Kieran, don't you?"

I wanted to believe her. Some of me did believe her, but another part was doubtful. She blurted out everything, then she shut up and waited for me to say something. You'd think I'd have been prepared for it, that I'd have been able to take it square on the chin and say some couple of words to save her from feeling so bad. But the quare fella was back inside me, uglier than before, hurt and wanting to hurt. What kind of a fool was I to imagine that the small, cosy world of our evenings in the car and the days working with Apollo would be enough for her as they were for me? There was a serious want in me, to make me imagine that Kitty, a girl who could crook her finger at any man and bring him running, would be content with me.

"Don't mind me, Kitty – you just think of yourself. Sure

the summer was just a bit of fun. You were handy for me. I was handy for you. Just as well you're moving on. We'd have run out of steam anyway."

"You played that card in Dublin," she said, cold as ice. "It doesn't work as well second time out. That sort of talk isn't you, Kieran. I'm sorry but you can't really carry it off."

"Suit yourself. That's the way I see it. Tough, if you don't agree with me."

"I don't take too kindly to this sort of act from you," she said, flaring. "There's no need for it, no need for it at all, Kieran. And I'm not taking it."

She stood up and reached into the pocket of her jacket. She took out a leather box, maroon in colour, about the size of a box for a watch. As it turned out, that's what it was but there was no watch inside it. I didn't know that then, though.

"That's for you," she said. "Though this isn't exactly how I imagined things would be between us when I was giving it to you."

"Not many things turn out as we expect, do they? I'm the living proof of that. Take that away with you. I don't need anything, especially not a watch."

"Did I say it was a watch?"

"Well, am I supposed to have X-ray eyes? I don't care what it is. Take it away."

"I gave it to you and I'm *not* taking it away. I don't care what you do with it. Shove it up your arse for all I care. It might be the best place to lodge it since you spend so much time talking through your hole."

With that, she went striding away up the earthen path. I felt like a proper tool. The box sat there. I was tempted to catch it and hop it off the wall. Instead, I sat there for a long time, thinking of Kitty and of what an eejit I was. Finally, I opened the box and looked inside.

30

Sally

Mammy believes in angels but not like the statues in the church with the feathery wings that could have been robbed off swans to stick out of their colouredy robes. She believes that angels are the people who are 'sent' to you at the very time you are in sore need of help: undercover angels sort of thing. If you follow that line of thought, there are some quare angels around the place, let me tell you. I'd prefer the ones with wings myself. I wouldn't be too pushed about a Guardian Angel from over the next ditch. Mammy declared Kitty an angel after she brought Kieran that going-away present and took off for England. I'm not so sure she would have awarded Kitty the angel title if she had hung around. Maybe she might have, but I'd imagine angels are harder to handle up close. Better to have them flitting in and out; better in Kitty's case, anyway, given that Mammy didn't exactly take a shine to her, to say the least of it, when she was around the place. She spoke a lot more highly of her when she'd delivered that boxeen to Kieran and vamoosed.

"For once in her life, that girl has done the right thing by Kieran," Mammy said to my father. "He's doing much better since she went to England. Though I thought he'd go into a decline when she left."

They were up in the stall at the milking. Myself and Tamara were drawing the buckets of milk into the dairy. Mammy seemed to forget we were there because we were in and out so often.

"There must be fierce power altogether in the foal's bit," Daddy said. "My father used to call it 'greim searraigh'. He got that Irish for it from the old people."

"It's the last thing you'd think had power," Mammy said. "It just looks like a shrivelled up bit of carrageen moss or dried-out seaweed."

We knew all about the power of the foal's bit at that stage. It's a wonder we had a trial of it at all because Kieran was going to give it short shrift after Kitty left. As luck would have it, Daddy had caught him just as he was going to tip it out of the box and into the range.

"What have you there?" my father asked, eyeing the leather box.

"It's some old mumbo jumbo that Kitty left me with a note," Kieran said. "She said her grandfather gave it to her before he died, and she had it stored away in a drawer. It looks like a fist of cobwebs to me. The foal's bit, she called it."

"Jesus, lad, give me that there!" my father said, grabbing the box as if the crown jewels were compressed inside it. "You don't know what you're doing. Are you gone soft in the head or what?"

"I think that was the approximate diagnosis in Dublin, right enough," Kieran said. "There's a consultant lost in you."

"Oh don't mind me, Kieran," Daddy said. "That just slipped out of me."

Daddy walked over to the window and held the box up to the light. He prodded the contents lightly with his fingertips. Myself and Tamara were up on our tippy-toes trying to see what all the fuss was about.

"Is it some sort of a relic?" Nana said. "Is there a cure in it?"

"It's the web from the Blessed Spider of Vienna, venerated since 1324 and stored in the convent of the Little Sisters of the Sacred Hernia," Kieran said. "The Donovans got a skelp of it from their aunt, the missionary nun in Jakarta."

Nana blessed herself. Mammy shot Kieran a dirty look.

"May God forgive you, Kieran, do you want to be struck down for blasphemy?"

"Again? Twice would be pretty hard going. I thought I'd got my allocation."

'Caustic' was the word Mammy used to describe our Kieran when he got her dander up. It was the perfect word for him. Did you ever see caustic soda burning its way down a blocked sink or drain, the white fumes rising off it? You wouldn't want to get a spatter of it. That was Kieran when he got stuck into something he didn't agree with. You'd stand well back, I tell you.

He cooled off when Daddy started explaining about the foal's bit cobwebby yoke that turned out to have a sort of power or cure. So Nana was half-right and half-wrong when she enquired if it was a relic or a cure.

"When a mare is going to have a foal, she goes away into some quiet corner where nobody can see her," Daddy said. "More often than not, she'll only foal at night. The foal is born with a class of jelly or little sponge in its mouth. When it falls in the grass, some grey crow or magpie could be waiting to swoop down and ate it. Even the mare herself might swallow it. But if you can get hauld of that jelly – the foal's bit – there's nothing a horse won't do for you. There's the height of luck following it."

I was studying Kieran, not obvious like but more from the corner of my eye. I was expecting a few sparks of caustic but he had a serious look on his face while Daddy was talking and, when he stopped, he pointed to the box and said, "Show it here to me."

He took the box and studied the contents with myself and Tamara at either side of him, looking into the box as well. I went to prod it with my finger but I ended up poking the air as Kieran swept the box back.

"Mind it," he said. "You might end up breaking it."

"That's gas coming from the lad that almost threw it in the fire," I said.

Kieran blew gently on the strange dusty-looking stuff.

"If the old people set so much store by it, maybe there is something to it," he said. "The proof will be in the pudding. Sure anything is worth a try."

"True words," Mammy said. "Kitty's grandfather must have had good reason to hold on to it. It was good of her to give it to you. All you have to do is to bring it out to the field with you when you're training Apollo. Nothing ventured, nothing gained."

"It will be like a science experiment," Tamara said. "It could just be tickety-boo. Let's try it soon."

Well, to quote my cousin Tamara, it did turn out to be tickety-boo. In our own words, it proved to be the 'rale dale' – that's the Cork version of the real deal.

What difference did it make? Well, to begin with, Kieran used the magic – if that's what you'd call it – only when there was some problem with Apollo: like when he'd be trying to learn some new moves, higher jumps or something. Kieran would bring it out to the field with him then. He'd open the box in front of Apollo's nose. He'd let him have a sniff of it – Apollo is very nosy. But he'd snap the lid shut then for fear that Apollo might think it was some sort of a treat or a reward and knock it back. Things did start to run smoothly. If we needed extra help, the foal's bit was the thing to get us out of a hoult, as Nana would say.

The biggest miracle it worked was that November when Apollo caught some kind of a virus and was thrun down in himself in the stable. Tom Dalton, our vet, was giving the horse this powder and that powder but he was left scratching his head at the end of it all. If Apollo wasn't moping around the stable with his head down between his knees, he was stretched out on the barley straw. The eyes were fierce dull in his head and he barely looked at the apples I brought out: he used to be red mad for the apples at any other time.

I was at Kieran to get out the magic box and give Apollo a sniff of the cobweb but he was haulding tough.

"We should give Dalton a chance first," he said. "I don't want to be pulling it out every time the horse sneezes. I'd be afraid we'd use up the power of it. If it is a power at all. Maybe I'm just more sure of myself when I know it's at my back."

Professor Tamara put in her tuppence ha'penny worth then, though this time her knowledge came from Earls Court rather than her 'research library' down in the parlour.

"Mummy told me once about trials done on people who were ill," she said. "Some of them were given actual pills, while others were given substitutes that looked like pills but had none of the medication in them. The substitutes or the fakes were called placebos. Some of the patients on the placebos improved as much as those on the real pills."

269

"It sounds like gobbledygook to me," I said.

Kieran wasn't too taken by what either of us was saying. He said he wanted to give Dalton one more try with his horse medicine.

"Apollo is too good to be fecking around with," he said. "Dalton is the best horse doctor going. There's fellas travelling from all over the place to him. He must have something else up his sleeve."

It was on the tip of my tongue to ask him again to chance the box while he was waiting for Dalton to come back but I knew if I pushed him he might go the other way. I was surer than anything that this was no time to be sparing it. Hard as it was for me to admit it, Tamara stood a better chance of getting a hearing than I did. I bided my time until I got her on her own and asked her to give it a go.

"He might listen to you more than to me," I said. "Just don't go banging on about that placy whatchamacallit lark. Tell him to try it this once. You must think the same as me. Don't you?"

She hesitated before answering me. That's all we needed: Tamara doing her looking-at-it-from-all-angles act. I took a deep breath and began counting to ten in my head. Thanks be to God, I was still at seven or eight when she spoke.

"Of course I agree with you," she said. "It's dreadful to see Apollo like that. But I trust Kieran's judgement too. Maybe he has a good reason for holding back and waiting for Mr Dalton."

"Please, Tamara, trust me just this once," I said. "I won't ask you again. Just say something to Kieran. He mightn't listen to you but at least we'll have done everything we could do."

270

When we went down to the stable, I was more shocked at the state of Kieran than I was at the sight of Apollo, though both of them were the picture of misery. Kieran's forehead was stretched tight with tension and his eyes looked as if there was a headache drumming behind them. I had half a mind to call Tamara off. I didn't want to be the cause of her blundering in on a minefield. Before I had a chance to give her a nudge and an eye signal, she was off. My stomach was swirling. To give her her due, she delivered the appeal in her own gentle way, much better than I could have done it. I was watching Kieran's face all the while; not one muscle relaxed. He didn't open his mouth for at least a minute after she stopped speaking. I was beginning to think he might say nothing at all.

"Ye think I have nothing to lose by trying it?" he said dully. "To be honest, I think that as good as Dalton is, he's struggling. But if I try the foal's bit and that doesn't work either, where do I go, what do I do? That's why I'm stalling."

His tone put the fear of God in me. Stupid, stupid me, I didn't realise how sick Apollo was. If anything happened to Apollo, Kieran would be in freefall again. I thought of Nana's words again. I was going to stand up like a brave young soldier.

"I know you think I haven't much sense, Kieran," I began, "and this is scaring the living daylights out of me as well as you, but there's a feeling inside me saying that it's right to try the foal's bit now. You know all those quare thoughts that go through your head in the mornings and keep you a prisoner in the bed? In the end, there's nothing for it only to jump out. Bite the bullet now. Go for it like a brave young soldier."

What was I after doing? If this went arseways, I'd be the

271

one blamed for it, for ever and ever. Well, I had no choice, had I? Something inside me was driving me on. I watched Kieran take the box out of his pocket. It was happening now, for better or worse.

Apollo was stretched out on the straw. He whickered and raised his head a little when he saw Kieran approach and sink to his knees beside him. We all had a hand in Apollo but he was Kieran's horse. Kieran was the only one for him, you could see it as plain as day.

He opened the box and set it between Apollo's ears. The horse twitched but he didn't shake his head as I expected him to. Kieran touched the foal's bit lightly with the tips of his fingers and rubbed Apollo's head from the forehead down to the tip of his nose. All the while, he was talking gently to Apollo, telling him what a great horse he was, how smart and clever he was, how proud Kieran was of him, how he made Kieran feel good about himself.

As Kieran spoke, I could see his forehead relax and the pain go out of his eyes. But kneeling on the one spot took its toll. As he sat back, he winced.

"Come on, the two of you," he said. "Take a spot at either side of Apollo and tell him why he needs to get his act together – for himself and for all of us."

That was a bit rich coming from a fella that gave half the year thrun on top of his bed but I was saying nothing. Tamara and myself stationed ourselves on either side of Apollo's neck. We started plaiting his mane, talking to him about everything we'd done together, how quick he was to learn, how much more we had to do together and what a great jumper he was going to be. I think we were convincing ourselves as much as him. Kieran was still stroking Apollo's face, touching the horse's bit in the box every so often. I was half-scared he might wear it away but I said nothing.

How long were we at that talking and stroking caper? I couldn't honestly say because I lost track of time. I was just concentrating all my thoughts on making Apollo better. We might have been still there when they came out from the house calling us to go milking but for the fact that, suddenly, Apollo stretched out his front legs, scattering us. He pulled himself up and shook himself like a dog before walking over to the water bucket and sinking his puss into it for a big, long shlurp. He pulled his head out then, the water streaming out of his mouth.

I wanted to jump around and shout 'Up Cork!' as if it was Munster Final Day but Kieran's face was still serious.

"I can't trust it yet," he said.

That night, he took his quilt out into the stable. Mammy said he'd catch double pneumonia – she said that when he was safely out of earshot. Tamara and myself wanted to stay in the stable with him but he wouldn't hear of it. Of course, we slept out the next morning and had only a bare minute to look into the stable before rushing for the school bus. Kieran was fast asleep in the straw and Apollo was standing over him as if he was a mare caring for a foal.

The hands of the classroom clock dragged themselves round every hour. When we got home that evening, Tom Dalton had been and gone. He had given Apollo an injection, though he didn't think he strictly needed it. He had pronounced Apollo as right as rain but advised Kieran to keep him in the stable for at least another week. He prescribed some molasses to be mixed with the oats as well.

"Those powders are powerful tack," he had told Kieran and Daddy.

No one contradicted him.

That night, Kieran said he would have to write to Kitty and thank her. Tamara stood over him and called out flowery things for him to say. I joined in with a few sentences of my own until he got right sick of us and cleared us out of the bedroom. I'd have given my right arm to have a good read of that letter. Mammy said I take after Nana. The flipping cheek of her.

31

Jenny

She was propped up on a bank of snowy pillows the afternoon Con and Tamara went to Cork Airport for Jack. My heart was nearly breaking at the sight of her: she looked so small lying there with the innocent excitement of a child waiting for Santy.

She had been saving the good pillowslips and the sheets for this – a trousseau in reverse, stored away at the top of the wardrobe. She had me airing her burial habit. That was no notice. The habit came out a couple of times a year to be hung on the back of a chair in front of the range to banish any dampness she imagined might be taking hold. In the beginning, we were all half in dread of the brown robe but, after a while, it was nearly as familiar as an apron to us. Nearly.

"Are you afraid you'll catch a cold in it?" I asked.

"I'm in no mood for yer jokes," she sniffed. "When I'm going on my journey, I want everything right."

For a woman so much in cahoots with the Man Above and his cabinet, my mother had a surprising lack of enthusiasm for the next world. I could never get my head around it. She used to floor me when she'd start suggesting that there might be no life after death. She was a different woman, though, when any priest called round: the devout

Catholic face went on then before you could say 'mantilla'.

Kieran used to tease her, "Yes, Father, no, Father, kiss my big toe, Father'.

'Twasn't too many were left in on her 'Doubting Thomas' routine apart from myself.

"Is there any heaven, at all?" she'd wonder. "I told Paddy Mahony to come back and tell me if there was. I'm still waiting on him."

"He might come yet, or maybe he won't be let," I joked. "Anyway, wouldn't it be lovely to meet up with him and all your friends and relations again?"

"I don't know," she frowned. "Your father wasn't always the easiest man to live with."

That was the bones of the chat we had a fortnight earlier, just before she had taken to the bed. There was no joking and no debating now. She scarcely made a dent in the pillows; she was so weak, she could only speak in fits and starts. I had told her that Jack was coming. I didn't want to her to get a shock. That was only part of the reason I told her. She was fading fast but I knew that if she would hold on for anything, it would be Jack. She was after waiting eighteen years. What was a couple of days to that? They say hearing is the last of the senses to go. If that were the case, my mother would have an ear for the grass growing to the very last.

"Is that a motor I hear going the road?" she said, startling me from a daydream of my imagined reunion with my brother. I was playing it every which way in my mind, inventing the right words to bridge the big space that had opened up between us all in the years since he'd left. I had talked to him on the telephone a handful of times since Tamara arrived but that was not the same.

Those calls were mostly to tell him how she was getting on, and I used to put her on the phone to him for most of them. I could imagine Herself down in the post office fattening on the conversations, so I rationed the information. My mother was right. It was our car going the road and, before I knew it, Jack was standing in the doorframe with Tamara by his side, holding fast to his hand. The child looked as if a lamp had been lit inside her. Had any of us the least idea how hard it had been for the poor child?

I had forgotten how tall my brother was, forgotten his way of stooping his shoulders to lessen that height. Here he was, a thinner, greyer version of the black-haired Jack who had headed down the lane, a duffle bag over his shoulder and hurt smouldering in his eyes all those years ago. I never forgot the sight of Lilac straining on the rope in the wooden Ford crate and keening like a banshee until every dog in the place was yowling in sympathy with her that day.

Kieran was so like him, the self-same brown eyes, the snubby nose, the lanky frame. Why hadn't I realised that Tamara was drawn to Kieran because he looked so like her father? All the words I had rehearsed shot out of my head like a flock of starlings bursting from a tree. He took my two hands in his and squeezed them, looking directly into my eyes. They were the old kind eyes, not a trace of bitterness in them. Not many people could imagine me – a woman known for the gift of the gab – struggling to string a sentence together: some things are just too big to fit into words. And then he was swooping over the bed, kissing Nana on the forehead. I jumped up from the chair and waved him into it, not taking no for an answer, though he protested. He sat there, arms resting on the eiderdown, one of her small hands dwarfed inside his.

"You came, Jack," she said. "Our Lady brought you. I knew . . ."

The tears were sliding down her lined face. Jack's eyes were welling up.

"*Shhh*, Mam, *shhh*," he said. "Don't be bothering yourself with talk. I'm here now. I'm an awful ape that it took me so long. You wouldn't meet a sorrier man in a day's walking."

I spoke for my mother. Nothing like the speech I had tried to prepare but I was too choked for anything more. "There's no need for 'sorry'. You're here. That's all that matters."

"Your lovely girleen," Nana said, looking towards Tamara, who was sitting on the arm of the chair.

My mother lapsed into silence again. My mother not talking, it was so strange. She lay back, smiling and smiling. Every so often she closed her eyes. Then she closed them for the longest time. Tamara's hand flew to her mouth. I blessed myself and began to cry.

The eyelids parted suddenly, and the faintest of smiles sparked in her rheumy eyes. "Still here," she whispered.

I left Jack and Tamara have their time with her. The kitchen was so silent. Sally had let the range go so low it had practically gone out: another job for me. Sally and Kieran were above in the stall with Con.

I looked around the room, my eyes coming to rest on the empty 'throne': another link going. How many more to break away before I'd pass myself? I shivered. In the fullest, busiest, chattering days in this kitchen, on days of the harvest or the making of the hay, a shadow would pass over me. Not often, mind you, and not for long, but when it did I used to think of the people who had crowded the kitchen before us and how we were all passing through, all part of the chain. I gathered myself together. Well, I was here now, wasn't I? And the kitchen wouldn't be empty for long.

Jack would be hungry. I went to the fridge to get out some cold bacon and tomatoes. I'd have to feed him up while he was here: put a bit of mate on those bones of his. Tamara could have scrambled eggs – again. How that girl survived without a mouthful of mate was a mystery to me. How she wasn't clucking like a hen at this stage was another mystery. She'd run a chape household if ever she met her equal.

My mother did hold on for Jack but even that mighty heart of hers couldn't keep her with us much longer that that. She did take such pleasure from seeing him that I began to hope she might rally. God help my poor deluded brain. She was conscious enough that evening to say a few sentences off and on. Jack sat up all night with her. We all took turns coming and going from her bedroom. In the morning, she had another small bit of chitchat with him up to half ten or so. He was hollow-eyed and stubbled but only agreed to lie down as long as I promised to call him after two hours.

Again, she greeted him with a smile when he returned to his station at the bedside with Tamara and Sally around dinnertime. I don't think the girls fully understood that mother was sinking. I didn't see the point in upsetting them more than they were already. Anyway, does anyone fully realise that the end is nearing for someone you love? You think you will have them for another few months, weeks, days. The mind plays its own tricks on you. It's always as if you have some more time in reserve: this hour and the next hour and the next. However would you cope otherwise?

Early that afternoon, she fell into sleeping with her mouth open. I know this might be a strange thing to say but she reminded me of nothing but a baby waiting to be born. Sleeping, sleeping through the evening and into another night with Jack and Kieran and myself at her side. I left Tamara and Sally stay up as long as they liked but the sleep got the better of them around two o'clock. Con had gone off before midnight. He needed his sleep for the cows.

It was a blessing in itself that she was peaceful. None of that terrible rasping and clawing for breath my father was tormented with when he went. But he had spent half his life pulling on his packets of Sweet Afton.

She slept through into the next morning. The doctor came and examined her. He called Jack and myself out to the kitchen. He said it wouldn't be long: a couple of hours at the most. It would be a miracle if she saw it through to the next day. Jack and myself stood there after he had gone.

"It's an awful bloody story at the end, isn't it," he said. "It never fully came home to me till I lost Ruth."

"And now – Mam," I said. "It's all too close for you."

"When you think about it," he said. "Finishing up. To be gone with no coming back. I always thought I'd end up mending our differences sooner. Pity to God I kept putting it off."

"You know what they say. Any of them are only a day ahead of us."

"I'm glad she had a bit of comfort at the end of her days. There wasn't much to be had when we were growing up. And my father wasn't the easiest to be putting up with, as I well know. I didn't help either, taking off like that and not coming back. Do you think she had much happiness at the end of it all?"

"Sure, happy or sad never raised its head for the old folk," I said. "They just took it all as it came, and it was a bonus to see old age. She was as proud as Punch of the family though, delighted to see them get on. Having Tamara here was the icing on the cake for her. She had prayed for that girl night and day since she was born."

There was no miracle unless you count the aisy way she passed over: gone on one shuddering breath into the twilight of a November day with the evening star hung like a bright lamp over the shoulder of the hill our house nestled into: the house she bawled her first cry in, drew her first breath in and the house from which she set out on her final journey.

Her work was done – with the help of Little Nellie and Our Lady of Perpetual Succour. Kieran was out of the bedroom. Jack was home. Tamara was talking. She was at peace.

32

Sally

It was Tamara that saw the star first. I looked up at it when she pointed it out, but I didn't put much pass on it. A star is a flipping star. Tamara was more gone on that kind of stuff than I was, maybe because she was from the city and you couldn't see the stars there with the dint of the smoke: imagine that. The first winter she was here, she was always craning her neck, staring up at them. When you can look up at a rake of stars any night of the week, you don't pay too much heed to them.

The sky was navy blue when Tamara spotted that evening star, not black, because the light was not long gone. It only strikes me now as I'm telling you that Nana went away round about the same time as the light was going from the day. That's sort of nice when you think about it, that they went together, nice but lonesome at the same time.

When Mammy made us go into Nana's bedroom to say goodbye to her, I thought it was going to be awful. To tell you the truth, I was scared out of my life. I never saw a dead body before, except on the telly, and that doesn't count. It was bad enough, but not as bad as I thought it would be. She just looked as if she was asleep. The weird thing was that she looked younger than when she was alive. Weirder again, she looked more like Mammy. I didn't want to think too much about that. I didn't kiss her but I touched her forehead and that was awful hard to do. Nana wouldn't want me kissing her. I'd never kissed her when she was alive, so why would I go doing that just because she was dead? That didn't mean I wasn't sad. The sadness didn't come all at once, like I thought it should have when I saw Nana, well, what was left of her now that her soul was gone to heaven. I was more numb, the way your face is after the dentist gives you an injection. Mammy said it would take a while to sink in. But when I saw Mammy crying and, worse again, when I saw Daddy crying, I felt lost in myself, really, really lost. That's when I told Tamara that we should go out to the stable.

There was something about the sound of Apollo eating hay — the *chomp, chomp, chomp* of his teeth in a steady rhythm that made you feel peaceful in yourself. The chomping and the horsey smell and the quietness of the stable were a medicine in themselves. The evening was getting colder but it was warm in there. We stayed there for ages and ages. It didn't mean we were forgetting that Nana was dead but it wasn't as hard as being in the house with all the commotion. The neighbours and the rest of the relations were arriving. A lot of them had this quare way of talking at you, like you were aged two instead of twelve. More of them acted as if you were invisible.

"Two funerals in the space of eighteen months was too much for any living soul, let alone a small girl," I had overheard one of the neighbours say about Tamara. I hadn't enlightened them as to the fact that Tamara's mother didn't really have a funeral, well, in the sense that we do funerals, not that I am taking from what she had to go through. I couldn't have stuck it, if it was me.

"What was yeer funeral like?" I asked her. "You don't have to tell me if you don't want to."

"Mummy wanted a cremation. She had it all planned out, right down to the invitation list. Very select, very small. She didn't want a fuss."

She explained that you had to be invited to a funeral in England. People just didn't turn up in crowds as they did here where the adults swore that a good funeral was nearly always better than a wedding, especially if the person had enjoyed a long life. All the English funeral customs seemed pure cracked to me, I told Tamara.

"Ditto for the Irish ones," she told me.

Ditto was a new one on me. I added it to my list of good names for horses. That was one of my hobbies, dreaming up names for horses. I got that from Nana, well, kind of. She never placed a bet in her life but she always had her nose in the racing pages. She'd pick out names she liked and tick them off with a pencil as winners. We'd read the results the following day to see if they had done any good. I had taken to cutting out the horoscopes too and reading them a week later to see if there had been any truth to them. Nana used to read them with me but they weren't of much use to either of us because they were mostly about romance and jobs. I got lonesome thinking that I'd never be doing that again with her.

The fields, the trees and the hill were all black by the time we forced ourselves to go back to the busy house, and I had to admit that the evening star was desperate bright altogether. Tamara called it a 'celestial lamp'. She would.

"Perhaps it's an old soul," she said. "Or do you think some of the light could be from Nana's soul shining out of it?"

"It's a flipping star. Anyway, Nana couldn't get all the way up there that quick."

"Oh yes, she could have if her soul was travelling at the speed of light."

I could feel a lecture on astronomy coming on, so I skedaddled down the yard ahead of her.

When Nana's coffin was carried out the following night, the light spilled before her through the front door into the dark night. The hill was nowhere to be seen. The darkness was all over it like a blanket.

The day she was buried was wet and windy and the ground was muddy under our feet in the graveyard outside the village. I looked up from the grave at one stage and saw a raggedy square of blue – as big as the Screen Field – open up in the cloudy sky. I like to think that Nana opened it up for us.

Uncle Jack was holding Tamara's hand fast. I was glad for her. Losing Nana made me understand in a small way how hard it was for Tamara when her mother died. I remembered how mean I was to her when she came over to us from London. I ground the heel of my black boot into the mud.

Nana was gone. I still couldn't bear to look at her empty chair in the kitchen. No one could bring themselves to sit in it.

"Died after a short illness bravely borne." That's what the parish notes in the local paper said. The priest said we were lucky that we had some warning, that we had time to prepare. Kieran muttered that the priest would find a blessing in anything, including the burnt arse of a pot. He might have listed other unlikely blessings only Mammy shot him a poisonous look.

Kieran is doing great now because Apollo is turning out to be such a mighty hunter and jumper. Three or four rosettes that he won in gymkhanas are pinned up beside the Sacred Heart lamp in the kitchen. In the middle of the reds and yellows of the rosettes is a short article cut out of *The Southern Star*. The headline says: '**APOLLO IS A RISING STAR.**'

Kieran still has his moods and his tiredness but we don't see too much of his temper. Tamara calls him 'The Volcano', dormant but bubbling away under the surface, only to erupt a few times in his lifetime – if we're lucky. I've seen enough of his eruptions to last my lifetime anyway.

Guess who Apollo's talented riders are? You have it in one. Tamara and myself. We have the fancy hats and jackets and all, like they have at the horse show in the RDS in Dublin. Kitty bought them for us as a going-away present. She wasn't so bad in the end. She seems a lot better when you don't have to be dealing with her. Tamara will be going back to London in January. Uncle Jack will go away after the funeral but he will come back for Christmas: his first one at home in eighteen years. Not than any of us have much stomach for decorations and all that lark now that Nana is gone. We are unfortunate with the Christmases. Last year, it was Kieran. Now it's Nana. To tell you the truth, I am a bit nervous about the one next year. They say everything comes in threes.

"Are you sure you want to go back?" I asked Tamara the other day. "This is kind of your home here now."

She was a bit slow about giving me an answer so I had another go at her.

"You are still kind of annoying but we've learned to put up with you."

"Ditto."

"You and your ditto. If you stay a bit longer, I promise

to send you back with a genuine Cork accent. Do you know what I mean, girl? Do you know, like? Sound as a bell, boy!"

She smiled but she didn't continue the jokey tone. That's our Tamara, serious to the core.

"I really belong with Daddy because he still has Mummy wrapped up in him," she said. "When I am with him, I feel I am still holding on to a piece of her. I love you all but he is someone of my own."

"You're right to want to go home to your daddy but you'll have to come back for loads of holidays."

According to Mammy, a big part of the blessing of Nana's gradual passing over a few weeks was that Uncle Jack had come back to make his peace with her and with everyone else. Mammy had thought he was sour with us because she got the farm instead of him. He explained that the place had too many bad memories because of his father but they weren't enough to have kept him away. He was always planning to come home 'next year' but it never happened. Ruth was afraid to come because she thought she wouldn't be accepted. He didn't want to come without her. You couldn't keep up with them: all that sort of quare thinking. And then Ruth got sick . . .

Before Nana died, she told Kieran she was saving the best of her blessing for him. But that was another story again.

33

Kieran

Who'd have thought that I'd be the first one to cop that Nana was on the way out. Maybe it was because I move slower than the rest of them now. I notice things more. And I'm not saying that I copped it all in one go. It took about a week for it to fully sink in. Even if she came up to me with it printed on a bit of paper in black and white, I would have told her to go way with herself, told her she was the creaking door that would never fall. This is how it began.

I was on my own out in the stable one day about a month or so before she passed away. I was brushing Apollo down. Don't ask me where the two were. Usually, I couldn't even stir without having one of them on my tail. Brushing Apollo was a job that suited me because I could lean against him whenever the bad leg started acting up. I liked it too because it was satisfying to get rid of the old hairs and bring the shine up on him. I was brushing away, happy out in a world of my own when didn't I hear my name being called. It was Nana. She was after hobbling down through the yard with her stick. That was odd in itself. There was an east wind blowing up the lane, and she hardly ever stirred out of the house when it was cold. Whatever way she stood against the light, I got a right land.

"Are you after losing weight?" I asked her.

"Do you think so?" she said, acting a bit too surprised. "If I am itself, don't go saying anything to your mother. She'd only be fussing."

The stable door was open. She came in and sat down on the kitchen chair I kept in there, her two hands clasped together on the stick in front of her. She was asking me this and that about Apollo, how the training was going and probably a score of other questions that won't come to me now. I knew she was going round and round the bush with the small talk and that she'd come to the point sooner or later, so I let on nothing only brushed away nice and steady. The thinness of her was picking at me, though. Nana was never what you'd call a big woman, but she was never scrawny either. Now she was as thin as a lath.

The look of her was one thing, but something else came back to me and gave me a quare auld feeling in the pit of my stomach. There was a robin haunting the front garden that week. I met him in the kitchen door against me one evening but I waved my arms and fecked him out again. I don't know how Mammy didn't notice him. Just as well. A robin was not good news in our family, not by a mile. If one of the cheeky little feckers got too fond of hanging around the house or trying to come in, it was a sign that someone was going to die. Now, I doubt very much if that'll ever qualify as an exact science that could be jotted down in a notebook but I know a fair few people who swear by it.

Maybe Nana caught me in a weak moment that evening. Or maybe there was something about the two of us being on our together, but when she asked me how I was, it all came out of me in a flood.

I did shrug her off the first time she asked.

"*Arrah*, I'm keeping the best side out like the cracked jug on the dresser," I said.

She smiled but rounded on me again with the same question.

"Sure I can't tell you anything you don't know yourself," I said. "I am up and down like a yoyo. It's as if there is something dark inside in the middle of myself coming on like a magnet betimes and dragging me down. In the middle of the night, I could get a mad rush of blood to the head, persuading me that I can get on with things. That makes me feel that I could take a crack at anything. Sleep won't come with the dint of all the ideas that come racing into my brain. Then, in the cold light of the morning, that magnet is going full pelt and everything turns to sh– everything turns to you know what, and I can hardly drag myself out of the bed. I am like the small lad at the seaside making the perfect sand castle. Then, some mad, bad thought catches hauld of him and he goes lepping all over it. After I give into the quareness and lash out at someone or something, I am sick to the stomach with the hate of myself for the damage I'm after doing."

"Your grandfather had the same auld divils pulling at him only he didn't have to carry the cross you are carrying," she said. "You're taking after him. Black cat, black kitten."

I was surprised to hear her say that and not too happy about it. The auld grandfather with all his moods wasn't exactly the person I wanted to have breaking out in me. As if she could read my mind, she spoke again.

"But you wouldn't meet a dacenter man if you walked all the way from here to Timbuktu. And he was a great man to get things done. That's running in your veins too, don't forget."

She was still talking when she reached deep into the pocket of her brown tweed coat and pulled out a small book. Her bank book, she told me. The plan was that I'd go to town with her on pension day and that she'd withdraw a big skelp of it for me to lodge in my post-office book.

"In case anything might happen to me," she said.

"Don't be daft, Nana. Nothing's going to happen to you."

There was no reasoning with her. Right go wrong, she wanted to do it. She had this notion that I should buy a mare and start breeding Apollo to make some class of a future for myself.

"They'll all say I'm robbing you," I said.

"Let them say what they want. Please yourself and that's one pleased anyway. I'm after telling your father and mother. It's my money and I can do as I want with it."

She was true to her word. The money was put into my account in the post office. I should have been happy but I didn't like the way she was making out that she wasn't long for this world. Mammy was after noticing by then that she was failing. Once the secret was out, she seemed to go downhill at the rate of ninety. The doctor was sent for. She took to the bed. It was so fast, woeful fast altogether. None of us could believe it.

I wanted to drink round the time of the funeral. The house was full of every type of a bottle winking at me. But I held tough, didn't taste a drop even though my tongue was hanging out for it. I'm tempted to break out some time, to get totally out of my fucken skull. The fear that I might never be able to put the brakes on myself is holding me back.

I'm tired now. The tiredness is a vise-grip squeezing any

bit of good out of me. But do you know what? I'll get over this too. I will an'all.

Before she died, Nana told me that some people can hand on a gift in their passing. She wasn't talking about wills or money or any of that stuff. It sounds daft when you talk about it, I know. She said she heard of one fella who got the most beautiful singing voice after his father died.

"It might sound like a cracked idea to you, boy bán, but I will do my level best to lave something good for you, if I can at all. Something that will make you able to take the bad stuff that happened to you and turn it to the good. Reach high, Kieran, like those astronauts. Ate the moon, the dark side and all, and spit out stars. Peg them stars up into the black sky into any shape that suits you. Don't be bothering with any plough or any other bit of scrap that was up there before. Make your own pattern."

It might have happened anyway. I was heading slowly in that direction, two steps forward, one step backwards. I was getting a bit stronger in the gammy arm and leg but, better again, my mood was lifting. That magnet wasn't pulling me down as deep or as often. Apollo was a class of a moon pulling me in the other direction.

I was standing out in the yard one night looking up at the full moon and Nana's words came back to me. For the first time in a long time, I felt right in myself.

This is the way things are, Kieran boy, I thought to myself, and you can dale with it.

And I fell to thinking what kind of a foal the mare would have.

293